Dear Readers,

Since we first sta[rted] ... had a lot of posi[tive] ... thought you migh[t] ... cover best fits each *Scarlet* title. Well, when we've chosen a manuscript which will make an exciting addition to our publications, photo shoots are arranged and a selection of the best pictures are sent back to us by our designers.

The whole *Scarlet* team then gets together to decide which photograph will catch the reader's eyes and (most importantly!) sell the book. The comments made during our meetings are often intriguing: 'Why,' asked one of our team recently, 'can't the hero have even more buttons undone!' When we settle on the ideal cover, all the elements that make up the 'look' of a *Scarlet* book are added: the lips logo, the back cover blurb, the title lettering is picked out in foil . . . and yet another stunning cover is ready to wrap around a brand new and exciting *Scarlet* novel.

Till next month,
Best wishes,

Sally Cooper

SALLY COOPER,
Editor-in-Chief – *Scarlet*

PS I'm always delighted to hear from readers. Why not complete the questionnaire at the back of the book and let me know what *you* think of *Scarlet*!

About the Author

Born in Lancashire, Lianne Conway has since lived in Yorkshire, Dorset and Buckinghamshire. She spent much of the period between the seventies and nineties in various permanent and temporary secretarial jobs, working in areas as diverse as engineering and personnel and, ultimately, for a well-known charity.

Lianne now realizes that her mobility was probably the result of a restless Sagittarian nature. Somewhere in between jobs, she produced a novel and discovered that she had probably always wanted to write without knowing it! It was as she tried – and tried again – that Lianne also discovered how difficult it was to get published. After giving up her day job a number of years ago, she had some short stories and poetry published, and *Starstruck* is her first published novel.

Married for twenty-four years, Lianne lives in Buckinghamshire, with her husband, cat and word processor and claims, 'I'm still trying to make sense of all three!'

*Other **Scarlet** titles available this month:*

SUMMER OF FIRE by Jill Sheldon
DEVLIN'S DESIRE by Margaret Callaghan
INTOXICATING LADY by Barbara Stewart

LIANNE CONWAY

STARSTRUCK

SCARLET

Enquiries to:
Robinson Publishing Ltd
7 Kensington Church Court
London W8 4SP

First published in the UK by Scarlet, 1996

A copy of the British Library Cataloguing in
Publication data is available from the British Library

ISBN 1-85487-710-0

Printed and bound in the EC

10 9 8 7 6 5 4 3 2 1

To Adèle and Phil, with love

PROLOGUE

It was a face that made you look twice, not because it was especially handsome or even offering the childlike appeal of the pretty boys being spawned by film, fashion and media industries. In tune with the height and build, the impression given was one of strength, a bump at the bridge of the nose betraying some early break of the bone. Yet it was the eyes that drew you in: a compelling, piercing blue. Even ice-cold with indifference, Fergus Hann demanded attention. And now, there was little doubt that Layne would be meeting him in the flesh.

To be starstruck as a cinema-goer was permissible, a necessary escape, but to be starstruck during the course of her working life was asking for trouble and, right now, she wanted to do the job to the best of her ability. She had quite enough on her plate, thank you very much!

CHAPTER 1

Opening her eyes, Layne side-stepped the spray from the shower and wrenched the setting to cold. Then, forcing herself forward, she lifted her chin bravely and allowed icy water to stream from head to toe.

If a cold shower was the only way to concentrate the mind, then she was willing to take the cure! But the freezing water pounding down upon her only seemed to emphasise her vulnerability, causing her to shiver with nervous apprehension.

Layne leaned back against the tiled wall and turned off the shower. Squeezing her wet hair over one shoulder, she took a deep breath and reminded herself she was competent and capable. There was no reason on earth why working alongside this international star should affect her . . . He was, after all, only a man . . .

The following afternoon, feeling tired, creased and crumpled, Layne fought to retrieve her hand

3

baggage. She made her way down the narrow aisle and stepped out of the aircraft to be met by a wall of heat. The airport buildings shimmered as she approached and a wave of nausea threatened to overwhelm her but she strode doggedly on. She did not intend to give her body a chance to complain.

Inevitably, her one small suitcase was the last to appear on the luggage carousel but at least someone had been sent to pick her up. A young Greek of about eighteen or nineteen was calling out something unrecognizable to everyone but herself.

'Layne Denham, Layne Denham!'

'Is it far to travel?' she asked, adding the words, 'Long way?' with hand gestures to help him understand.

He shrugged. 'Fifteen, twenty minutes,' he said, adding some flourishing gestures of his own before throwing her bag on the worn back seat of his very used car.

Layne sighed, pushing stray strands of damp blonde hair away from her forehead, then took a deep breath and slid herself into the passenger seat.

She wished she could feel the same zest for life as her driver. No sooner had he swung himself in beside her, started the engine and got the car throbbing with eastern pop music, than they were off with a squeal of tyres in a cloud of dust.

After a time, she could no longer bear to look at the crucifix swinging wildly from his rearview mirror, so she followed his example and wound her window right down to watch the passing scenery, in preference to the narrow, twisting road ahead. He clearly believed they were in the hands of God and she was too weary not to fall in with this philosophy.

At first, her change of attitude did not prove fruitful. Unfinished concrete-block buildings with reinforcing rods sprouting heavenwards announced the curse of the fast-developing tourist trade and the remaining landscape consisted of a dusty, arid plain. Layne closed her eyes and tried, without success, to doze.

The forward lurch of her body with the slamming on of brakes and a loud blast of the car horn soon re-awakened her will to survive.

An old man on a donkey was quietly making his way round a tight bend in the road and her driver, certain of his divine pact, had been taken by complete surprise. Several more blasts of the horn were followed by much shouting and gesticulating but, for the first time on her journey, Layne smiled, both at the donkey's stubborn refusal to be intimidated and the old man's admirable indifference.

This turn of events seemed to herald a change in their surroundings. The bend negotiated, they found themselves travelling through a town and, though the buildings looked haphazard and run-down, to their left twinkled the blue sea of the harbour. Expensive boats moored at the harbour wall contrasted strongly with the dilapidated air of the town itself.

In her side mirror, Layne could see lorries queuing for the ferry. Greek parents were watching over-impatient children and an orthodox priest in his black robes was organizing a group of volunteers to help him on board with his new furniture: a round table and set of four chairs.

Tourist gift shops spilled onto the opposite side of the road with their sun hats, tan lotion and postcards on stands. Displays of Greek ornaments beckoned from their windows.

The town itself did not last long. Soon they were flying along a straight stretch of road looking down on a vast plain of olive groves. The mood of the music had changed, too, to a plaintive eastern wail. Layne sank back, spirits a little revived, and relaxed into the atmosphere. It was still hot but the air funnelling in through the open windows of the car beat a pleasant tattoo on her forehead, sending her hair streaming out over the back of her seat.

Her companion's incoherent words of anticipation were, therefore, greeted with mixed feelings when the car turned off the straight into the drive of an extensive new villa, beside which a number of temporary buildings had been erected.

Layne decided that no one should have to think in such heat in a location like this, let alone work, or rather rework, a pivotal scene of her screenplay, 'The Thorn Field'.

In no time Rowan, assistant to Axel Miller, the director, was apologizing for the short notice as he led Layne across the paved front of the villa, decorated with huge pots of red geraniums, and on round the back. Layne brushed against a purple bougainvillaea, passed a tempting turquoise swimming pool and followed Rowan across a dirt track to a small room in one of the temporary buildings.

Painfully aware of the lack of air-conditioning and her travel-weary state, Layne looked reluctantly down on a wordprocessor that had seen better days. She would not have been surprised to find an ancient manual typewriter but still found it difficult to be grateful for this blessing of modern technology.

'I'd really benefit from a shower, Rowan,' urged Layne. 'My brain feels stale after the journey and I wasn't expecting such heat at this time of year.'

'I know.' Rowan shook his head apologetically. 'You wouldn't believe it but the water went off this afternoon. A bottle of mineral water is probably about the best I can do just now.'

'No chance of a swim?' suggested Layne.

'Pool's off limits until after the shoot. Jerry's orders.'

'Jerry!'

Rowan looked distinctly uncomfortable. 'This is as much to do with Inge Jensen as it is with Jerry. She is insisting the mother's role should be strengthened and, to be truthful, Layne, Jerry hasn't been able to take his eyes off her since she arrived.'

Layne let the flat of her hands drop loudly onto the desk in front of her. 'Brilliant.' She sat back and studied Rowan through narrowed eyes. 'And what does Fergus Hann have to say about it?'

Rowan rubbed his chin, then shoved his hands deep into the pockets of his jeans. 'Ah, well . . .'

'Ah well *what*?' pressed Layne pessimistically.

'He doesn't know. We've been filming around him for the past week. He's flying in later today with his daughter.'

'It's nice to know how important this is to him,' grumbled Layne.

'I'll get that mineral water,' offered Rowan hurriedly and disappeared.

Taking a huge deep breath, Layne tossed her hair over her shoulder. She was not in the mood for massaging Inge Jensen's ego. Had Fergus Hann been warned about the script changes, Layne might have had a chance of fighting Jerry over this but, of course, the so-called 'star' of the film had swanned off, hadn't he?

What was she thinking about . . . 'so-called star'? No bones about it, he was one of the industry's most courted leading men. He could pick and choose exactly what he did. Layne? She was the barely heard-of writer of the screenplay. Fergus Hann could not know she had written the main role for 'The Thorn Field' with him in mind, just as she could never have imagined her wildest dreams coming true when he was cast in the part.

To say she admired his work would hardly have done justice to her feelings. Oh, she knew all the failings he was supposed to have as a human being from women's magazines but, on screen, he could have you believe anything. Those eyes could freeze the soul or melt the heart at will.

Layne sighed heavily, deciding that in real life, he would appear a huge disappointment and that media opinion would prove true. All that was left was to be professional and do what was being asked of her. Get down to the job in hand.

She waited for Rowan to return with a giant bottle of spring water. Then, together, they went through the workings of the wordprocessor and where everything could be found. Already her head was throbbing with the responsibility, though Layne assured Rowan she would put together a meatier alternative to the mother's role. His look of relief was soured by Layne's plea that, not only should Fergus Hann still have the last say, but that the actor playing the role of his son should be warned of changes at the first opportunity.

By the time darkness had descended, anger had stung Layne into offering any prospective viewer new insights into the nature of the boy's Greek mother.

The original scene had centred on the boy giving his father a long-harboured piece of his mind, after having to save the man from drowning in the swimming pool. Inge's latest intervention resulted in Layne's extinguishing the sympathetic light with which her character was viewed. The boy's mother now assumed a whining, shallow selfishness, almost equal to that of the father's.

As Layne printed up the third copy of her rewrite, she realized the effort had drained her of what little energy she had. Rowan had the sense not to interrupt her and Layne became gnawingly aware that she had eaten nothing since the unappetizing lunch on the aeroplane.

As the printer spewed out the final sheet, Layne heard a girl's voice coming from the track outside.

'There's a light on, Daddy. What was that noise?'

'Shall we have a look?' came the conspiratorial

response, in a voice that made Layne jump. It was unmistakable. How many times had she heard it?

'Yes, yes!' urged the girl.

'Oh no!' groaned Layne to herself.

There was a small knock and the door opened. A large moth flew straight in and fluttered round the light. Somehow, Layne found the strength to turn slowly and calmly towards the newcomers.

Her attention was unexpectedly drawn first to the prettiness of the little face looking up at her and, without thinking, Layne smiled openly.

'Hello,' said the pretty face, whose blue, blue eyes shone happily at this surprise.

Layne squatted down to the child's level. 'Well, hello, flower. And who are you?'

The question had Layne's eyes moving upwards from the child to the parent, who was looking quizzically down on her with equally blue, blue eyes. 'Hi,' he said, knowing no introduction of himself to be necessary, but warning her, 'This is Trouble, with a capital T!' He squeezed his daughter's hand.

The child, in her turn, shook her head in denial. 'It is not! It's Hanna!'

Of course, remembered Layne: Hanna Hann! 'Hello, Hanna, then,' she said, finding the strength to straighten up and look Fergus in the eye. He was taller than she'd expected, so she had to lift her chin. 'I'm Layne Denham.'

There was a just perceptible flash of surprise in the blue eyes as they compared the mental picture of Layne Denham with the woman in flesh.

A sense of shame flooded through Layne as she remembered her unwashed state. If she could ever have foreseen meeting Fergus Hann while looking like a wrung-out dishcloth, she would have curled up and died. She would still make time for that. Now, there was no option but for a small smile of resignation at this irony to play on her lips.

He found the self-possession to hold out a hand. She looked at it carefully before putting her own, much smaller, neater one into it. As he squeezed a greeting, Fergus said, 'Jerry told me he wasn't having er . . . how shall I put it . . .?'

Withdrawing her hand before it betrayed her embarrassment, Layne raised an eyebrow and suggested, 'Any damn writers cluttering up the place?'

Fergus acknowledged the truth of this with a smile and Layne persuaded her tired body not to swoon. She was not a teenage hero-worshipping fanatic.

'It's not the usual practice,' he reminded Layne.

'Well, he changed his mind, at short notice.'

Fergus reached down and swung Hanna up into his arms. 'When did you arrive?'

'This afternoon.'

12

Layne stepped sideways as Fergus looked past her at the papers piled on the printer. He frowned. 'And what's so important you've had to plough straight in?'

There was a whimper from Hanna. The moth had scorched itself and was now flapping around the small room, making her anxious.

'The confrontation scene between Dale and . . . his father, in the pool.'

'What!' Fergus's eyebrows shot together.

'Daddy!' complained Hanna in a wail.

Layne gave him credit: He fixed his attention firmly back on his daughter. 'You, young lady, should be in bed by this time. Come on, we'll get you back to nanny whatever-her-name is.'

'She's Heidi! But I want you!'

'Want, want! I know just what you want, Horrible Hanna . . .'

Fergus pretended to drop the girl but caught her just in time. Hanna giggled. He turned on his heel, warning Layne: 'Don't go away, I'll be back.' And then he was gone.

'No, Daddy . . .'

Layne heard his voice trail off in the distance: 'If Daddy doesn't work to earn money, Hanna will starve away to nothing . . .'

Sinking down onto her chair, Layne noticed her fingers were trembling. Not only had he seen her in this appalling state, but he was coming back!

The last thing she wanted was more aggravation. On the other hand, if it were to be aggravation from Fergus Hann . . .

Still musing on the possibilities, she looked up to see Rowan approaching. He skipped up the steps. 'You must be in need of a break by now.'

Layne lifted the sheaf of papers. 'All done, Rowan. Inge isn't going to like it but at least she can't complain she has nothing to say.'

'I'm sure you've done your best. I'll take them for Jerry to read through.'

Layne got up and sorted them into sets. 'Just leave me this one. Fergus Hann is coming to take a look.'

Rowan's face sank. 'He knows, does he?'

'He and his daughter were walking past and spotted the light,' explained Layne, adding, 'It's probably just as well, Rowan. I think there could have been an almighty blow-up if he'd just been presented with this tomorrow.'

Rowan gave a sigh of resignation. 'You're probably right. I've mentioned it to Tim, the boy playing Dale, and he's not happy.' Rowan clapped a hand to his forehead. 'Oh, oh. Look who's coming.'

Fergus could be seen striding purposefully down the track and there was no escape. Layne tried a soothing smile but her mouth felt dry and tight. She folded her arms across her chest for support.

14

Rowan took the bull by the horns and stepped into the doorway. 'So you're back, Fergus? Good journey?'

Fergus sprang up the steps, threatening the small space and its occupants with his presence. 'No flannel, please, Rowan. What the hell's been going on?'

'It's just that Jerry felt we weren't . . . utilizing Inge's talents to the full.'

Layne watched the blue eyes glitter at Rowan with all the meaning in the world. Fergus corrected Rowan, saying, 'You mean Inge has no intention of taking a back seat? Isn't that more like it? Perhaps Jerry would like the whole screenplay rewritten just to suit Miss Jensen?'

'Now, hold on, Fergus. Have a heart . . .'

'Like Jerry's, you mean?' Fergus waved a hand in Layne's direction without favouring her with a look. 'Good old Jerry, who only demands the presence of a writer when he wants to make a hash of an essential scene. Look! He drags this woman over from England, sticks her in a room so hot you could fry an egg on the wall and without so much as a chance to change her clothes by the look of it and . . .'

Layne sank back into her seat through shame but Fergus took it for weariness. 'Look at her!'

Irritated, Layne managed to complain, 'Layne! Look at Layne! The one the cat dragged in!'

15

Fergus looked suitably contrite. 'I'm sorry. Layne.'

She glanced from one to the other and, pushing her hair away from her face, sighed, 'At least read the rewrite, both of you. Don't decide until you've read it.' Getting to her feet, she reached for her bag. 'Now, if you don't mind, gentlemen, I'd be most grateful for somewhere to lay my scruffy, travel-worn head.'

Fergus pulled the bag from her hand. 'I'll take that. Where've you put Layne, Rowan?'

'The portakabin has a single bed in it . . .'

'Just for while she serves her purpose?' suggested Fergus, angry now.

'No, I didn't mean . . .'

'Anywhere will do,' emphasized Layne, swaying on her feet. 'So long as there's some water on.'

Fergus frowned at Rowan. 'What about our floor of the villa? Not all the rooms are occupied.'

'Not yet . . .' Rowan hesitated.

'Right, the villa it is,' decided Fergus. 'Any complaints from Jerry can be delivered to me personally. And you can tell him I'll be seeing him about *this*.' Fergus waved the rewrite in his hand.

Layne smiled sympathetically at Rowan and patted his shoulder. 'It's not fair your taking all the flak!'

Rowan allowed himself an answering smile.

16

'Just occasionally it is worth it. Sleep well, Layne. And I do appreciate what you've done, even if some people think I don't.'

Layne stumbled behind Fergus in the dark until they reached the light of the villa. He turned into one of the doorways and led the way upstairs. Had she not been so weary, Layne would have savoured these moments, following that admired back and having her pathetic little suitcase carried by the arms that had held more leading ladies than she wished to remember.

She was unaware that she chuckled aloud until the back stopped and turned, so that she almost collided with it.

'What's so funny?' demanded Fergus.

Layne felt drunk with emptiness. She smiled a little stupidly and said, 'I do like a man to take charge.'

He raised a disbelieving eyebrow, just the way he had in the film 'Touch The Trees', and carried on. She wanted to say, 'Yes!!', quite as emphatically as any Wimbledon Championship winner. After this, life could only go downhill.

She allowed him to inspect two vacant rooms and choose one on her behalf.

'This one's got a good view,' he said. 'The mornings will be quite something.'

Layne was sure she agreed. She found herself staring longingly at the bed and blinked herself quickly awake, mumbling something meaningless like, 'That'll be nice.'

He threw her suitcase on the bed and disappeared through a doorway. Within seconds, she could hear rushing water.

When he reappeared, she was standing in the middle of the room, awkwardly wringing her hands.

'Water's on and just right,' he announced.

Layne cleared her throat and forced out a thank-you.

Fergus Hann had turned on her shower. It wasn't going downhill just yet. He took a step towards her and seemed to be searching for words. In the end, he said, 'I didn't mean to be rude, you know. About your . . .'

She watched his eyes move to her body. 'About my . . . bedraggled state . . .?'

Fergus took another step closer. 'No. Well . . .' He shrugged, realizing he couldn't win. 'I'm sorry.'

Layne smiled sympathetically. 'I know you meant well.'

The blue eyes shone gratefully, straight into hers. She was frozen in the glare, unable to blink. 'Can you manage now?'

Giving herself a mental shake, Layne looked down at herself, at her dishevelled blouse and the inch of cleavage, at the creases in her striped cotton trousers and the scuffs on her white shoes. She nodded. 'Oh yes.'

As she looked back up at Fergus, she found him favouring her with an affectionate, crooked smile, as if she were a kitten that had been up the chimney.

'Right,' he declared. 'You get into that shower and, if Hanna the Horrible's drifted into dreamland, I'll read your rewrite with interest . . . not that this whole business doesn't make me angry.'

Too tired to be grateful, she told him, 'Don't waste your energies. Read the script first.'

Layne dared to put a hand on his shoulder and urge him to the door. Though it would have been beyond the comprehension of any devotee of Fergus Hann, just at that moment the temptation offered by the running shower proved the greater of the two.

Glancing briefly back at the room he had chosen for her, she remembered to say, 'And thanks for your help.'

The words sounded final and she found his eyes twinkling with humour, though all he said was, 'I'll let you know what I think of it,' flicking the script with his fingers.

Layne closed the door and, dreamily, began to peel off her clothes. She almost wished she could not manage . . . that she had broken her wrist or something and needed help undoing her buttons and wriggling the trousers from her legs. She crushed the thought before it took flight.

A short time later, luxuriating in the shower, Layne reached out and wrenched the setting to cold. It did not comply. The water remained exactly the same lukewarm temperature offered by the hot setting. Layne was forced to merely imagine the cold drenching, instead, in an attempt to screw down the lid on her emotions.

At last, when she considered herself to be suitably sensible and sober, Layne wrapped herself in the white, fluffy towel provided by the villa and brushed the moisture from her long, blonde hair with determined strokes.

After applying a layer of cooling, perfumed body lotion, she slipped into her thin, satin-finish wrap and spread-eagled on the bed in an ecstasy of relaxation. The fatigue had left her limbs. She felt clean and alive again.

Forty minutes later, Layne realized she was far *too* alive. Chunks of 'The Thorn Field's' screenplay kept appearing in her head. Then, if she closed her eyes tightly, the face of Fergus came to disturb her as well.

Resigned to wakefulness, Layne got up and slid back the glass door to the small balcony. A heavenly scent from the garden hung in the night air. She breathed it in and was filled with a sense of well-being. High-pitched chirrups from the local cricket population serenaded her and, now and again, the fleeting rustle of a scuttling lizard could be heard.

A tapping on the door drew Layne from her reverie. She tiptoed across the tiles in her bare feet and turned the door handle, allowing only a gap of a couple of inches to observe her caller.

'How could you do it?' came Fergus's voice from the dark.

Layne let the door drift back another two inches. Now she could see the flash of a smile.

'It's Inge to a T,' he agreed, clearly delighted.

Too late, Layne realized that flattery got you anywhere. No sooner had she stepped back in pleasant surprise, than he was in the room. Fergus had changed his clothes, too. He was in tight jeans and a blue shirt, the sleeves rolled up.

He smacked the script in the palm of his hand, still smiling, said, 'You did an excellent job on her! Of course, I'm not sure we can allow it. Let's go somewhere to eat and talk about it.'

'Well . . .' Layne pulled the collar of her wrap up high. 'I'm already . . .'

His eyes finished the sentence for her, casting a seemingly casual eye over her state of undress. He pressed on: 'It isn't late and you haven't eaten.'

21

Her stomach agreed by uttering a treacherous, famished groan. Layne hung onto the tie of her wrap but was forced to allow a smile of resignation and the words, 'Oh, dear.'

'Exactly,' said Fergus. 'There's an excellent small eating place off the main street in town. You can always have something light but you'll probably find, after a large brandy, you'll sleep like a baby.'

Layne looked down and noticed her bare toes wriggling nervously. 'All right,' she said quickly, in the hope he had not looked in the same direction.

Fergus was not an actor for nothing. He pretended he had not, offering instead, 'I'll wait by the pool. Throw any old thing on.'

Listening to his steps disappear along the landing, Layne put her hands on her hips and seethed. 'He thinks I always go round like a ragbag!' She turned on her heel and looked through the few contents of her suitcase hanging off a chair. Picking some of them up and examining them, Layne began to suspect he may have been right. At this rate, she thought, he's going to be proved right.

She was sure she had thrown in a thin dress and was beginning to get desperate when it occurred to her to look under the bed. To Layne's relief, the very plain, sleeveless black dress had slipped down by the wall while she was unpacking.

After throwing this on, running a brush through her hair and applying a touch of red to her lips, Layne slipped into sandals, grabbed her handbag and headed for the pool.

'Not bad for such short notice,' remarked Fergus, studying his watch. He looked back up at her and did a double-take. This time, the repeated 'Not bad at all' was directed at Layne's appearance.

She smiled broadly. 'Well, it is just *any old thing*.'

'I did it again, did I?' Fergus reached out and took her hand. 'Sorry.'

Too taken aback to resist the pressure of his fingers, Layne allowed herself to be led along the dark path towards the hire car parked in the drive. He released her to open the passenger door and said, 'Hop in.'

'It's a shame we can't walk on such a lovely evening,' complained Layne, sliding onto the seat.

'Town is a long, dark walk and you are in no state for that tonight.' He slid in beside her, reaching for the ignition as he spoke, so that Layne had no idea how to take the words, 'Maybe when we get to know each other better.'

She concluded it was the sort of practised line forever falling from the lips of men such as Fergus Hann. To be on the safe side, she threw cold water on the suggestion, and said stiffly, 'I expect I'll be flying home in the next twenty-four hours, if it's anything to do with Jerry.'

'Jerry,' said Fergus determinedly, reversing the car onto the main road, 'is not a subject for discussion this evening.'

Layne felt the warmth of his hand brush her leg as Fergus changed gear. She looked quickly away into the blackness of the olive groves.

The soft night air filtered through her part-open window and Layne felt, as the car purred along, that she could easily curl up right there and fall asleep. Fergus had other ideas.

'I may not like the way this has been handled but I'm glad you've come, Layne. I can pick your brains about Joseph Lennox.'

Layne was pretty sure there was nothing she could offer this talented actor concerning the character she had invented for him but she accepted the implied flattery graciously.

'I'll be happy to help if I can.' Not eager to discuss his own character just then, she changed the subject. 'So you think the rewrite could be a bit over the top?' She sensed his smile.

'It's perfect for Inge.'

'But?' urged Layne, studying the profile she knew so well, unable to believe there was no celluloid barrier between them.

'You don't need me to tell you. It's not for the film.'

'No way,' she agreed. 'Nothing should detract from Dale's confrontation with his father.'

The car turned into one of the narrow bends leading into town. 'All we have to do is convince the two unmentionables, Inge and Jerry,' said Fergus casually.

'That's like saying all we have to do is climb Everest and jump off the top!'

'No problem.' She caught the flash of a wolfish grin as the car rolled between street lights. 'It's fine to pretend to live dangerously, just as long as you keep a parachute up your sleeve!'

Once in town, Layne was sorry to feel the car veer away from the main street and the winking lights of the harbour but she knew Fergus would not go out of his way to arouse public interest. On the other hand, she had not considered the use of a disguise.

As the car came to a halt, he reached for the glove compartment, apologizing, 'Forgive me but it helps to take certain precautions.'

Layne watched as Fergus slipped on a pair of black-rimmed spectacles. He climbed out of the car and ruffled up his hair, before coming round to unlock her door. Obediently, she climbed out, blinking at him.

'Your mouth is open, Miss Denham. The idea is to deter people from staring.'

'I'm sorry. I was just trying to think who you remind me of.'

Fergus put a supporting hand beneath her elbow. 'Your favourite uncle or your elder brother?' he suggested. 'In fact, any Tom, Dick or Harry.' Fergus led her in through the doorway of the small restaurant. 'Now, what can I get you to drink?'

'Mineral water, please.'

He looked downcast behind his lenses, repeating with mock dismay the words, 'Mineral water.'

Layne stood her ground. 'If I'm to finish on a large brandy, I think I'll stick to mineral water, thank you.'

'As you wish. Find us a discreet table, will you?'

This was not difficult. The lighting was dim, the tables few and the existing customers Greek. Layne chose the corner furthest from the doorway. As he approached, her eyes flashed recognition.

'Clark Kent!' she declared.

He pretended to trip and spill her water, making her laugh. She felt pleased to witness his chameleon qualities in the flesh.

All at once, her expression turned to one of horror and Layne clapped a hand to her mouth.

'Don't tell me I forgot to change my tights!' blinked Fergus.

'I haven't any money!' declared Layne, clutching her bag tightly. 'Only a bit of English. I was

26

going to change some travellers' cheques tomorrow.'

He shrugged. 'It's hardly the end of the world. I think I can run to a couple of aubergines.'

Layne gave a wan smile. 'I am sorry. I wouldn't just come out . . . expecting a man to pay.'

There was a twinkle in his eye as Fergus spoke. 'No. I could tell you weren't that sort of girl.'

'I do feel awful,' she insisted in earnest. 'I'll pay you back tomorrow.'

Fergus picked up the menu and surveyed it over his spectacles, mumbling, 'That's all right then. I can't do with a woman who doesn't stand her corner.'

Despite herself, Layne had to smile. 'Stop pulling my . . .'

'Never on the first date,' he interrupted. 'It pays not to let things get out of hand.' All at once, he took off his spectacles. 'Pay? Did I say "pay"? Heaven forbid!'

'You're terrible!' complained Layne, smiling despite herself.

They shared a Greek salad while waiting for the main course to arrive. Layne had asked for a simple omelette, while Fergus chose the grilled swordfish.

It was not long before Layne realized the swordfish was not the only thing being grilled. By the time they were halfway through the meal, she had answered questions on her struggling career and was fighting hard to remember the details of the script on which he was quizzing her.

He was surprised she had risked her new-found success by strenuously arguing for a child with a real disability to act the role of Dale.

'I knew the real-life frustrations would bring an edge to the acting of that part,' she explained. 'Besides, these young people need every chance to show they can do any job they set their minds to.'

She found his blue eyes seriously searching hers. 'I understand "The Thorn Field" was conceived out of your own personal experience?' he questioned, gently.

The unexpected joys that occasionally sprang from her late sister's trials with life enabled Layne to talk openly about her fate. 'My younger sister, Lizzie, was born with damage to her brain. She spent what years she had with the minimum of mobility but she was still Lizzie, a person and not a cabbage. She knew more than she could say, she had quite a sense of humour . . . and we loved her.'

His expression was grave. 'But she died.'

Layne nodded. 'Three years ago. We just managed to celebrate her fourteenth birthday.'

'Was it hell?' The expression of genuine concern in Fergus's eyes disturbed Layne. It was unexpected . . . unlike anything she had ever seen in his film roles. Something that made her realize she did not know him at all.

Tears pricked her eyes but she forced a smile and shook her head. 'It seems terrible to say we felt relief but, after months of watching her deteriorate in health, we simply knew that she was free . . . that the fetters of her disability had fallen away and she was whole. I remember her with enormous admiration. She was a fighter.'

'Well, Tim, the actor playing Dale, may have very different problems but he seems to bear out everything you say.'

'Does he? I hope I can see him in action.' Layne felt reassured by what appeared to be genuine interest on Fergus's part.

'We'll make sure you do. It was an eye-opener for me and, if we can relieve ourselves of Inge's ego, we should have a pretty explosive scene on our hands.'

'I must warn you, Fergus, not to blame Jerry for my absence until now. It's true he doesn't have much patience with writers but I did ask for special leave to work on a commission from a television company and, in the end, we had a clause written into the contract to suit both us and the director. I can't say I like the way he handles things but I can't have it both ways.'

'Even so, there is such a thing as common courtesy. And it is useful to have writers accessible, though I have to admit you've been well out of Inge's way until now.' Fergus beckoned the waiter, ordering Metaxas, while observing, 'She has been known to eat people and spit them out.'

'I hope you're exaggerating,' Layne said laughingly, but he merely grinned.

'You certainly landed the boy with parents from hell too! I hope *that* isn't your own experience.'

Layne shook her head. 'Thank heavens, no. I couldn't wish for better.' The subject reminded her. 'You have a beautiful daughter, Fergus.'

He feigned surprise. 'What? Hanna the Horrible?'

'You could have another Shirley Temple on your hands.'

'Heaven forbid! Hanna's dramatics are strictly in the amateur league.'

By the time the white car pulled into the villa drive, its occupants were feeling at peace with the world.

'I certainly ought to sleep easily now,' admitted Layne. 'Thank you for a very pleasant meal, Mr Hann. I intend to repay you.'

Fergus turned, one eyebrow rising suggestively. 'You do?'

Layne looked quickly away, pulling down the hem of her dress. 'As soon as I get my travellers' cheques changed.'

'Ah,' he said.

A sudden silence made her turn. He was studying her quizzically. Just to look at him had her stomach tightening. She tried to sound casual. 'Well, I don't know about you but I'm ready for bed.'

Too late, she bit her tongue. Fergus did not hesitate to agree. 'I've never been more ready.'

There was a dare in his voice. He could have been having fun at her expense or he could have been realizing the role of womanizer preferred by the gossip columns.

A sudden need to escape from this man and the feelings he aroused in her had Layne fumbling in her lap, then leaning forward, feeling around her feet.

'Lost something?' he asked.

Layne had a horrible feeling she had. Her handbag was back at the restaurant. 'Oh no!' she wailed. 'I have. My bag! Damn!'

'No? And with all those travellers' cheques? I'll never get paid now.'

He was still playing with her but Layne looked up at him in desperation. 'I'm sorry, Fergus. Can we go back? Would you mind? I could really kick myself.'

Fergus sat back in his seat, stroking a hand back and forth along the steering wheel. 'Mmmm . . . well, I don't know.'

Layne changed her tone to one of firmness. 'What don't you know?'

'You could give me a little encouragement.'

The nerve!

'What sort of encouragement?' she demanded, presuming she knew very well.

Layne was the recipient of a piercing blue gaze. 'What do you suggest?' He smiled.

She swung the door of the car open. 'I suggest that I go indoors and telephone for a taxi. I am quite capable of retrieving my own handbag without having to – ' she searched for words, concluding – 'prostitute myself!'

His hands dropped from the wheel. 'That's a bit strong, isn't it? I wasn't asking for your body, Ms Denham. Just a goodnight kiss.'

Cross with him for confusing her and cross with herself for misjudging him, Layne exercised a woman's prerogative and made things worse. 'I should imagine you've had enough goodnight kisses to last you a lifetime, *Mister* Hann!' She swung her legs hurriedly out of the car, hissing, 'Goodnight!' before slamming the door shut and stumbling away along the dark path to the villa.

The burst of light from his headlights to help her on her way had Layne cursing with irritation.

No sooner had she got nicely back to the safety of her darkened room, closed the bedroom door and leant back against it, taking deep, deep breaths to calm a treacherously thudding heart, than there was a tapping from the other side of the door.

Layne sighed heavily, switched on the light and turned the handle.

Fergus, one elbow casually resting on the frame, was holding up her bag. 'I think this must be what you were looking for?'

Layne blinked. 'Where was it?'

There was an evil twinkle in his eye. 'I found it on the back seat.'

Layne stated the obvious. 'You knew it was there all along!'

Fergus dissembled. 'After you'd gone, it all came back to me. I remembered lifting it off the back of your chair as I followed you out to the car. I must have thrown it on the back seat and forgotten about it.'

'Forgotten about it?' Layne arched a sceptical eyebrow.

He feigned innocence. '*Yes*, ma'am.'

She shook her head. 'Well, don't you forget that I've seen that look in too many of your films to be taken in by it.'

He leant in towards her. 'You've seen a lot of my films then, have you?'

A turmoil of embarrassment, annoyance and desire boiled within Layne's breast as the blue eyes, lit with amusement, searched her face.

All at once, she flung her bag to one side,

straightened her shoulders and pronounced with determination, 'Oh yes. I worship the very ground you walk on, didn't you know? I am the number one Fergus Hann fanatic.'

'That must be very difficult to say.' He pretended to be unaware of the obvious sarcasm in her tone.

Refusing to be side-tracked, she kept her momentum going. 'I shall just lie back, shall I? Then you can ravish me and notch another one up on the bedpost?'

Suddenly his amusement had died and been replaced by a certain wistfulness. His voice was quiet and not a little disturbing. 'I shouldn't have thought the gutter press had much place in your reading matter.'

Layne swallowed but stood her ground. 'My reading material comes from every facet of life.'

Something made him look up. He moved her aside and strode across the room. Layne stared open-mouthed as he slid the open glass door across to cut off the balcony and night air. 'That was unwise,' he said.

'I may have forgotten to close it but it's a warm enough evening. I like fresh air.' She was affronted that he felt he could do as he pleased in her room.

He shook his head as if she were a hopeless case. 'So naïve. I hope you have some repellent.'

'Repellent?' she repeated, crossing her arms. 'No, but I'll be sure to get some.'

Fergus came back towards her. 'Where were we?'

Layne pointed at the door. He ignored her, studying her face. 'Did anyone ever tell you? You've got green eyes.'

Layne refolded her arms and tapped her foot. 'Just about every man I've ever known.'

'Ah.' Fergus cleared his throat. 'And is that many?'

Her arms stayed folded and her foot kept on tapping. Fergus came to the obvious conclusion, acknowledging, 'I appear to have made nanny angry again.'

The foot stopped tapping, as Layne haughtily tossed a handful of hair back over one shoulder. 'Goodnight, Mr Hann.'

He reached out a hand, tucking some of her hair behind one ear. Layne hung onto her sanity for dear life. Imperceptibly, he moved closer. She felt his fingers brush their way down her cheek and forced herself to stare hard at a button on his shirt, while every nerve in her body was begging her to give in.

The pressure of his fingers beneath her chin, tilting her head up, made it impossible for her to avoid his eyes. At first they seemed to be drinking her in, then they moved to her lips.

'I promise you.' His voice was gentle and persuasive. 'My sole intent was an innocent kiss.'

Layne had trouble finding her voice. When it came, the words were little more than a whisper. 'That wouldn't be wise.'

The back of his finger had begun stroking her throat, up and down, up and down. 'Why not?'

Using all the will-power in the world, Layne forced out the platitude, 'One thing leads to another.'

'Only if you let it.'

Unable to bear much more, Layne shut her eyes tightly. '*Goodnight* . . . Fergus.'

There was a long, hesitant silence, then a quiet sigh of resignation. His hand fell away. 'Goodnight, then.'

Once she heard the turn of the door handle, she found the courage to look at him. He gave her a reluctant smile and voiced the parting shot, 'Sleep well, *if you can.*'

As the door closed behind him, Layne slumped onto the bed, emotionally drained. The trip was already turning into a nightmare. She had expected that meeting this man in person would be a trial but never in her wildest dreams had she dared hope he would show any interest in either her body or her mind.

An already restless night was hardly improved

by the realization that his remarks about repellent had not been facetious. In fact, by the time she had just splothered her third whining mosquito on the plain magnolia walls of her room, they had begun to make horrible sense.

She had, indeed, been naïve. She had always connected midges with Scotland and mosquitoes with Africa. She had expected the Greek night air to hold neither terrors nor nuisance. Greek mosquitoes, she decided, belonged somewhere between the two.

The irksome knowledge that Fergus kept being right did, at least, help in one respect. She was able to wreak bloody vengeance on the insects with far greater accuracy.

CHAPTER 2

As a result of all her early-morning ambushes upon the Greek insect population, Layne was still deep in luxurious, dreaming sleep at eleven o'clock, when consciousness of the outside world began to intrude. The odd shout or rumble into life of a distant car engine permeated her brain and, slowly, Layne curled and stretched into reluctant, semi-wakefulness.

The scampering patter of small feet on the landing had her fumbling for her alarm clock and pulling it towards her. Somewhere among the tousle of hair and sheets she spotted the hour hand. With a shriek of horror, Layne leapt out of bed and pulled back the glass door. Down beneath her balcony she could see Jerry take his glasses off to jab them at Rowan, complaining vehemently about something.

Convinced she was the cause, Layne scooted off to wash and change, achieving a record time. Once at the bottom of the steps, she doubled over, panting, only to look up and see Fergus and Inge, arms linked, with their backs to her at the far end of the pool.

Inge looked sensational in sunglasses, with her dark hair swept back in a long pony-tail, a low-cut red top emphasizing her ample assets and the tightest, shortest shorts Layne had ever seen. Fergus was wearing shorts, too, and Layne cursed his tanned long legs, his muscles bursting with health, and, above all, the latent power in those wide shoulders. A woman could afford to be helplessly feminine with a man like that at her side.

Layne turned quickly away. If the man could make a pass at her, how could he possibly resist the more obvious charms of a woman like Inge Jensen? Of course he could not. This was probably the reason they did not appear to be at loggerheads over the rewrite of the script.

Heading off in search of Rowan, Layne nearly bumped into him rushing round the corner of the villa. 'Oh, thank goodness, Rowan. I overslept. I'm so sorry.'

Rowan was equally apologetic. 'That's the least we could let you do after yesterday. I understand you got something to eat with Fergus. Our hospitality left a lot to be desired, I'm afraid.'

'So what's happening?' asked Layne, filled with a sudden enthusiasm to take on the world to the exclusion of all else.

'Axel decided to do a couple of set-ups with Tim, who, as you know plays Dale, so Jerry's been tied up. He's holding a script meeting over lunch in the villa in about an hour. Why don't you come with me and meet Tim?'

'I'd love to, Rowan. Lead the way.'

Tim had his blond head down puzzling over a crossword as Layne arrived. He was about to scratch his ear with a pencil when Rowan spoke, making him look up.

'Hi,' he said.

Layne was struck by the boy's pale complexion and the blank stare from his wide, light blue eyes. On being introduced, he jabbed his pencil accusingly towards her, shaking his head. 'I don't like the changes and I'm saying so.'

She smiled with relief. 'Good. Neither do I.'

Rowan cleared his throat uncomfortably and quietly made himself scarce.

'Why bother, then?' persisted Tim.

'Other people felt differently. Sometimes we have to compromise, I suppose.'

'That's not a word in Dale's vocabulary, is it?'

Layne laughed, warming to this real-life character, mature beyond his twelve years. 'You obviously know him well.'

For the first time, she detected a glint of humour in his eyes. 'I ought to. I've already learnt every last word off by heart.' The pale face was strangely transformed by a smile as he pointed a finger. 'I hope you know you've made my life very difficult. It's not easy getting your mouth round some of those sentences!'

'I do apologize,' she volunteered, adding, 'but I have it on authority you're more than capable of delivering them to great effect.'

He blinked long eyelashes at her, admitting, 'I enjoy it on the quiet. It helps to work out my frustrations.' He cocked his head, looking past her. 'At last! Here comes Max with the Coke.'

Layne turned to see a good-looking, dark-haired man in his early twenties approaching. He held an armful of cans against his chest.

'This is Layne,' called Tim. 'She wrote the whole thing! Max calls himself my enabler,' he explained.

'Pleased to meet you, Layne.' Max nodded an apology that he was not free to shake hands. 'It's like feeding the five thousand! At least these should keep the boy quiet. I might as well be serving Cleopatra, except, of course, Cleo took *herself* to the toilet.'

'Talking of which . . .' smiled Tim horribly.

Max flapped a hand at him. 'You haven't even drunk anything yet!' He shook his head and made to follow Tim's wheelchair.

'Excuse us,' said Tim, calling back over his

shoulder, 'I'll see you at the meeting and stick to your guns!'

Layne waved after them, only able to guess at the extent of Tim's disability. One thing she saw immediately was why he had been picked for the role.

She viewed the prospect of the script meeting with mixed feelings. On the one, practical, hand, she was starving and in desperate need of food after her late start and, on the other, she was apprehensive in the face of probable opposition from the producer and his favourite star.

It was regrettable that the director, Axel Miller, rarely showed any interest in the actors' lines. His specialities were cinematography and editing, so actors soon learnt to keep any questions on characterisation to a minimum, or to direct these elsewhere. However, knowing she had Tim on her side was reassuring and Layne could only hope Fergus was a man of his word, despite her treatment of him and the obvious temptations offered by Inge.

Determined that, at least, no one should suspect her feelings, she presented herself on time and began to fill her plate with cheese, bread and salad from the buffet.

When Jerry and Rowan walked in, their heads were down in earnest discussion, the rewrite papers stuffed under their arms. Layne took a deep breath and initiated the approach. Jerry's dark eyes darted upwards to peer over his glasses at her.

'It's me,' she explained, still put out at his handling of matters. 'Layne Denham.'

He managed to nod, scratching at unruly curls of black hair, before conceding, 'Good of you to rush over, Layne. I suggest we get lunch and take it through to the annexe. Keep people moving, Rowan. We don't want this to take all day.'

The inevitable wait took its toll on Layne's nervous system. She munched through her food until the others filtered into the annexe. There was a lot of self-conscious throat-clearing, except from Tim, as chairs were lifted from a stack and seats placed haphazardly round an old rectangular table.

Layne was favoured with an unexpected flash of smile from Inge. The scent from her expensive perfume drifted into the room with her. Fergus was the last to arrive, rushing in without any lunch.

Jerry opened the proceedings with a casual reference to the general appreciation to Layne coming out to work on the script at such short notice. He then promptly passed the buck by saying, 'Can we have comments on the rewrite, please?'

Rowan kept his head down, fidgeting with a piece of cotton that was unravelling from his short-sleeved shirt.

Inge was the first to speak. 'I'd like to do it. I think it's what we need.'

Layne felt her mouth fall open. Why it should be what they needed remained unexplained.

'I don't,' said Tim, rolling his chair forward. 'It loses the power of the central action if someone is prattling away on the sidelines and taking her clothes off at the same time.'

Layne tried hard not to smile as Inge shook her head vehemently and said, 'She's the boy's mother. She *has* to be involved. It helps to focus attention on the other two.'

Inge sat back, crossed her bare legs and looked to Jerry for help.

'I agree with Inge,' he said, albeit looking uncomfortable. 'The mother should have some input . . .'

There was a bang as Fergus slammed the flat of his hand down on the table. Everyone jumped. 'You can't do this, Inge. I'm sorry, but this rewrite makes you look more like some shallow tart parading the swimming pool for business!'

Layne swallowed. Was she dreaming or was everything turning out just the opposite of her expectations? Inge was supposed to make that complaint and Fergus should have been upholding the values of the original. Fergus went on. 'Diane Lennox has some depth. This – ' he looked at a loss for words – 'does not.'

Layne realized her mouth was open again. She shut it tightly. Was this his revenge for rejection?

Rowan came to her aid. 'I'm sure Layne didn't intend it to look that way.'

Fergus glanced across at Layne and then it hit her. He was acting for all the life in him. Suddenly, she wanted to laugh. She had no Thespian abilities that she knew of. All eyes seemed to be on her, as this time it was she who cleared her throat.

Taking a deep breath, she managed to keep her voice firm and flat. 'I was asked to do a rewrite and I did the job as best I could under the conditions. Everyone will understand that my preference is for the original. The son has far more to reproach his father for than his mother. I did sense as I was writing last night's script that justice was not being done to Diane Lennox's character . . . and I wonder if it would be better to develop this at a later stage, or have a new scene follow the one in question?'

She forced herself to look at the faces round the table, ending with Fergus. He rewarded her with a wink.

'What do you think, Inge?' urged Jerry. 'They do have a point.'

Inge looked less sure of herself. She certainly did not want to come across to the cinema audience as tarty or shallow. Uncrossing her legs, she leaned forward, encouraging Jerry to peer over his glasses into the depths of her cleavage. 'If Layne could take another look at the later scenes, perhaps she could give Diane a . . . bit more to bite on,' she ventured.

Layne forced a smile. 'I'm sure I could.'

'Yeah!' came the undiplomatic cry from young Tim.

'Well.' A self-satisfied Jerry sat back. 'That seems to be agreed, then. I'm afraid Rowan and I will have to press on but if any of you have any questions for Layne, then this is your chance.'

After Rowan and Jerry took their leave, Layne headed for Tim, but, feeling a warm hand on her shoulder, turned to find Fergus whispering in her ear. 'I think we make a good team.' Before she could make any reply, he had gone.

After receiving a few words of encouragement from Tim, Layne was buttonholed by Inge, who had a few recommendations for the development of Diane's character. They were interrupted by Hanna, who came running into the annexe, sobbing. 'Daddy. I want Daddy!'

Layne rushed towards her. 'Hanna? What's the matter?'

The child looked up with a tear-streaked face. 'Where's Daddy? Nanny Heidi won't wake up.'

Layne turned to Inge. 'D'you think you could find Fergus? I'd better go back to the villa with Hanna and see what's happened.'

46

Layne had to give Inge her due: she walked quickly and calmly outside in pursuit of Fergus, her manner placating the child somewhat.

'Daddy's coming, Hanna,' Layne reassured her. 'Can you show me where your nanny is?'

Hanna nodded and took her by the hand, leading her to the stairs of the villa, and explaining in breathless pants, 'She was sick. Then she went to sleep on the floor.'

They both ran up the stairs and to the far end of the villa, passing through Fergus's suite and Hanna's smaller room, into the nanny's suite. Heidi was lying on the shower-room floor, unconscious but apparently still breathing.

Layne pulled off the scarf she had been wearing to protect the back of her neck, ran to the wash basin and soaked it under the cold tap. 'Nanny will be all right,' she soothed Hanna, as she held the scarf to Heidi's hot temple. The girl began to groan. Layne sighed with relief, dabbing at her neck and cheeks. 'Can you sit up?' she urged.

'Feel sick,' came the dull response.

'Hang on, I'll get some water.'

Layne found a bottle and glass by Fergus's bedside, next to a framed photo of an attractive brunette.

By the time Fergus arrived, Heidi had succeeded in getting some of the water down. He

47

was out of breath but relieved not to see any dead bodies.

'What's the problem?' he asked.

'I don't know,' said Layne. 'Maybe too much sun.'

'What can I do?' came the offer.

Layne decided Heidi felt as if she had a temperature. 'Maybe she'd be better in my room. It's so stuffy in here. Can you lift her?'

Fergus had no problem with that. He swung Heidi into his arms and, though she moaned, Layne was relieved the effort did not make her physically sick. She imagined that Fergus would not have appreciated it.

He deposited the girl on Layne's bed and told her, 'Someone's fetching a medic.'

Layne quickly removed Heidi's shoes, plumped up the pillows behind her head and closed the shutters to cut down on light and sound. 'You go and settle Hanna,' advised Layne. 'I'll stay with Heidi till someone comes.'

Fergus did not argue. He got to the door and turned, announcing, 'You're a brick.'

Layne was still contemplating the lack of romance in this statement when the doctor arrived. She was relieved to find that there would be no communication problem as he was not Greek but a bearded Irishman called Grady, employed to deal with health problems for the duration of filming. She left Heidi alone with him.

When he rejoined her at the top of the stairs, Dr Grady pronounced the cause a virus, with which Heidi had apparently battled some months ago. Being of an especially virulent nature, it had returned to haunt her. The only effective treatment was a further course of antibiotics and avoidance of the searing heat of the day.

A thought struck Layne. 'She's nanny to Fergus Hann's daughter. Is there a chance she may have passed it on to the little girl?'

'We can't be sure but children are surprisingly resilient when it comes to adult illnesses. And if the little girl does show signs, they may well manifest themselves in a completely different way. I wouldn't worry too much . . . just tell Fergus to keep an eye open and make sure she boosts her Vitamin C intake.'

'Thank you, doctor.'

The doctor smiled through his beard. 'No one calls me that. I'm Patrick. And you are?'

'Layne, the writer.'

His eyes lit up and he scratched his beard. 'Really? I once fancied myself as a poet. It's a mercy to everyone the fancy passed. I envy you, Layne.'

'It's not a very practical skill.'

'A good book often has anti-depressant qualities,' he remarked, taking a couple of steps down. 'I'll be back with the antibiotics shortly, or I'll send someone over.'

'Thanks again, then, Patrick.'

He gave a brief wave, leaving Layne to look thoughtfully out at the countryside around her. It was time she started making some notes on likely script revisions. She, too, made her way down the stairs and across to the heat cell that housed her wordprocessor.

Despite starting work in this half-hearted fashion, it was not long before re-reading the script got her imagination moving. She found there were more possibilities for delving into the character of Diane than she could have hoped. It was easy to get carried away and was quite suddenly evening before Layne realized it was time to call a halt. She still had to see if she could hitch a lift into town and find a bank or money exchange. She needed to become solvent.

Just as Layne was leaving the 'office', she heard a car revving in the drive and ran to see if someone was on his or her way out. She was in luck. Max had been given a few hours off by his taskmaster and cheerfully told her to join him.

The town was beginning to liven up following the afternoon siesta. Shops and businesses had reopened and the older Greek men, in their neatly-ironed short-sleeved shirts, were gathering together on seats or at pavement tables to drink coffee and watch the world go by. Wives, sisters and aunts were doing their shopping, accompanied by children and babies.

Like Layne, Max had business to do, but arranged to meet her on the quayside in an hour and then find somewhere to eat. By that time, Layne had been able to relax in the cooling evening air and watch the boats rocking on the water as the tide slapped against the harbour wall.

She began to wonder if Fergus owned an expensive boat. There was one, in particular, that took her eye because of its equally expensive-looking owners who were up on deck. The man was in evening dress, resting one arm on the rail and holding a champagne glass in the other hand. There were also two women deep in conversation, one still wearing dark glasses, dressed in a green top and white trousers, her hair tied back with a matching green scarf. The younger woman, possibly her daughter, smoothed a self-conscious hand down her tight-fitting lemon dress.

At the opposite end of the deck was a man, so casually dressed that he could have been an employee, possibly even the skipper.

Yes, thought Layne, there would be a good story here. The owner looked shifty, as though he could be living off immoral earnings. The scene would go down in the index file of her memory for storage, to be examined for further possibilities at a later date.

* * *

Max proved to be a highly entertaining companion. His clear sexual preferences gave Layne an added insight into her new colleagues and by the time the meal arrived, he had already given her his own lovingly jaundiced view of key members of the crew and cast. Where Fergus was concerned, she found she had competition.

Such was the combination of a good wine and Max's phraseology that when he spoke the words, 'I'd die for an affair with that man. I watch him in action and everything, I tell you, *everything* melts. Mmmm . . . those eyes, the charisma, the cut of his jib. If he asked for the top off my egg, I'd give him a hundred omelettes . . .' Layne almost choked but Max was not to be stopped. 'I tell you, Layne, at a time like this I'd die to be a woman. You don't know how lucky you are. He goes for blondes, too. That isn't a wig, is it? I could borrow it, you see.'

Layne wiped tears of laughter from her eyes and tried to suppress the onset of hiccups but every chuckle brought on another spasm. 'Oh Max! You are . . . you are . . .'

'A One?' he suggested, leaning forward, eyebrows arched to the heavens.

She gave a dreadful snort that brought on another volley of hiccups.

On a sudden change of mood, Max speared a tomato, declaring, 'Oh, don't take any notice of me, dear. I'm all talk.'

She took a deep breath, followed by another glass of wine and was relieved not to be assailed by more hiccups. 'How long have you been with Tim?' she managed.

'The boy? Oh, since he seriously wanted to act, I suppose. About three years. Tim doesn't like to admit it but we're cousins. He's too young to see that acting is camping it up with the best of us.'

'Just how limited is Tim? In mobility, I mean.'

'What you see, basically, is what you get. He wasn't born with disability. A car knocked him off his bike when he was six, injuring his spine. There's no feeling in his legs but the last few months he's had sensation below the waist. There's reason to hope he may improve.'

'I imagine he is determined to.'

'He wasn't before he got this part. *You've* done that for him, Layne.'

Layne was taken aback. 'I had nothing to do with Tim getting the part.'

'Of course you did. You wrote it for a start. How many writers give disabled kids the chance to play opposite a megastar?'

She shook her head. 'Max, I had no idea Fergus Hann would take the role.'

Max jabbed his fork at her. 'I don't believe it! It's tailor-made . . . the womanizing, hard-drinking, fast-living egocentric who farms his kid out to nannies . . .'

Layne was horrified. 'That's Joseph Lennox you're talking about. A *fictional* character.'

'He and Fergus are interchangeable. Couldn't give a damn. That's what I love about him, I suppose.'

She bit her lip. 'Perhaps,' she ventured, 'you shouldn't believe everything you read in the tabloids? Fergus loves his daughter. Everyone can see that.'

Surprisingly, Max gave in. 'Yes. Of course he does. I'm just being a bitch.' He stared hard at Layne's seafood platter. 'You know it's a crime to eat that. You should save it and wear it at Ascot.'

CHAPTER 3

Max returned Layne to the villa just after nine-thirty with the comment, 'We'll have to do this again and start people talking! Hope to see you at the boy's Big Scene.'

'Is it scheduled for tomorrow?'

'There was some frantic rehearsing today.' He shrugged. 'I assumed he wanted me out of his hair tonight so that he could let fly with his lines.'

'Hurray!' Layne rubbed her hands excitedly, before skipping up a couple of the steps and turning to say, 'Thanks for making the evening so enjoyable, Max. You should be in entertainment yourself.'

Already on his way, Max waved a hand and called, 'I doubt people could swallow two megastar helpings in one decade ... Fergus Hann *and* Maxwell Maurice Davy!'

'Probably not,' agreed Layne and ran up the steps, chuckling to herself.

Once outside her room, she was taken aback by

55

the DO NOT DISTURB notice on the door handle. A scribbled note had been stuck to it. It read: *Layne, Fergus has your belongings.*

Swept along by the evening's merriment, Layne had forgotten all about poor Heidi but she could not see what her belongings had to do with Fergus.

Layne might have viewed the prospect of facing him now with far greater reluctance, had Max's avowed obsession not cast him in a more human, more accessible light. Besides, it had all made her laugh. She took a deep breath and strode out along the landing. Once at Fergus's door, she gave two very loud raps.

To her surprise, there was a scamper of small feet and then Hanna's piping voice called, 'Who is it?'

'It's Layne, Hanna.' She hesitated, then repeated, 'Layne Denham.'

The door opened and Hanna, dressed in a long, white nightie with puffed sleeves, rubbed a sleepy eye and said, 'Hello. It's all right to answer to you.'

Layne relaxed. 'I'm sorry, Hanna. I didn't mean to wake you. You go back to sleep.'

Hanna reached out, took Layne's hand and pulled at it. 'You have to come, too,' she said, drawing Layne inside the door. 'Look.' Layne followed Hanna's eyes. Her suitcase was on Fergus's floor. Hanna opened the wardrobe.

What few clothes she had brought were hanging there. 'And look,' said Hanna proudly, fingering the thin pink shift with a cat on the front that Layne used for nightwear. It lay on Fergus's pillow with the waist pinched in, as if laid out by a hotel maid. 'I did that!' announced Hanna.

'It all . . . looks very nice,' managed Layne, while confused thoughts tumbled about her brain.

Hanna drew her on through the next doorway to show off her own bed. 'This is mine. Will you read to me?'

Layne held back the sheet for Hanna to slide in and asked, 'Have you been on your own for long?'

Shaking her head, Hanna told her, 'Dr Patrick stayed with me for a while and I showed him my books but he had to go because someone else's poorly. He's gone to find Daddy but I told him I wasn't frightened.' She informed Layne of this fact with an emphatic shake of the head.

A book of fairy-tales was waved expectantly beneath Layne's nose. There was no option but to give in. She smiled. 'Which one's your favourite, then?'

Layne decided Hanna showed signs of becoming a great organizer. She scrambled for the bed and pulled at Layne, so that she had to perch on the edge. Then Hanna threw over the pages until she got to the right story. Layne took the book from her and cast an eye over the pictures as

Hanna huddled up and peered sleepily over her arm.

Sometime later, when Fergus crept back into the room, he was greeted by the appealing sight of an angelic daughter contented and asleep on the shoulder of a not-so-angelic, dozing Layne Denham.

It was not until she became aware of Hanna's weight being eased off her that Layne's eyes flew open to find Fergus on his knees, tucking his daughter beneath the sheet. Layne was on the point of speaking when he looked up and put a finger to his lips. Together they crept out of the room and Fergus pulled the door to.

'I'm sorry about that,' he said quietly. 'I got delayed. Thanks for putting up with her, especially when you're all in yourself.'

Layne decided Fergus must have an honours degree in making a woman feel at her worst. She bristled and waved a hand towards her suitcase. 'Could you explain the meaning of this?'

Fergus looked round the room. His eyes fell on her nightie so delicately arranged on his bed. 'It doesn't look as if I need to. I can see you've made yourself at home.'

Layne went over to the bed and snatched up the offending object. Her voice rose. 'I didn't put it there. Your daughter is obviously nursing an ambition to become a chambermaid.'

'I shall have to speak to her about that.' A smile lit his eyes. 'It doesn't reflect too favourably on our life-style, does it?'

He saw little humour, however, in Layne's face and explained reasonably, 'It's just until Heidi recovers.'

'Is it?' Layne asked sceptically. 'And what's wrong with the other empty room we looked at?'

'Axel's mother has arrived.'

Layne had not considered this possibility. She persisted. 'What about Heidi's room?'

'Hardly wise, do you think? It's bad enough Hanna having to sleep next door. There's no point in asking for trouble, surely?'

This, too, was horribly reasonable. And yet, Fergus Hann's bed was not. She watched his eyebrows draw together.

'You didn't think . . .? You couldn't have thought . . .?'

'What was I supposed to think when I find I've been removed wholesale into your bedroom. My clothes are in your wardrobe.'

'But – ' he pointed out, with something resembling a smirk – 'mine are not.' To demonstrate, he crossed to the wardrobe and opened the doors. She had no alternative but to acknowledge, silently, the truth of this.

Fergus came back and stood before her, thumbs hooked in the waistband of his jeans. He spoke down to her using a tone he no doubt employed with a recalcitrant Hanna. 'I know this will come as a surprise to you but I don't actually expect women to fall into bed for my favours. I believe the choice should be mutual.'

Layne still managed to maintain one sceptically arched eyebrow. 'You hadn't thought to replace Hanna's nanny either, then?'

His hands fell to his sides. The blue eyes searched hers and seemed to find her wanting. 'All I can say is,' he concluded, stabbing a finger at her, 'I am glad I only have God for a judge and not the almighty cynic, Layne Denham.'

Satisfied to see pain register in the sea-green depths of her eyes, Fergus turned to make for the door. He was halted by the pressure of her hesitant hand on his arm.

Layne bowed her head. 'I'm sorry. I've been ungracious. It is kind of you to let me have your room.' She ventured to look up. 'I appreciate it.'

He glanced down at his sleeve. Layne let her hand drop.

'Still don't trust me, though, do you?' His eyes raked her face for some betrayal of feeling.

She spoke with sincerity. 'I hardly know you, Fergus.'

He reached down and took the elusive hand between his fingers, smoothing out its nervous flutter with repeated stroking. 'I'm easy to know. You're the one with the ice barrier raised.'

She felt the heat of his other hand at her waist. Its pressure brought her within inches of his body. His breath whispered into her hair, 'I don't think it would take much effort to start a thaw.'

Fergus squeezed her hand, drawing it behind his back as he did so. Layne tried not to breathe, with her chin so close to his chest, but her heart betrayed her, bumping so hard and fast she was sure he could feel the urgent beat of it.

'What d'you say?' he urged, so that she was forced to look up into eyes that first smiled encouragement into hers, then fixed firmly on the fruits her lips might have to offer.

It would not have mattered what she said. Her body was already lifting off the ground, her mouth victim to an uncompromising kiss that stifled the words in her throat, crushing her lips. It was a kiss that drained the very lifeblood from her, yet the only thought in her mind was that she never wanted it to end.

When her feet did touch the floor, she swayed with a luscious limpness, so that he had to steady her. She expected to find him viewing her with infuriating amusement but his expression once more reminded her she was confusing the real Fergus with his screen alter ego.

He looked apologetic, almost shocked. Raking a hand through his hair he said, 'Are you all right? I didn't expect total meltdown!'

Layne knew her hair was in disarray, her cheeks were burning and her green eyes were shining unashamedly back up at him. She gave a slightly hysterical laugh. 'What exactly does the man expect when he tries to kiss the life out of Fergus Hann Fanatic Number One?'

He gave her a hard smile. 'A true fanatic would have had me on the floor by now trying to relieve me of my underwear.'

Layne blinked, apparently surprised. 'You mean I've been deluding myself. I'm not really a fan at all?'

His expression relaxed into one of amused indulgence. 'I don't know what the hell you are, Ms Denham . . .'

'Miss,' she emphasized.

'*Miss* Denham, then. You didn't kiss me back, I do know that.'

'I can't recall any opportunity.' Layne put a finger to her throbbing lips. 'Though it is all a bit hazy.'

He caught the finger. 'I'm still here, aren't I? You could wish me goodnight.'

'I do wish you goodnight.' Layne withdrew her hand. 'If you knock me for six with your acting tomorrow, then I may be forced to kiss you back . . . but not before.'

'As a reward for good behaviour? You really

should have been a nanny.' He made for the door and turned. 'Talking of which, you won't mind keeping an eye on my daughter while you enjoy the luxury of my bed, I hope?'

By the time Layne's hands had flown to her hips, the door had closed behind Fergus and she could hear his steps pounding away along the landing.

At last, allowing herself a small smile of triumph, she floated towards his shower room as if on air. Surely she could be permitted this small luxury?

Layne made no attempt to freeze beneath the shower this time. She would hold onto the last ten minutes forever if she could, for there was now no doubt. From here, things had no option but to go downhill.

After patting herself dry, Layne let the towel drop and stared critically at her naked body in the mirror. It wasn't that bad, really. She pushed the damp blonde hair back across her shoulders and swung sideways. Her breasts may have been half the size of Inge's but Layne did not have the rounded hips to counterbalance such curves. She was altogether straighter and slimmer. Her best asset, she knew, was the shape of her legs, and she had that on the greatest authority.

Her father had always told her she had better legs than any model or TV starlet. In fact, he had claimed legs like hers went out with black and white films and he had never expected to see their like again. Layne smiled to herself. She thought of Max and wondered if he would 'die' for her legs as well as her 'wig'.

When Layne opened Fergus's wardrobe to put away her clothes, she saw his sheets piled in the corner. The man had even changed his bed for her. He was getting more wonderful by the second.

The cool expression on the face of the brunette in the photoframe took the edge off her pleasure as Layne peeled back the sheet and slid her legs into his bed. She had heard little of the woman she imagined to be Hanna's mother and, though she began to wonder what her name was and where she was now, Fergus's soft pillow and the perceptible tang of his aftershave tempted Layne to close her eyes.

For a minute or two, she tried to luxuriate in the experience that had been his kiss but, in failing to replay her response in every tiny detail, she drifted into a restful, dreamless sleep.

The last thing Layne expected was to be rudely awoken at five in the morning, firstly by Fergus shaking her into consciousness with questions on his role, and then by Hanna's arrival to demand the cause of the commotion.

Fergus groaned at the appearance of his daughter

and, after failing to coax her back to bed, warned her she had no option. Even in her sleepy state, Layne saw it was too early for heavy-handedness to do the trick. As Fergus marched Hanna back to her room with a tight grip on her wrist, Layne called, 'Hanna, when Daddy's gone to work you can come in to me, if you like. Go back to bed and I'll let you know.'

Hanna glared up at her father with a 'so there!' kind of look, detached herself and retreated behind her door.

'You'll regret that,' warned Fergus, returning to Layne's side.

He was wearing shorts and no shirt but Layne was almost too tired to care. On a stifled yawn, she asked, 'What on earth do you want at this hour? I thought there was a fire or something.'

She felt the weight of his body depress the mattress. 'It's all right for you lie-a-beds. Some people have to be in make-up by five-thirty, you know.'

Layne pulled herself up. 'How vain can you get!'

'That's the acting profession for you, darling!' came the response but any humour soon disappeared. 'There are a couple of things I wanted to ask.'

Layne rolled onto her side to lean on her elbow, sticking her knees in him as she did so. He shifted slightly. 'Sorry,' she said, hitching herself higher

65

up the pillow and fixing him with a glazed green gaze.

'I meant to speak to you about it last night but got distracted,' he said.

She smiled, deliberately playing stupid. 'By what?'

He sighed, as if she were past hope. 'What do you think?'

'Not a lot at this time of the morning.'

'Well, force yourself for a few minutes. Yesterday, Tim and I tried pushing Lennox and son to their limits. It seemed to work.'

Despite herself, Layne found she was concentrating. 'You mean you went further than the written page?'

He nodded. 'Fine,' she said.

'You don't mind?'

'No,' came the flat response.

'I suggested he use a few expletives.'

Layne rocked forwards with greater interest. 'Where exactly?'

'Dale,' he explained, 'is coming round after the asthma attack. He's used up most of his vitriol in the swimming pool, so now he's growling, "I don't want your help" et cetera. It struck me a string of expletives could have Lennox raising a hand to him, stopping himself just in time. It's the first fatherly gesture Dale has ever witnessed. It gives him the chance to react in a number of ways.'

Layne's eyes lit up. 'It would certainly add to the emotional tension,' she agreed.

'We pushed it all the way and it felt right.'

'Then you have my blessing.'

He studied her with some humour. 'You're not just saying that so I'll leave you in peace to snuggle back down in my bed?'

She casually reached down to scratch her foot, acknowledging, 'Well, that, too. But I do know you'll do it right.'

'You can't possibly know. Your interpretation may not remotely resemble mine.'

Layne shook her head exaggeratedly. 'It doesn't matter.'

'Of course it matters. The writer's vision is invaluable; you know that.'

She blinked up at him, then jabbed a finger into the pulp of the pillow, causing a deep depression. 'I think Jerry would take issue with you there. As I see it, I've supplied the virgin words. They're yours to handle as you will. No one has been there before you.'

'*You* have!' He sighed heavily. 'Why do I have the distinct feeling we are going round in circles?'

Layne shrugged. 'You ask for free rein with the script and I say it's your interpretation I want, anyway. What more is there?'

Fergus frowned. 'You could be more explicit? I feel as if you're withholding something I should know.'

She rolled onto her back, cradling her head in her hands, as if that were an end to the matter. His eyes were drawn to the cat stretched across her breasts. Layne wore a smug smile as a thought occurred to her. Was it the gas advertisement that said it was good to have control?

Reluctantly, Fergus got to his feet. From where Layne was lying, he looked a long, long way up. 'You have to be the most infuriating woman I've ever met. And I've met a few, believe me.'

Layne grinned. 'That's an appalling piece of dialogue!'

Fergus smiled a not-very-nice smile. 'I have acted out a lot of romances with excruciating lines and infuriating heroines, who always seem to get the upper hand these days.'

'That's nice to know,' observed Layne cheerfully.

'I tend to prefer the old-fashioned way of dealing with them.' He leant across her, a hand either side of her neck, so she had nowhere to go. The smug smile left Layne's lips. 'Would you like me to elucidate?' he offered quietly.

Finding a voice from somewhere, she managed, 'Not just now, thank you.'

The smile broke into a wolf-like grin. He reached out, tidying a stray strand of her hair, as he explained, 'There were two ways you could force the heroine into submission.' His fingers wandered to the sleeve of her nightdress. He smoothed the material between his finger and thumb.

Layne cleared her throat, forcing herself to sound casual. 'No doubt both a bit politically incorrect today, Fergus.'

His eyes fixed on hers like blue lasers. 'So what would your solution be, Ms Screenwriter?'

'Well . . .' Her brain battled for a way of ridding herself of this disturbing presence. At last, she announced, 'In my book any hero worth his salt would sacrifice his feelings in favour of a better man and ride off into the sunset, to star again another day.'

To her relief, Fergus withdrew, though she still did not like the look in his eye. It occurred to her to suggest, 'Isn't it time you got made up?'

The unpleasant smile returned. 'Don't worry. I'm going.'

'By the way, you've left your shaving things in the shower room.'

He rubbed his chin, concluding, 'I think Lennox will look more convincing with a bit of shadow, don't you?' Layne had not thought of that.

Fergus crossed to Hanna's door and gave a light tap. There was no response. 'You're in luck. You may get an hour's peace.'

Layne looked offended. 'A promise is a promise,' she maintained.

He shook his head as if she were hopeless and made for the door.

'Break a leg, Fergus,' offered Layne.

'I suspect,' he said, opening the door, 'you really mean that.'

Layne dared to sit forward and shrug, giving a shiningly innocent smile. He left without another word.

CHAPTER 4

By nine-thirty that morning, Layne had played Happy Families with Hanna and taken her down to a breakfast of hot, buttered rolls and orange juice. Hanna did not like coffee or the jam that masqueraded as marmalade. Layne was wondering what to do with her charge, when Max appeared. He told her Axel would attempt a shoot of the 'boy's Big Scene' around midday; meantime Tim, Inge and Fergus were working on something else.

'I need to see Rowan and have a word with Heidi before I do anything,' Layne told him.

Max looked down at Hanna. 'Well, I'm going down to the beach for a swim. How do you fancy coming, too, gorgeous?'

Hanna's blue eyes shone hopefully up at Layne. 'Can we all go?'

Layne thought for a minute. 'Well . . .'

'Oh, come on, Layne. You can't come all this way and not sample the Med,' coaxed Max.

Highly tempted, Layne suggested, 'I tell you

what. Hanna and I will get our bathing things together and we'll call on Heidi on the way down. Then, if you and Hanna start making your way to the beach, I can follow on after I've caught up with Rowan. How does that sound?'

'Fine by me,' said Max.

Hanna looked from one to the other and then nodded sagely.

'I'll ask Rowan to let your dad know,' offered Layne.

Ten minutes later, bags in hand, Layne dared to contravene the DO NOT DISTURB order on her door. She knocked lightly. When there was no response, Layne opened the door carefully and looked in.

'Hi,' managed Heidi, just surfacing above the sheets.

'How are you?' asked Layne, holding Hanna back from entering.

'Not as bad as yesterday. Just physically exhausted. I think I need to sleep it off.'

'Well, don't worry. Max and I are taking Hanna down to the beach this morning. Fergus is working all day. You get as much rest as you can. Is there anything you need? Food or water?'

'Don't think so. I've two bottles here and I'm not hungry at all. Besides, Patrick said he'd pop in later today.'

'OK. We'll leave you in peace.'

'I beat Layne at Happy Families this morning!' shouted Hanna proudly.

Heidi managed to wave an acknowledging hand and Layne closed the door quietly.

On her search for Rowan, Layne bumped into the actors taking a break from filming. Seeing Hanna was not with Layne, Fergus asked where she was. Layne felt, as her father, he should already have made it his business to know but she said, 'We're all going down to the beach. Hanna's gone ahead with Max and I'm joining them shortly.'

'With Max?' Fergus looked none too pleased.

She nodded. 'Heidi isn't fit to look after her and I do have work to discuss with Rowan first.'

She felt irked at having to explain herself. She should hardly be answerable for his daughter's welfare. After all, she wasn't the child's replacement nanny. Layne dug her heels in. 'There isn't a problem, is there?'

'What do you think?'

Layne stared at him. Was he saying he did not trust Max with Hanna? She answered determinedly, 'I think there is no problem at all, Fergus. You think what you like. Now, if you'll excuse me, the sooner I see Rowan, the sooner I can join them.'

The walk to the beach was long and hot. By the time Layne got there, she was spitting mad. She might not be the world's greatest judge of character but she recognized Max, at heart, as a kindly-natured man, whose job, after all, was caring for a child.

Whether Fergus had some personal dislike of Max or held some wider prejudice, she had no idea but, in any case, much as she liked the little girl, she had no intention of bearing the responsibility for Hanna.

The beach had a wide sweep so that the score of people already sunbathing seemed to blend into the sands, making it appear almost deserted. As she pushed her feet deep into the soft, white sand and headed for the sparkle of the sea, Layne felt her bad temper dissolve away. She wasted no time in changing into her swimsuit and joining Max and Hanna, who were standing still in water up to Hanna's waist, pointing at their feet. Hanna looked up and giggled as Layne approached. 'The fish are tickling my toes!'

Sure enough, as Layne got into sea about knee-depth, a small shoal of pale fish came darting about her feet, as if in curiosity. 'I wonder what they are?' Layne said aloud to herself.

'Sticklebacks!' came Hanna's decisive answer.

'I don't think sticklebacks can live in salt water. Besides, these haven't got stickles,' pointed out Layne.

Hanna swooped down and tried to scoop the fish

in her hands but they were way ahead of her, scattering and then regrouping when the danger was over.

'I think I'll try getting out of my depths for a while,' said Max. 'I may meet a dolphin and have my life changed forever.'

Layne and Hanna watched Max go, carving his way through the clear, almost waveless water.

'Can I go and meet a dolphin?' asked Hanna.

'Well, I didn't like to disappoint Max,' said Layne in a conspiratorial voice, 'but I don't think there are any dolphins out there just now. You may need to have a boat ride to see the dolphins. Perhaps your father will take you one day.'

Once Max had returned, Layne was free to strike out to sea. The water soon felt pleasant to her body, despite the occasional cool brush of an undercurrent. Eventually, she rolled over and allowed herself to float, eyes closed, beneath the sun's hot rays. All tension evaporated and soon she was drifting aimlessly, enjoying the pure sensation of sea and sun on her skin.

When, at last, she walked back, dripping, to join Max and Hanna, Layne felt at peace with everyone and everything. She hoped now that the icing on the cake would be Tim and Fergus acting their socks off.

The start of the set-up was, in fact, delayed for an hour owing to a fault with some of the equipment. This gave most of the cast, crew, extras and onlookers time to take a more leisurely lunch-break and Fergus took the opportunity to reassure himself that his daughter had been properly looked after.

Hanna told him excitedly about the fish and asked him if they could try and find dolphins. He gave Layne a sideways glance and told his daughter to wait and see.

Layne did her best to keep her distance but, just before he left to change out of his clothes for the take, Fergus caught up with her and tried to make amends. 'I was short with you earlier,' he said, 'and it wasn't your fault. I was just a bit wound up about something. Hanna says she wants to watch, Layne. Do you think you could stay with her? You may need to clap a hand over her mouth. She has a habit of sneezing violently at the wrong moment.'

'All right,' promised Layne, feeling soothed by his attempt at an apology and aware this must have been a time of some tension for the man. A lot could go wrong and the onus to achieve the required results with the minimum of takes weighed heavily on Tim and Fergus. 'Don't worry,' she assured him.

He squeezed her shoulder gratefully and made off.

At last, after a couple of false starts, the action was underway with the character, Dale, already in the

76

swimming pool when Joseph Lennox, his father, emerged in trunks and sunglasses, smoking, coughing and heavily hungover. Somehow Fergus's assimilation of the character had affected him outwardly. Layne could understand how the haggard face could be achieved but his body actually looked thinner, less healthy.

Lennox picked up a yellow inflatable bed from the side of the pool and launched himself from the shallow end, unaware of Dale watching him.

Layne found herself particularly enjoying the subsequent action of Lennox falling asleep with the cigarette still between his lips. This appeared to drop onto the plastic, melting a hole that caused a leak. The inflatable was clearly specially doctored but seemed to genuinely shrivel as a result.

It was not until Lennox's body was half-submerged that he awoke in panic, unable to swim. Dale ignored his cries and watched him go under twice before swimming to help his father. So convincing was Fergus, that Layne felt the need to jump in and save him herself. The attraction of watching him on screen had always been the element of danger in his performance. He always played 'on the edge' and it made for exciting viewing.

Lennox screamed at his son not to let go but the boy released him anyway, informing him in disgust, 'It's only three feet. You're in three feet of water!' Spluttering, with water plastered to his forehead, Lennox accused his son of almost letting him drown and, furious, Dale puffed out his chest in aggression, shouting, 'I wish I had! You get into the pool with a hangover and you can't swim. You've got two working legs but you still can't swim! If I'd been drowning, you couldn't have saved me.'

'I'd have got help, dammit!'

'You're a slob . . . a boozing nicotine addict . . . a wreck!'

'Just hold on a minute . . .'

'No. You hold on . . .'

Layne was only half-aware that Hanna was quietly snoring into her chest, so convinced was she by the gut feeling being vented on the father by Dale. Later, when the child found himself gasping for breath in the throes of an asthma attack, she became aware of her fellow onlookers, all holding their breath. It was a silence you could cut with a knife.

They all watched anxiously as the father carried his boy from the pool and called for a maid to bring his asthma spray. Then, as the spray began to ease Dale's breathing, they experienced both players' emotions in the final interchange of words. The look of triumph on the son's face, as he succeeded in inflicting deep hurt, and the father's expression of shock touched something inside Layne. She suddenly realized tears were sliding down her cheeks and dripping into Hanna's hair.

When Axel finally called a halt to the filming, there was a burst of spontaneous applause. Hanna awoke to find Layne dabbing her cheeks with a tissue.

'Why are you crying?' she asked, concerned.

Layne managed a watery smile. 'It's a sad film.'

'Sad? I'm glad I missed it,' declared Hanna, scrambling to her feet. 'Where is Daddy? Has he finished?'

Layne could see members of the film crew patting both actors on the back, then Inge ran out and kissed Fergus on the cheek.

'I think he'll have to get changed first, Hanna,' said Layne.

But Fergus did not change first. As people drifted off, he picked his way across to Layne and Hanna. He had ruffled a T-shirt through his hair and thrown it over his shoulder but his body was still glistening wet. He had shed the Lennox skin and now walked straighter, broad shoulders held back.

Hanna ran to him, catching hold of his legs. She gave a loud cackle. 'I fell asleep.'

He smiled down at her. 'That's good.' The blue eyes left his daughter and fixed themselves on Layne.

Hanna informed on her. 'Layne's been crying.'

'Has she?' He looked closely at her.

A lump of emotion found its way into Layne's throat. She bent her head and fumbled quickly for a handkerchief. He came closer. 'You OK?'

'Will you make a happy film next time?' demanded Hanna.

'If you're a good girl and fetch me a big towel from upstairs. You'll have to be quick, though. I might catch pneumonia.'

'Two seconds,' agreed Hanna, happy to be of use, and she scampered off.

'Sorry,' Layne managed. 'You both, sort of, knocked me for six.' More bravely now, she looked Fergus in the eye. 'That was . . . breathtaking.'

'I presume that was your intention . . . trying to first drown me and then asphyxiate Tim!' joked Fergus.

She gave a limp smile. 'You know what I mean.'

'We'll have to do a retake though,' Fergus suddenly said.

'What!' Layne couldn't believe it. Their performances had seemed flawless.

He shrugged. 'Glare off the water.'

'I don't know how on earth you can act it again.'

'Well, I wouldn't want to almost drown again until tomorrow! You're happy, that's what matters, apart from being sad, I mean?' he assured himself.

Layne managed a broader smile. 'Lennox is perfect. I'm more than happy.'

'If you're so happy, maybe I should remind you. You owe me!' he informed her.

Layne thought for a minute, then gave a quick gasp. 'Oh, sorry. I'd forgotten. I can give it you now.'

Fergus looked happily surprised. 'You can?'

Layne opened her bag and got out her purse. She withdrew some notes. 'Will that be enough? I'm not very good with drachmas.'

Fergus sighed heavily and took the notes from her hand. He leant them against his damp chest and rolled them up very tightly. Layne blinked in surprise when he pulled the front of her top away from her chest and shoved the notes, none too gently, down between her breasts.

'You have a short memory, Layne Denham. You made me a promise and, as I think you said yourself, a promise is a promise? I'm looking forward to it.' He gave an evil wink, then waved up at Hanna, running down the steps, trailing a large white towel behind her. 'I'll relieve you of my daughter's company in the meantime. Just let me know when I'm wanted, won't you?'

Layne bit her lip. She watched Fergus wrap the towel round his shoulders and lead his daughter away. Why had she opened her big mouth?

Nevertheless, a more important consideration at

that moment was Tim, whom Max had helped straight back into the pool, where the pair whooped and splashed around, relieved that the drama was over, at least for the time being.

'You should come and join us,' called Max, as she approached. 'It's warmer than the sea.'

Layne shook her head but got down to their level, dangling her feet in the shallow end. She was soon joined by Tim.

'What did you think?' he beamed at her, as if he already knew.

'You were nothing short of wonderful,' Layne acknowledged happily, stretching out a hand to shake his. 'I think you'll go far.'

'I think you will, too,' grinned Tim, catching her hand and giving a sudden tug that took her completely by surprise. Her body lurched forward and Layne made an ungainly entry into the swimming pool with water flying up in all directions. Tim laughed his head off, while Max swam to her rescue. Not that this was needed in such shallow waters.

'Are you all right?' Max's hands at her waist steadied Layne as she got, dripping, to her feet. 'I shall write to the little whippersnapper's mother about this!' promised Max.

Layne smoothed a hand over her wet face and up into her hair. 'I take it all back,' she complained, unable to keep the humour from her eyes. 'You're a terrible ham!'

'Apologize, boy,' suggested Max. 'While you've still got the chance.'

Tim splashed his arms, keeping himself afloat. 'Why? I enjoyed it,' he laughed.

'Don't worry,' Layne whispered to Max. 'I'll get him.' She plunged forward and went chasing after Tim. Delighted, he turned and swam away from her. She had almost caught up to him when there was a shout from Max. Both she and Tim turned to find wet bank notes bobbing up and down on the surface. Layne felt herself blush as she realized what had happened.

Between the three of them, they managed to recover Layne's drachmas and, at length, she climbed the steps of the pool. Her wet shorts and top clung tightly to her figure as she emerged.

'Aphrodite,' proclaimed Max, swimming alongside Layne as she walked.

'Never mind Aphrodite,' smiled Layne, squeezing water from a handful of her hair. 'Tell that young man I'll deal with him later.'

She stopped suddenly short, nearly walking smack into Fergus, now wearing a dry T-shirt and shorts. There was one infuriatingly raised eyebrow hovering, as he spoke. 'He should be so lucky. Did nanny get a bit wet?'

Layne pushed the wet notes into the equally wet pocket of her shorts. She longed to shove Fergus in the water and take the smirk off his face but decided the balance of weight was in his favour. Still, she was sufficiently irritated to prod him in the chest. 'As for you.' The promise was a threat. 'Upstairs in sixty seconds or not at all.'

Fergus watched her stride past and sprint up the steps of the villa. Glancing down at the watching Tim and Max, he gave a wink of anticipation and sprinted after her.

Layne held the door back for him as she dripped on his bedroom floor. As soon as Fergus was inside, she closed it. 'Your performance was good,' she said, matter-of-factly. 'I promised a reward . . .' She beckoned him closer. 'So here's a kiss.'

The prospect of her literally damping his ardour spurred Layne into reaching her arms round his neck, pressing her wet top against his dry T-shirt and drawing his mouth onto hers. He remained surprisingly amenable, allowing her to kiss him in a manner that was hard and punishing. 'There,' she announced, releasing him just as briskly.

Pulling away, she found herself backed up against his hands. Their heat penetrated the now cool damp of her top.

Fergus shook his head. 'No,' he said.

Layne tried to push back but the hands blocked her. 'What do you mean, "*No*"?'

His voice was ominously gentle but the smile seemed sympathetic enough. 'We've got our wires a bit crossed, nanny.'

'Don't call me that! What do you mean?' she insisted.

'There was not an ounce of congratulation in that kiss is what I mean. You told me you found my performance *breathtaking*. It made you *more* than happy.' His hands forced her forwards. 'I thought you meant it.'

'I did mean it,' protested Layne.

'Then the least you can do is show it. Try again.'

As his hands urged her forwards, she reached out to stop herself bumping against him, fingers splaying against his chest. She could feel his heart thumping. Half of her wanted to succumb to the luxury of making love to this man, the other half had no wish to see her own desire exposed. 'I've paid my dues,' she maintained, staring ahead.

'You were smacking me down and don't deny it.' His tone was so reasonable and understanding that her stomach did a double somersault.

Layne curled her fingers into her palms, forcing the nails into her flesh. 'You asked for it. You can be very irritating.'

'I understand that, nanny, and I could reform with a bit of strict discipline,' he teased. 'But just this once, I think I deserve the carrot rather than the stick. I was good, after all. You did say I was good,' he persisted.

Layne forced herself to face his blue gaze. She sighed heavily and felt his fingers fan out across her shoulders. The sooner she got this over and done with, the sooner she could get out of her uncomfortably wet clothes. 'All right, but don't ever call me "nanny" again,' she warned.

He did not answer. She had to stretch up to put her lips to his. This time she was far less sure of herself and it proved to be a case of 'she who hesitates'. He moved a hand up to caress her throat, as though she were some delicate piece of porcelain.

Layne's will-power ebbed as he slowly but surely took control, bringing her body into his, parting her lips beneath the coaxing pressure of his mouth. She tipped back her head, at last willing not only to oblige but also to share in the experience of mutual discovery and sensation.

Her hair was smoothed over her shoulders, leaving her neck fully exposed and ripe for exploration. The feel of his lips trailing upwards along the bare flesh lit a fire of anticipation, so that by the time his hot mouth reclaimed hers, desire burned deep. Their kisses grew frenzied and greedy until both knew they were close to spinning out of control.

Drawing apart for breath, only half-seeing each other through lowered eyelids, it seemed the most natural thing in the world for Layne's barrier of wet clothing to be removed. Fergus wasted no time in peeling the clinging top from her body before wrenching it over her damp hair and casting it aside with impatience.

His eyes went from her bare midriff to her breasts, thrusting through the wet film of bra, then up to her smile of impatient welcome. This time when he reached out and caught her, she bumped against his chest.

Her fingers were curling into his hair, bringing his head down to her, when Hanna burst through the door, shouting excitedly, 'Daddy!'

'Hell's teeth!' he hissed, turning slowly in an attempt to obscure Layne's state of undress.

But Hanna had already cottoned on. She had a hand clapped over her mouth.

'What is it?' demanded Fergus.

Hanna's hand fell away and Layne caught a haunted look in the child's eye, as the child concluded sadly, 'Doesn't matter. Bad timing.'

The door slammed behind her and they both listened to the echo of her footsteps as she ran off down the corridor.

As Fergus turned to face Layne, she side-stepped him and lifted her wrap from the door hook. It felt as though a well-deserved bucket of ice-water had been tipped over her.

He shoved a weary hand through his hair, watching regretfully, as Layne shrugged into her wrap.

'I'm sorry about that.'

She spoke coolly. 'The child is entitled to use her own room.'

'That's hardly the point.'

Lifting her damp hair and throwing it over her collar, Layne observed, 'I think the timing was perfect, Fergus. Things were getting . . . out of hand.'

Fergus caught her arm. 'This was something more than "out of hand".'

She pulled it free. 'Well then, something more than "out of hand" must happen to you all the time. A child Hanna's age does not come out with the words "bad timing" without having had previous experience of bad timing or without being warned about it.'

He stepped forward, eyeing her critically. 'Layne, I don't believe you can turn feelings like that on and off like a tap. And Hanna's seen a lot of things on set. She's having to grow up quickly but sometimes she doesn't differentiate between real life and film life.'

Layne blinked at him, wide-eyed. 'You're not trying to tell me you restrict yourself to on-screen relationships! I'm not a complete fool.'

His features relaxed. 'You're by no means a fool. You drew your own conclusions about my private life before you met me. I don't see what has suddenly changed.'

Layne could not trust herself to say anything

other than, 'I think you should go after Hanna.'

'So do I,' he agreed. 'But I don't intend leaving things here.' He moved to the door.

'I'm afraid I do,' she managed. 'I'll vacate your room so you can be with Hanna.'

'No. I'll make other arrangements for her.'

'That's not necessary.'

'You'll keep the room?' His voice was insistent.

Impatient, Layne waved him away, snapping, 'Yes, all right!'

Fergus gave a brief inclination of his head and left.

It had been desperately difficult but Layne knew she had done the right thing. She wasted no time in stripping off her remaining wet clothing and heading for the shower. As water streamed from head to toe, she refused to relive the pleasure she had taken in those minutes of . . . she hesitated to apply the word passion because it seemed so old-fashioned, yet some force beyond herself had overwhelmed her and swept her beyond any awareness of her actions or responses. Passion or not, it was the picture of Hanna's face that now consumed her thoughts. Layne wondered how many times she had worn that haunted look. Despite Fergus's denial, how many times had she seen her father with a different woman, not one of whom was her own mother?

It would be easy, Layne told herself, for Fergus to find solace elsewhere but the knowledge did not reassure her. She was concerned to find it painful.

Realizing, at length, that Hanna had run off with the bath towel, Layne glanced down at her naked body and saw, like her mood, it looked damp and dejected. How she could be so ecstatically happy one minute and so bitterly empty the next, she could not imagine. The most difficult thing of all for her to accept was that Fergus Hann in the flesh was proving infinitely more disturbing than any one of his screen images.

CHAPTER 5

Rowan had his head down when Layne found him, poring over legal documents in one of the trailers. He glanced up when she knocked and gave a smile of relief. 'Oh, it's you. Come in, Layne.'

She approached his desk. 'I just wondered if you'd had Jerry's verdict on the latest rewrite, Rowan? If I'm not going to be needed here, I really ought to sort out my return travel. There's work waiting at home.'

Rowan got to his feet, stretching his back and shoving his hands deep into the pockets of his jeans. 'I'm pretty sure he was discussing it with Inge over drinks last night. I'll let you know as soon as I can.'

'Thanks,' said Layne. 'I'd appreciate it.'

'I'm sorry if we've rather left you to fend for yourself.'

'That's fine with me, though Max . . . and Fergus have been very kind.'

Rowan relaxed into a broad grin. He gave a

slight shake of the head. 'Sorry, it's not usual to hear Fergus and "kind" put together in the same sentence . . . irritable, nit-picking, self-centred, maybe,' he offered.

'Good at his job, though?' urged Layne, trying to maintain an inscrutable expression.

'One of the best,' conceded Rowan, adding a note of caution, 'but, if he is being "kind", take it easy, Layne.'

Layne looked Rowan hard in the eye. 'He must have something of a reputation, if I understand you rightly.'

'I don't think you do. He's not casual about these things. In fact some leading ladies get a decided cold shoulder off set.' He shrugged. 'It's just that the few he goes for never seem to last the course.'

'I wonder why I'm not surprised?'

'It's really nothing to do with me. Maybe the right girl just hasn't come along,' suggested Rowan. 'He may be looking for something extra special.'

Layne allowed herself a smile. 'Or something that doesn't exist? Well, there's no need to worry, Rowan. Life's complicated enough without getting involved with a . . . self-centred nit-picker?'

Rowan relaxed, admitting, 'Maybe I was being a bit cruel. You say you're busy on some other project. What is it?'

'A commission from a TV production company . . . a thriller. At the moment, it gets nowhere fast.'

'Well, it's good to know we haven't put you off writing for life!'

Layne shook her head hopelessly. 'It seems to be in the blood, for better or worse.' She made her way to the door. 'Don't work too hard,' she recommended.

Rowan slumped back in his seat. 'Ha, ha,' came the response, as he waved an ironic farewell.

As she left the trailer, she saw Ari, Max and one of the film crew climb into a jeep and roar away, throwing up clouds of dust. They were heading into town.

The sun had almost set and Layne decided to take the other direction, making for the taverna at the top of the hill. Dressed down for walking, in thin trousers and flat shoes, Layne felt comfortable as she made her way up the rough, winding road. There was the hint of a breeze, moving the still balmy air around, which made walking pleasant and cast a cloak of calm about the thoughts that occupied her mind.

In less than fifteen minutes, she had reached the top of the incline and turned to look out across the dark contours of the hills down to the winking lights of civilization and back to the wide sweep of the bay. It filled her with a sense of peace until, at length, the aroma of Greek cooking drifted by on the breeze, whetting her appetite and reminding her why she had set off.

Layne chose a small, outdoor table overlooking the bay and ordered an Ouzo while she studied the menu. It was still early evening and only two other families were patronizing the taverna.

When her meal of grilled lamb and salad arrived, Layne asked for a glass of red wine and settled down to eat, watching two fishing boats patrolling the dark water's edge, each with its one beam of light trained on the surface.

As time went on, the taverna began to fill up with people. Layne decided against a brandy, paid her bill and headed off back down the road. She had not thought to bring a torch and, except for the occasional passing motorist, the way was pitch dark. She stumbled several times on loose stones, so was not in the greatest of humour when a car burst round the bend and passed her at high speed, causing her to spring onto the rough grass verge for safety.

Layne was even less pleased when the same car squealed to a halt some distance ahead, swung round in a dangerous U-turn and came speeding back towards her on the wrong side of the road, sending stones flying to right and left. By now, the windows were down and she could hear voices shouting and see the outlines of three young men, two of whom leant out, waving their arms at her. All she could make out was the drunken confusion of a language she did not understand.

It did not occur to Layne to fear for her own safety, so concerned was she that they were on the wrong side of the road, but before she could issue any warning at all, a car swung round the bend and was forced to take instant evasive action. It narrowly missed them but skidded across the far side on the loose stones, bumping into the rough grass and just failing to miss a telegraph pole. There was a screech of brakes, a dull bump and a tinkle of glass as one headlamp went black.

Layne sped across the road, hardly caring that the first car was already accelerating away up the hill. Hearing cries, she pulled open the rear door to find a little girl sobbing and screaming at the same time. It was Hanna.

The 'Daddy' for whom she was screaming had thrust his car door open and was climbing out slowly, cursing beneath his breath.

'Are you all right, Hanna? It's Layne. Daddy's coming now.'

Concerned that the little girl may have sustained some injury, Layne carefully helped her out. Finding she was just in shock, she gathered the child in her arms. 'What the devil are you doing here?' snapped Fergus.

Layne glanced up and sucked in her breath, reaching a hand to his forehead. There was a streak of blood running from his eyebrow to his cheek.

Fergus ignored this, lifting Hanna out of her arms and attempting to examine his daughter in the dark.

'What the hell was going on?' he demanded.

'Just a bunch of idiots,' said Layne. 'Thank God you weren't going any faster.'

By now, Hanna was sobbing heartily into Fergus's shoulder.

'I think,' decided Layne, 'if this will drive, we'd better get Patrick to look at you both. You could have concussion. Get in the back and hold onto Hanna.'

'No!' screamed Hanna. 'Not getting back in!'

'Hush,' said Fergus, jogging her up and down, comforting her, as if she were a baby. 'Layne's right. Daddy wants to see Doc Patrick, even if you don't. If we have to walk I may not have any blood left!'

Hanna cast a horrified look at the cut by his eye and Fergus lowered himself into the back with her. She gave a long 'hmmmmm' of dread at first but kept up a brave silence, apart from the odd hiccuping, tearless sob, as Layne found reverse gear and manoeuvred the car back onto the road as gently as she could. The lack of a headlamp forced her to go slowly, so Layne was more than relieved when she turned the limping car into the villa driveway.

She immediately leapt out, giving Fergus the order to get Hanna upstairs to her bedroom while Layne rushed off in search of the doctor. She did not hear him mutter, 'Anything you say, nanny.'

Twenty minutes later, Hanna had been put to bed and Layne was reading to her, while Patrick, Fergus and Rowan discussed the now plastered cut over Fergus's eye.

'Give it a day, Rowan,' Patrick was saying, 'He's got away without stitches but it needs protection.'

Rowan raked a harassed hand through his hair. 'Jerry's going to be really pleased about this. It won't occur to him to thank the gods his lead man is still alive.'

Fergus was equally concerned. 'Can't make-up cover it up?'

Patrick shook his head. 'Even if they could, simply messing with it could start you bleeding again, so it would be wasted effort.'

'Maybe Layne could write something in? Lennox could fall off a chair, drunk, or his wife could throw something at him. Inge would love that. Let Layne sort something out,' suggested Fergus.

'Good idea, except Axel's scheduled to cover scenes preceding the confrontation,' pointed out

Rowan. 'The appearance of a scar could be explained away but the sudden disappearance is something else.' He shook his head. 'There's nothing else for it. You'll be having a day off, Fergus, and I'll have to hope Jerry's well lubricated when he gets back. Axel's probably got enough to shoot round you for one day.'

'I still don't understand how it happened?' enquired Patrick.

'Don't ask me,' said Fergus. 'I swerved to avoid a car but where the hell Layne appeared from, I've no idea.'

'I'll get Ari to exchange the car tomorrow,' volunteered Rowan. 'You're going to need one if you're at a loose end.'

'Hmmmm.' Fergus was already turning back into the doorway but remembered to acknowledge Patrick. 'Thanks, doc.'

'A good stiff brandy, Fergus,' he recommended, adding, 'And a restful night.'

Inside, Fergus found Layne throwing what few clothes she had on the bed. 'What's this?' he asked.

'Hanna will want you nearby tonight,' explained Layne, offering, 'I'll swop with you.'

'No need. I thought I might use Heidi's room.' He held up his hands in self-defence. 'Just for tonight. Patrick has prescribed a restful night,' he assured her.

Layne tried to ignore the meaning in his eye.

'It's time you had your own room back, Fergus.
The last thing you want is to catch Heidi's virus.'

'Too late to worry about that now,' he said
dismissively. 'Besides, Heidi's being packed off
home on doctor's orders, so you can have your
room back tomorrow.'

Layne dropped the blouse she had in her hand.
'What will Hanna do, without a – ' she hesitated to
use the word – 'nanny?'

He shoved his hands into his pockets, regarding
her quizzically. 'She'll have to make do with her
father . . . a poor substitute, I realize.'

'You know I didn't mean that!'

'Do I? I'm not quite sure what goes on in that
head of yours. Now, if you'll throw me the sheets
from the wardrobe, I'll make up my bed.'

Layne fetched the sheets and offered, 'Look, I
can do this. You go and get the rest of your things.'

There was a pitiful whimper of 'Daddy' from
the next room. Fergus smiled and took the sheets
from Layne. 'I'm not one of those helpless men
who expect women to slave for them, though I
appreciate the thought. I should only have to
disturb you a couple more times, then we'll leave
you in peace.'

Fergus pulled the door to behind him and Layne
could hear him soothing Hanna in gentle tones as
she hung up her clothes. She forced down the
feelings of sympathy and affection that had been

bubbling their way to the surface, ever since she saw he was hurt.

Five minutes later, he reappeared with the news that his daughter had nodded off and then he left to collect his things.

When Fergus returned, bag slung over one shoulder, he apologized for the bottle of brandy in his hand, explaining, 'Doctor's orders.'

Layne allowed him a twinkle of humour. 'I believe you.'

He got to the doorway and turned. 'You never did say what you were doing at the scene?'

'I'd eaten at the taverna and was on my way home.'

'Alone?' he enquired.

'Alone,' she acknowledged, 'until assailed by a car full of idiots.'

'You could have ended up a lot worse than us, then.'

'I can look after myself,' she said defensively.

He came back towards her. 'What if we hadn't caused a distraction?'

Layne narrowed her green eyes accusingly. 'You want me to be grateful you almost killed yourself?' The blue eyes returned her accusation and understanding dawned in Layne – 'Ah! *I* was the reason you almost killed yourself, was I?'

He backed down. 'Perhaps we could both have been more cautious.'

Layne's lips tightened. She almost spat the words, 'I take no responsibility for the actions of mindless, drunken youths. I was simply walking home, minding my own business. And I almost wish I'd carried on doing just that.'

Fergus's features relaxed. 'I'm glad you didn't,' he conceded, giving a wave of the bottle. 'Fancy a nightcap?'

Still rattled, Layne folded her arms and shook her head.

'No, of course not,' acknowledged Fergus, recognizing the warning signs. 'I'll wish you goodnight, then.'

Layne maintained her stance, snapping, ''Night.'

As soon as the door closed between them, she gave a huge sigh and let her arms drop to her sides. Too soon, it seemed, for the door reopened briefly. Fergus's voice was almost a whisper, as he pointed out, 'You forgot to toss your hair.'

When she was sure he had gone for good, Layne could not prevent a smile creeping to her lips. If she was not very careful, he would soon know her better than she knew herself.

The sound of a door opening wakened Layne. She had no idea what time of the morning it was. It could have been anything from two to three-thirty. There was the shuffle of feet and then a child's laboured breathing close to her bed. Layne spoke quietly, 'Hanna? Is that you?'

'I want a cuddle,' came the words in the form of a whining demand.

'Daddy's sleeping in Heidi's room, Hanna,' Layne told her. 'He'll give you a cuddle.'

There was a loud, unfeminine sniff. 'You're softer and more snuggly than he is,' pronounced Hanna. 'Well . . .'

There was the sound of movement in Hanna's room and then the voice of Fergus enquiring from the doorway, 'Are you in there, Hanna?'

'Yes,' decided Hanna, jumping onto Layne's bed.

'Well, come out and leave Layne in peace,' he ordered quietly.

Hanna threw herself down, clutching Layne determinedly round the neck.

'It's all right,' managed Layne, trying to breathe. 'I don't mind if you don't.'

He took a couple of steps into the room, peering down at them through the dark. 'You sure?'

'Yes. She just wanted a cuddle.'

Fergus directed the words 'Five minutes, then,' at his daughter and warned Layne, 'Tip her out when you've had enough.'

'Don't worry,' she assured him.

They heard him stub his toe and curse on the way back to his bedroom. Both girls giggled and

Layne managed to rearrange the burden on herself more comfortably, before giving Hanna a reassuring squeeze.

'You smell nice,' observed Hanna.

'Good.'

Hanna shuffled her legs, deciding, 'Daddy likes you.'

Layne sighed inwardly. She said, 'I like him too. Now, shall we try and go to sleep?'

'Hmmmm.' There was a bit more shuffling, then silence. A short time later, quite out of the blue, came a little voice and an accompanying squeeze. 'I love you, Laynie.'

Layne stared into the dark. She felt a tear come from nowhere and slide slowly back into her hair. 'I love you, too, sweetheart,' she said softly.

CHAPTER 6

Fergus had never known his daughter sleep so late. He was already washed and dressed when he ventured into Layne's room and found Layne almost hanging out of one side of the bed. Hanna was facing the other way, quietly snoring into the pillow. He managed to creep past and escape the room undetected.

It was only when he returned some time later with a tray of hot coffee and rolls that he found signs of activity. Hanna had rushed off to the bathroom and Layne was in the process of yawning and pulling the sheet about her, pleased to have the bed to herself again. The arrival of Fergus brought a look of horrified recognition to her face.

'What time is it?' she demanded.

Fergus put the tray down on the table and poured her a cup of coffee. 'Don't worry. You deserve a lie-in after putting up with the Horrible. It's nearly nine.'

Layne ran a self-conscious hand through her

hair as he passed her the coffee and lowered himself onto the edge of the bed. The crispness of his shirt and the tang of aftershave made her want to dive beneath the sheets and hide. Why did he always make her feel like a ragbag?

'Nine?' It sank in slowly. 'To you I suppose that's the best of the day gone?'

The coffee, at least, smelt delicious and reviving. 'Thanks for this,' she managed, answering his gaze shyly over the cup as she drank.

'Hanna and I are having a day out, courtesy of my battle scars.'

Layne glanced up at the dressing above his eye. 'How is it today?'

'Fine. I wondered if you'd like to join us?'

Hanna came skipping back into the room and was about to fling herself onto her father's knee, when he warned her sharply, 'Layne doesn't want hot coffee spilling down her front!'

Hanna stopped short and pushed out her lower lip. 'Sorry,' she mumbled, her blue eyes asking him to love her in spite of it. Few men could have resisted.

He reached out and pulled her gently onto his lap. 'I was just asking Layne if she'd like to have a day out with us.'

Hanna's eyes lit up and Layne could cheerfully have emptied her coffee all over him. He would know as well as she did that this was tantamount to blackmail. 'I probably have work to do,' she said, preparing an escape route.

Fergus squeezed his daughter tightly to stop her twisting her body with excitement. 'No, you don't,' he said. 'I had a word with Rowan. He said Jerry was very pleased with what you'd done and the day was yours.'

Layne knew she was scowling. 'You had a word with Rowan? Did he have anything else to say?'

Fergus shrugged. 'He just said he'd see us this evening. Ari is bringing a car for our use, so there's no problem.'

'Hurray!' shouted Hanna, succeeding in jiggling up and down.

Layne was already shaking her head. 'I don't think so, Fergus.'

Hanna wriggled free of him, appealing to Layne directly. 'Please come, Laynie.' She turned suddenly on her father, eyes alight. 'Can we take a boat to see the dolphins?'

He smiled right into the scowl on Layne's face and said, 'Of course we can.'

She made a mental note to pay him back for this later but, right now, Layne was outnumbered. The coffee cup was carefully removed from her hands by Hanna, so that she could put an arm round Layne's shoulder and assure her, 'We can see the dolphins!'

Only Fergus and Layne knew there was no

guarantee there would be any dolphins but there was no arguing with Hanna's certainty. 'I seem to have no choice,' she concluded flatly.

Hanna turned to Fergus and they exchanged blue-eyed looks and conspiratorial smiles.

By eleven thirty, all three were on the top deck of the ferry from town, heading out towards one of the islands. Layne looked across at Fergus hanging over the rail, pointing things out to Hanna, and appreciated how the simple additions of sunglasses and a hat could reduce him to the ranks of the ordinary man, if he so wished.

The sun beat relentlessly down on a bejewelled, turquoise sea and, despite her qualms, Layne was glad she had been coerced into getting out and seeing the raw beauty that Greece had to offer. Hanna ran from side to side, frightened she might miss the arrival of her beloved dolphins, until Fergus told her to keep still or he would throw her in with them. Layne saw that the little girl knew where the boundaries were. Hanna recognized from the steel entering his voice that no further excesses of behaviour would be tolerated and she had no more wish to challenge him.

Layne found herself wondering how Fergus would cope when Hanna reached her teens. She quickly quashed the thought that, by then, he could have a permanent woman in tow, who would take over the burden of Hanna's adolescence. It worried her that this was not a matter she wished to contemplate. The sooner she was on that flight home, the better for her sanity.

A shout from Fergus had Hanna rushing to his side and Layne made her way along the rail to join them. He was pointing to a boat, holding a dozen or more tourists, some distance away. Accompanying it, as it carved its way through the waters in the opposite direction to the ferry, were anything from five to seven dolphins, some speeding alongside before diving out of sight, others propelling themselves into the air in great leaps.

'Ah, dolphins,' sighed Hanna, a little disappointed they were so far away and not swimming with the ferry.

'Aaaaah.' Fergus pulled a face, mimicking her.

Hanna pulled a face back, smacked him on the leg and then giggled.

'They don't look real,' observed Layne. 'They're *too* perfect.'

Fergus edged down his sunglasses, peered over the top, then pushed them back so that she could not see his expression when he said, 'They're a good omen.'

'What's an omen?' demanded Hanna.

'They're lucky,' he told her.

Her eyes shone up at him and she smiled back out to sea.

'If only everyone could be so easily pleased,' he whispered to Layne.

But, as the day passed, all three were more than easy to please. Fergus hired a car and had Layne direct them to the areas of interest on the island using the map he had borrowed from one of the crew.

First, the car grumbled its way up the steep, winding slopes to the ruins of an old monastery with spectacular views across a plain of olive groves to the rocky outcrops of coast, hyphenated by stretches of white sand, lapped by the blue waters of the Mediterranean. Layne took photographs of Fergus and Hanna, dwarfed beneath a giant yucca, but refused to be photographed herself.

On the coast road, they stopped at a fishing village to admire the coloured boats and silver shoals of fish flashing like jewels below the surface of a crystal clear sea. Layne thumbed through the postcards on stands while Fergus and Hanna disappeared inside a gift shop, only to emerge five minutes later with their hands behind their backs.

'We've got you a present,' Hanna advised her, smiling.

Layne immediately fixed Fergus with a look of suspicion.

'I've got one too,' Hanna reassured her.

Fergus stepped forward and, with a flourish, presented her with a huge floppy sunhat in a red that shouted so deafeningly it made everyone blink. Hanna then waved her own smaller, but equally loud, version triumphantly.

Layne accepted it, laughed and pulled it down over her eyes . . . too late to stop Fergus snatching a quick snap of her with Hanna's automatic. This had a sobering effect and Layne did her best to retrieve some decorum by readjusting the hat to a less ridiculous angle.

After making their way along the shoreline and clambering up a hard slope, shiny with dried grass, to look out across the sea, Hanna pronounced herself unimpressed and hungry. Fergus mimicked the whine in her voice accurately but did not argue as they headed towards one of the seafront tavernas to share the seafood speciality.

Hanna pretended to be horrified when Fergus dangled some cooked tentacles before her eyes but soon gave way to giggling, picking up two circles of grilled squid and peering at him through the holes. Layne loved the infectious hiccup in Hanna's giggle and soon found herself joining in.

It was Fergus, who, finally embarrassed by the attention drawn by the two hysterical women at his table, brought an abrupt end to the meal by getting to his feet.

Layne immediately jumped up, announced, 'My

shout,' and disappeared inside the taverna to settle the bill.

'Why's Laynie going to shout?' demanded a puzzled Hanna.

'Why do you think?' asked Fergus.

'Mmmmm.' Hanna tapped her lips, thinking for a plausible reason, and came up with, 'Because the testacles were tough?'

Fergus grinned. 'It's as good a reason to shout as any.'

The beach they decided on was so deserted, Fergus set aside his hat and sunglasses and threw himself back on his towel.

Hanna stood over him with her hands on her hips. 'Take your shirt off, Daddy!'

He opened one eye. 'Take yours off first.'

'I haven't got one on.'

'Layne has,' he observed with the one eye.

Layne pushed the red floppy hat to the back of her head and smiled smugly at him through her sunglasses. She began to unbutton her blouse with pride. Fergus reached out for his hat and dropped it over his face. He didn't remove it until he heard Hanna's voice offering the compliment. 'That's nice.'

Seeing Layne had been wearing a black and white swimsuit underneath all the time, he complained, 'That isn't fair.'

She put her hat and glasses next to his, announcing, 'Last one in the sea's a slowcoach.'

Already Hanna was struggling to pull her dress over her head but Layne did not wait, streaking across the hot sand and splashing through the shallow water, before thinking to cast a casual backward glance. Hanna was now standing over Fergus with folded arms while he rummaged in the depths of a beach bag. The child was wearing red bikini bottoms but appeared to be waiting for the top. Layne smiled to herself and ploughed on into the cooling sea, making an early dive to acclimatize her body quickly.

Being enveloped by the Mediterranean soon proved therapeutic and Layne basked in the experience, enjoying the feel of the sand giving way beneath her thrusting toes and the relaxing sound of lapping waves.

Fergus, it seemed, had forgotten to pack the vital bikini top and was now making his way towards the water's edge, holding his daughter's hand, trying to joke her out of her disgruntled mood. It did not take long, once Hanna's toes touched the water. Layne thought it surprising that, despite her unusual upbringing, Hanna was, essentially, a naturally happy child.

Fergus still wore his shorts but had discarded the shirt on his daughter's instructions. He looked up to see Layne studying the pair of them from a distance, her head bobbing just above the surface, her hair floating with the gentle movement of the tide. She gave a wave and a contented smile. Making sure Hanna was not looking, Fergus pointed at the child, drew a line around his own nipples, shook his head and then drew the same finger sharply across his throat.

Hanna had chosen this moment to glance up. Layne pointed toward her and Fergus caught on quickly, pretending to smile soothingly down at his daughter. Hanna was not taken in. She bent down, scooped up two palmfuls of water and threw them at him, chuckling to herself.

Layne struck out, swimming parallel with the shoreline, aware that Fergus's body already had an even tan in comparison with her own white skin, untouched by the sun for so long. The simple observation seemed to emphasize the contrast in their life-styles and Layne reminded herself that, though today, far from everyday pressures, they may take pleasure in each other's company, there would always remain a huge gulf of life experience between them.

She would enjoy what she could but prepared herself, at the end of the day, to parcel this time up and keep it apart, putting it on the shelf of her memory, only to be taken down and peeped into when it could be safely viewed as a small but valued piece of her past. She knew she couldn't wish for more.

As she swam back to free Fergus from entertaining

Hanna, she realized it was not going to be easy. He was sitting at the water's edge, his broad back towards her, getting his shorts wet, as he pointed something out in the sand. At that moment, Layne recognized she was the luckiest woman on earth, and that tomorrow, things would definitely deteriorate.

'I'll stay here if you fancy a swim,' offered Layne, as she drew near.

He pushed himself to his feet and said to Hanna, 'You'll be all right if I have a swim with Layne, won't you?'

Hanna nodded and smiled up at them, still poking her finger deep into the sand as she sat with the waves lapping over her legs.

'Come on,' said Fergus. 'Last one to reach Atlantis is what Hanna would term a "Go-slowch" . . .' With this, he splashed off through the water leaving Layne staring.

'Go on,' waved Hanna. 'Quick!'

Layne took a deep breath and made off after him, knowing she could not possibly keep up the pace Fergus was already setting, propelled, as he was, by his long legs and powerful shoulders. Instead, she swam in his direction but did not attempt to race, happy to exercise her body without bursting her lungs with exhaustion.

When he eventually looked back to find a great expanse of water between them, Fergus turned and swam slowly back toward her. 'You'll never make Atlantis that way.'

Layne grinned. 'I was rather hoping a friendly dolphin would give me a ride.'

He rolled onto his back. 'You have a lot in common with my daughter.'

'It's important to have a dream, as the song says,' remarked Layne, following suit, wafting the water through her fingers and casting an eye to shore to reassure herself Hanna was safe.

Fergus floated closer. 'More than most, if you write, I imagine.'

Layne tipped her head back and closed her eyes. 'Too many,' she agreed.

There was a long, restful silence and then Fergus's words, 'You have a natural beauty.'

Wafting the water madly to prevent herself sinking, Layne's eyes flew open. Fergus was circling her slowly. 'You see,' he said. 'You don't even know it.'

She gave a strangulated, embarrassed laugh. 'Is this from the man who has the gift for making me feel like a sack of potatoes?'

'That was never my intention.' He floated closer, reaching out to enclose one of her hands in his so that Layne was forced to make her legs work harder to keep afloat. 'The truth is,' he said, his hand tightening on hers, drawing her nearer. 'I have a very strong fancy for you, Layne Denham.'

Her legs gave way and she only just managed to close her mouth in time to avoid having it filled with water. His arms were suddenly around her, lifting her, his legs intertwined with hers. She found it hard to force the words from her throat, 'We must go back.'

Fergus glanced across to his daughter, then met Layne's eyes with a challenge. His hands left her waist to slide inside the shoulder straps of her swimsuit, peeling them slowly back and down, as if she were a slender fruit ripe for the eating.

The surrender of her breasts to their watery fate, swaying in the palms of his hands, sent a rush of urgent desire flooding through her veins. Layne's fight to stem it was almost undermined by Fergus's savage kiss of desire.

'Please!' she gasped, pushing at him as soon as his lips left hers. 'Let me go, Fergus.'

He allowed her to float away, retrieving the wayward straps of her swimsuit as she did so. Intensity deepened the blue of his eyes as he spoke, his voice almost a growl. 'Don't be afraid to enjoy yourself!'

'Be honest!' Layne hissed back at him, 'What you want is sex, Fergus. Not me. I'm going back to Hanna!'

He gave a sad smile and rolled sideways. 'You're going back to safety. It's not the same thing.

That's twice now you've used Hanna to escape your own feelings,' he called after her.

Speechless that he could suggest such a thing, Layne struck out for the shore but Fergus kept pace with her, saying only, 'We can all be hurt by the truth as others see it.'

Normal service had to be resumed speedily for Hanna's sake and both parties were prepared to admit to themselves that there was a grain of truth in what the other had said, so, although the first five minutes of sunbathing was distinctly subdued, it was not long before Hanna had persuaded Layne to oil her shoulders, while Hanna herself squirted suncream on her father's chest.

At least, Fergus thought he had packed the suncream. It did not take long for all three to notice that the 'cream' was not being absorbed and had a distinctly minty smell.

'Oh no!' shouted Hanna in delight, holding up the tube.

'Daddy's brought the toothpaste!' She collapsed in a heap of giggles, while Layne was unable to halt the smile creeping to her lips.

Resigned, Fergus eyed the white patch setting in the sun among the hairs on his chest, sighed heavily and reached inside the beach bag for wet wipes.

Suddenly, Hanna got up and skipped away to the shore, laughing her little head off.

'I'm changing her name from Hanna the Horrible to Hanna the Hysterical,' he announced, applying the third wet wipe. 'At least I shouldn't have halitosis of the chest.'

Layne finally snorted with uncontrolled laughter and he threw his hands up, doing an impression of a frustrated tennis player, 'Why does no one take me seriously!'

An hour later, an invasion of human life in the form of two noisy young couples had Fergus, Hanna and Layne packing up at the double, with Fergus reaching for his hat and sunglasses. Aware they were being watched as they left, Layne allowed Fergus the liberty of draping his arm fondly about her waist. Hanna, whose legs were draped round her father's neck, nearly gave the game away by clinging too tightly to his hat and nothing else but Fergus managed major readjustment without losing either hat or daughter.

After deciding it was too hot to do much more in the way of sightseeing, all three plumped for the return ferry and a meal in a taverna on the way back. Halfway through that meal, Hanna suddenly put her head down in the middle of the salad and began to snore.

Layne and Fergus smiled at one another over the child's head and the smile lingered long enough for each to recognize they were sharing something special.

Fergus shifted Hanna onto his knee, so that her head lolled against his chest.

'I'm so glad the dolphins came to see her,' said Layne.

'They didn't have any option,' he informed her.

Layne's green eyes shone with gratitude. 'Thank you for a lovely day.'

'It isn't over yet,' he promised, stroking his daughter's hair, as he considered Layne's features carefully, concluding quietly, 'You were wrong, you know.'

Layne raised an eyebrow in curiosity. 'Wrong about what?'

'The sex.'

She blinked incomprehension.

'I've decided it's you I'm after, not the sex.' Fergus gave a casual shrug but there was a twinkle of humour in his eyes. 'I can get that anytime.'

'I don't doubt that,' she remarked sourly, choosing to ignore the joke.

He persevered. 'You think I could be attractive to the opposite sex, then?'

Layne gave a wry smile. 'It's just possible. But I wouldn't want you to get too conceited about it.'

'Would it be conceited to suggest I could be ever so slightly attractive to you?'

She sat back, scratching her chin and pretending to eye him objectively, 'Well . . .'

He leant forward, holding Hanna tight, and speaking in a half-whisper, said, 'Forget the fact, of course, that you allowed me to fondle your breasts, which was purely an aberration on your part . . .'

'Fergus!' hissed Layne, her eyes flying to Hanna and then the surrounding tables. At last she threw an angry glare in his direction. 'Do you mind!'

'Not at all.' His voice grew louder. 'I'd do it again quite happily but you haven't answered my question.'

Deciding she needed to shut him up for once and for all, Layne smacked a hand down on the table and said, at equal volume, 'All right. You have a wonderful body and eyes to melt stone but I'm sorry to inform you that I only want YOU for the sex.'

With a slight smile, he conceded, 'It's a start.'

There was a long moan from Hanna, changing Layne's look of triumph to one of guilt. 'I think it's time we went,' she recommended.

'Have another drink first,' offered Fergus.

Layne shook her head. 'My tongue has been loosened quite enough, thank you. Who knows what I might say next?' She did not give him a chance to answer. 'Come on. Surely Hanna needs to be tucked up in bed?'

Fergus sighed. 'If nanny says so.'

She got to her feet and scowled down at him, before declaring coolly, 'I'll settle the bill.'

He surveyed her with admiration. 'Twice in one day! Now that's my girl!'

Layne spun on her heel, ignoring the infuriating wink.

At the car, Fergus laid Hanna carefully across the back seat. As he straightened up, Layne reached out to open her door but he put a hand out to stop her. 'Layne, I'm glad you came. You made Hanna's day. It is appreciated.'

A little overcome by the sincerity of these remarks, Layne kept her eyes on his shirt collar, flapping repeatedly in the stiffening evening breeze. 'I've given up all thoughts of revenge for being coerced,' she admitted, before forcing herself to look at him. 'Though I doubt I made Hanna's day. The dolphins did that.'

'You made mine, then,' confessed Fergus.

'Stop saying nice things to me!' Layne's complaint was not without humour.

He smiled. 'Why?'

'I just . . .' She shrugged. 'Don't deserve any attention from you at all.' Her words belied her reaction when she saw the kiss coming. She fell into it, a willing partner. It seemed a perfect end to a perfect day until, that is, she managed to ruin it all on the last stage of the journey.

A combination of curiosity and conscience had her asking him, 'Just how much that is written about you is the truth, Fergus?'

'The same as with anyone, I imagine. Very little.'

'So tales of your wild past are pure fabrication?'

He gave her a quick sideways glance. 'To which aspects of my "wild past" do you refer, may I ask?'

'I'm not sure I dare say,' she replied, suddenly unsure.

There was humour in his voice. 'There's a first time for everything, I suppose. Do you want me to say it for you? Fast-living, hard-drinking and broken hearts scattered in my wake?'

'Well . . . I don't think I'd have put it quite like that.'

Fergus did not seem to hear her. He ploughed on, 'Money and fame came early. I was too young to handle it with maturity and too vain to see through the flattery. It's a great age to have your ego massaged and you revel in it. Only too late do you realize you've screwed up a fair chunk of your life. Even so, I doubt I behaved really badly all that often . . . but you know as well as I do, those are the times that provide the mire in which the press swine love to wallow.'

'It does seem as if there are no ethics any more,' agreed Layne, as if talking to herself. 'Everyone's considered fair game, no matter what the consequences.'

'Oh, don't get me wrong. I'm not saying there aren't plenty of puffed-up celebrities who simply beg for some reporter to deflate their egos with the stab of a sharpened pencil . . . but premeditated character assassination is something else.'

'I suppose the wise ones soon learn to be discreet,' murmured Layne, surprised to find the car slowing.

Fergus pulled on the wheel and the car rolled a few yards off the road. Layne threw him a questioning look as the handbrake creaked on. He turned to face her, one hand still on the steering wheel, apparently continuing the conversation. 'Or reform, Layne. People do reform. They usually mature with age. All that was a long time ago, now,' he pointed out.

'I know,' she conceded gently. 'I'm sorry. I shouldn't have brought it up.'

'I expect I should be pleased you're showing interest.'

Somehow there was a question left hovering in the air but Fergus released the handbrake. As the car moved off, he added, 'And I really wouldn't like you to think I bore any resemblance to the monster you've created in Lennox.'

They hadn't travelled very far when Fergus jammed on the footbrake, this time bringing the car lurching to a halt. He turned once more to face Layne but his expression had changed. She was convinced he was about to say something extremely unpleasant when a voice piped up from the back.

'Are we home, Daddy?'

Fergus managed to keep his voice level with reassurance, saying softly, 'Nearly there, chicken.'

'Quack, quack,' said Hanna sleepily, snuggling down again.

Instead of smiling at the absurdity of his daughter's logic, Layne and Fergus stared at each other. She knew he had stumbled across an unwanted discovery and that her own carelessness had brought it about.

'That's it, isn't it!' he concluded, trying to keep his voice down.

'What?' The question was miserably unconvincing, defeated before it was spoken.

'All this business about "play Lennox however you like"! Dammit, you really think he and I are one and the same person!'

Angry now, as his own words sank in, Fergus put the car firmly into gear and drove away up the road. His foot weighed heavily on the accelerator for the remainder of the journey.

Layne was at a loss for words. She took one look at the way his jaw was set and dared not look again.

Only when they swerved off the road and into

the villa drive did Fergus announce, 'I believe choosing the right to silence can now be construed as guilt.'

'Fergus, listen to me . . .'

He opened his door but turned on her sharply, 'And you have the nerve to talk about "ethics"!'

Layne did not wait for him to remove Hanna. She made her way along the track, slowly at first, then broke into a run. By the time she got to the top of the steps, she had an overwhelming desire to cry but swallowed it down and rushed ahead to his room.

The important thing now, clearly, was to erase any reminder to him of her existence and Layne threw herself into packing her things as quickly as she could.

Fergus had to practically climb over her to put the sleeping Hanna into bed. When he closed the door on his daughter, he approached Layne, who was frantically throwing things out of the wardrobe onto the bed.

'That is childish,' came the rebuke.

'I'm saving you the trouble of kicking me out,' she stated flatly, continuing unhindered.

'You don't intend to explain yourself, then?'

The green eyes glittered up at him. 'I doubt it would do any good. You've clearly made up your mind.' She returned to the job in hand but he caught hold of her arm, swinging her round to face him.

125

'You don't exactly paint a flattering picture, Layne. Is that how you really feel?'

'I didn't think you found "flattery" desirable any more?' responded Layne, pulling her arm away.

His eyes narrowed. 'Now you're fencing with words.'

'It's my job, isn't it?' she snapped, soon realizing he thought she was being too clever for her own good.

Fergus sat down on the bed in front of her, separating her from the clothes she was trying to pack. 'Would you sooner I was like the flamboyant Max, hmmm?' He tossed his head and held up a limp wrist, presenting an appalling caricature that horrified Layne, not least for its hint of accuracy that produced instant recognition and thus guilt.

'I don't know what the hell you . . .'

'You went out with him, didn't you?' Fergus employed his own voice for this accusation.

'Now who's being childish?' retorted Layne, wrenching away at a pair of trousers trapped by Fergus's weight.

Reluctantly, he got to his feet, voicing the suggestion, 'Maybe you're secretly disappointed I haven't lived *down* to your expectations, is that it? You'd have much preferred me to want you for the sex, just so that I didn't upset your preconceived ideas. What a disappointment I must be!'

126

Fury boiled in Layne's breast. She turned on him, waving the trousers in the air for emphasis.

'Well, that really is rich! If you were honest with yourself, you'd see the disappointment is yours. You seem to have spent every day since my arrival trying to worm your way into my knickers!'

Fergus caught hold of the waving trousers and held on tightly, jerking her towards him and growling with menace. 'The only good reason for wanting to get into your knickers right now would be to smack your smart arse good and hard!'

There was a loud howl from Hanna's room and Fergus shoved Layne out of his way as he strode off to calm his daughter, muttering a string of expletives under his breath.

Layne wasted no time. She grabbed what she could in her arms and kicked her case back along the landing to the room vacated by Heidi.

There was no way, she knew, she would ever sleep, still spitting, as she was, with vengeful anger.

After throwing her things on the bed, Layne did an about-turn and headed back downstairs. There was supposed to be a bar in one of the trailers. She intended to drink herself into oblivion.

On finding the place, Layne suddenly wished she had made a less dramatic entrance, for the only people drinking were Max, Inge and two of the make-up girls.

'Ah, come in, Layne,' called Max, waving her over. 'Had a good day? We missed you.'

She opened her mouth to speak but, to her shame, was shaken by a sudden, convulsive sob. In no time, hot, uncontrollable tears were coursing down her cheeks.

Inge and Max stared at each other, before Max drew Layne into the seat next to him, trying to coax out the trouble. All Layne could manage to get out was a tearful, 'I'm sorry!'

'I'll get her something strong,' promised Inge, moving to the bar.

'Come on, dear,' soothed Max. 'It can't be that bad, can it?'

At first Layne nodded, then she shook her head and forced out the name 'Fergus' on a hiccup.

By the time Inge returned, Max imagined he knew the possibilities. Either Layne's attentions to Fergus had been rejected, or Fergus had used her and then rejected her. When Inge placed the colourless liquid in front of Layne, Max leaned over and whispered the Fergus word. Inge and Max exchanged knowing looks.

'Drink this,' he urged Layne, holding up the glass, and, grateful for aid of any kind, Layne took it and drank.

Firewater raced down her throat and through her veins, making her gasp for air. She coughed.

'I must try some of that,' Max told Inge.

Inge took a seat across from her, fixing Layne with dark, knowing eyes. 'You don't have to tell us, Layne,' she sympathized. 'Fergus is a difficult man.'

A small voice somewhere in the depths of Layne's soul wanted to say she was wrong but it was fighting against the bluster of anger and hurt pride, tempered only by sadness that she had been the one to bring it about.

It proved unnecessary to go further, anyway, as Inge and Max were making it up as they went along. 'You can't have a genius without gaping flaws in character,' decided Max. 'It simply isn't possible.'

'He's an egotist, not a genius,' Inge explained. 'Some people feed off the camera. I've seen it often. The knowledge they are being looked at drives them to extremes of performance.'

Layne found herself wanting to smile at the irony of this remark and took another gulp of the firewater to stifle her responses.

'You couldn't rustle up another couple of those?' Max asked Inge.

'I'll give it a try and I think one more will put Layne back on track,' she said, and soon returned with three glasses of firewater, one for each of them.

'I don't think I should,' whispered Layne, trying to find her voice through the flame licking her throat.

'Nonsense,' said Max. 'you need all the Dutch courage you can get. Are you still supposed to be sleeping with him?'

Layne blinked, horrified. 'I never have slept with him!'

Inge slammed her glass down, disgusted. 'Well! There you are! What sort of man lures you into his room and *then* rejects you!'

'You've got it wrong!' insisted Layne.

Inge patted her hand sympathetically. 'Here, you are among friends. I tell you, if a woman lying in his bed cannot persuade Fergus to release his passions, then what can?'

Max offered the arch suggestion, 'A man?'

At last, Layne found her humour, unable to keep it from her voice, as she desperately tried once more to put the record straight, 'I have never lain in Fergus's bed in an attempt to "release his passions"! No doubt he'd rather I had,' she added on a sour note.

'No doubt,' agreed Inge. She looked down at her ample assets. 'If I poke him in the eye with one of these, I think he would have to notice.'

Layne had difficulty controlling the smile curling her lips, as she pictured the scene. She took another mouthful of the drink and ventured,

'It would serve him right.' It smacked of sweet revenge. She heard herself giggle.

All three lowered their heads and giggled like children cooking up mischief. A thought struck Layne, 'Where is Jerry, anyway?'

Inge sat back. 'Would you believe it? He's deserted his darling Inge in favour of Axel's ageing mother! Rowan, Axel, Jerry ... three men to entertain one woman!'

'It has nothing to do with the fact that Axel's mother's money is financing a third of the movie,' said Max drily.

'Hmmmm,' agreed Inge. 'I know on which side my butter's breaded.' She got to her feet. 'My trouble is I do like dark men. Still, perhaps I should go and wish Fergus a goodnight.'

Layne looked from Inge's staring dark eyes into her glass and held it up. 'Just what have you put in this?'

Inge swayed a little and tapped the side of her nose, saying nothing but, 'Ah-Ha! Wouldn't you know to like?'

'Don't go to Fergus tonight, Inge,' advised Layne, trying to be serious. 'He's ... best left.'

'Tonight,' concluded Inge, 'you, Layne, are not the best left judge of this.'

Max and Layne watched her swing away and disappear through the door. Max's hands flew to his face. 'Dearie me!' he snorted, but there was a twinkle in his eye that made both of them burst out laughing.

Layne forced herself to admit, 'I've done a terrible thing.'

'What?'

'Sent Inge to her doom. She's got the wrong end of the stick.'

'Heaven help her then,' announced Max to an explosion of helpless laughter.

It was only when this had thoroughly subsided that Layne sobered herself up mentally.

'Max?'

'Yes?'

'Can I ask you something?'

'I'm not too good as an agony aunt, Layne. I usually give the wrong advice.'

'No. I don't want advice.'

'Well, fire away, then.'

'Does Fergus . . . like you?'

'I wish!'

She had to smile but persevered. 'No. I mean have you two ever had a disagreement?'

He shrugged. 'Not to my knowledge. In fact, I once asked him to pass me Tim's make-up when one of the girls had fallen sick. When I'd finished doing the boy's face, Fergus told me I was in the wrong job. I took it as a compliment.'

'I expect that's how he meant it,' murmured Layne, uncertain in her own mind.

'Why do you ask?'

'Oh . . . it's only that he threw it in my face that we'd been out together, that's all.'

Max viewed her sympathetically. 'Hmmmm. Sounds like the green-eyed monster might be dripping poison, don't you think? Even so, he knows I'm not exactly straight. But then, if you won't sleep with him, maybe he's worried you're not, either.'

The thought cheered her up. 'I had never thought of that, I must admit.' On impulse, she kissed Max on the cheek. 'I love you, Max.'

He wagged a finger at her. 'Only because you know you're safe, madam.' Getting suddenly to his feet, Max announced, 'Come on, it's time we got you back. Besides, I'm beginning to despair of finding Inge Jensen alive!'

By the time they reached the side of the villa, they could hear loud splashing noises.

'You didn't write a hippo into the screenplay, did you?' enquired Max.

Layne shook her head. Then the same thought occurred to them both at the same time. Max and Layne exchanged a long stare, then ran round the side of the villa to the swimming pool.

They had no idea how to react to the sight that greeted them. Fergus was acting as lifeguard, hauling a spluttering, soaking Inge backwards through the water to the shallow end. As he pulled her to unsteady feet at the bottom of the steps, he warned, 'Now for Pete's sake don't ask for the kiss of life.'

Max let out a loud 'Ohhhh!' as Inge flung out a hand to slap Fergus's face, destabilizing herself, only to sink down into the water again. This time, Fergus let her flounder her own way out and dripped his way up the steps ahead of her.

As he came level with Max and Layne, he still could not quite believe what had happened. 'How the hell was I supposed to know she couldn't swim? I should have let her drown, throwing herself at me like some wanton . . .'

'You didn't chuck her in!' gasped Max, eyes alight with humour, following the bedraggled figure clambering out of the pool . . . her dress firmly stuck to all the wrong places, hair plastered flat against her head, completely covering one eye.

Fergus glared down at Layne. 'She picked a bad time,' he claimed in his defence.

Layne glared back. 'She'd been drinking, that's all.'

Fergus looked over his shoulder at Inge. 'I think you'll find she's sober now.'

Max skirted the two of them, feeling sorry for Inge. 'I'll go and see she's all right.'

Layne sighed. It looked as if she would have to accompany Fergus up the steps. He did not wait, intent on finding a towel to dry himself off. Only at the top of the steps did he turn as if to say something, then thought better of it, shoving a hand through his wet hair. She watched him drip his way along the landing, shirt clinging to his broad back, feet squelching in trainers, and slapped a swift hand to her mouth to stop the bubble of amusement bursting out loud.

At that moment, he swung round, pointing an accusing finger at her. 'Don't you dare. Not one word!' he threatened.

It was some relief to find he, too, saw the humour in the situation and, as the door slammed shut behind him, Layne dropped her hand and allowed the bubble to take flight and then disintegrate in one almighty explosion of mirth.

By the time she'd managed to fling herself inside her room, helpless hysteria had taken hold and had her slowly sliding the length of the door to the floor, body convulsed, silent tears coursing down a severely aching face.

CHAPTER 7

The next morning, things did not seem so funny
. . . not funny at all. Workmen were demolishing a
tower block in her head, not in the usual way, but
by drilling, hammering and chiselling all at the
same time. One by one a great slab would be
dislodged and thud to earth, in turn releasing a
blunt shaft of pain that soared from the base of her
skull out through the crown of her head.

Layne had never known anything like it. It had
been years since a hangover had held her in its
vice-like grip but she was convinced it had never
been as miserable as this. The only time she felt
nausea was when she succeeded in shifting her
body, so she stayed in one place. Her body had
proved difficult to shift, anyway. It was like a dead
weight and totally detached from the alien war
battling in her head.

There was no sense of time or place. Just
survival in a hell, which was, she suspected, of
her own making and no less than she deserved.

What she thought to be another dread thud turned out to be a knock on the door. She did not care. No voice volunteered an answer, even when the door opened and there was the rustle of whispering somewhere on the outer limits of her sensitivities.

Layne did try hard to flutter her eyes open when she felt a draught from the cover being lifted and a girlie voice crying in anguish, 'Daddy, Daddy! Laynie's dead!'

There was the blurred image of a man's face surrounded by blinding light. Layne groaned, screwing her eyes tight, half-aware she had seen him in dreams or on the telly. His voice came nearer, at the same time calming the child's cries.

'It's after one, Layne.'

What was he telling her for? She wasn't Layne, was she? What was he doing there, anyway? Shouldn't he be in make-up?

God, was it Fergus? That's who it was. And it was after one. What? In the afternoon? Why wasn't she up? She tried to move her head and body at the same time but everything spun round at top speed. She felt hot, sick, sticky and now everything was aching. 'I'm dying,' Layne whispered, but no one was interested and she was glad. It was all right because a welcoming cloak of darkness floated down to envelop her.

★ ★ ★

Eventually she was disturbed by men's voices in conversation and the clatter and clink of something beside her bed, but still she had neither the inclination nor desire to investigate. The material world meant nothing so long as she could have the heaven of sleep, where dreams of her mother building up the bedroom fire, taking her temperature and tucking her in, made her feel cosy and safe.

Or was it Lizzie she saw in the bed? Was it Lizzie she was undressing and washing, feeding and joking with? Of course it was Lizzie. Why would it be her? Both Layne and her mother were tucking her in, then Layne huddled up on the bed to read to her, and Lizzie's lips tugged down at one corner, her sign of a smile. Dear Lizzie . . .

Tears slid down Layne's face, so she pushed her nose hard into the pillow, too weak to oppose the voiceless sobs that heaved upwards and outwards. She cried silently and bitterly, aggravating the blinding pain in her head, but nothing could stop her, not even the gentle stroking of her hair or the hand tidying stray, damp strands behind her ear, trying to soothe a hurt it did not understand.

At length a squeeze at her shoulder urged her to stop. A low voice close to her ear murmured, 'Hush. Let it go, Layne. Save your strength.'

The effort of her turning was made easy by Fergus, who took all her weight and tipped her body towards him. Her limp head slipped into the crook of his neck and her hand fell splayed against his chest. His gentleness and warmth only served to bring more tears helplessly and hopelessly splashing down Layne's face and soaking the neck of his T-shirt. His handkerchief could do little to stem the flow. She felt the soothing movement of his hand sliding back and forth along her arm and once he kissed the top of her head.

It took a long time but the tears did subside, yet still she was reluctant to leave the comfort of his arms, so he had to help her, pulling up her pillow and shifting her sideways. She lowered her eyes, ashamed to look at him, but he took her hand and squeezed it. 'You've got the dreaded virus. Patrick has left you some pills and I want you to take them with some water.'

Eyes still lowered, she gave a careful shake of her throbbing head. The prospect revolted her. She knew she would throw up. She heard him pour water into a glass, then the velvet-gloved steel in his voice. 'I'm not leaving here till you've taken these pills.'

Layne forced herself to look up at him and wished she had not. The thought of him *ever* leaving her sent a single tear trailing down her cheek. He shook his head, then squatted down, making a detailed, if puzzled study of her sad features. 'What *am* I going to do with you?'

The light of humour in his blue eyes brought a reluctant, watery smile to her lips. He smiled back sympathetically and, despite all the headache, nausea and weakness, Layne felt a desperate want for him, which went way beyond physical need. She wanted all of him more than anything she had ever wanted in her life. She had to stop herself from saying, 'I love you more than anything else in the world.' Not that he would have believed her. He would have put it down to diminished responsibility as a result of illness.

He recognized a weakening of some kind and took advantage, insisting, 'The pills.'

She sighed heavily and nodded. 'You win.'

After she had just about managed to down the capsules Patrick had left her without heaving, Fergus moved to the door, satisfied. Layne wanted to say so much but left it at, 'Thank you for . . . coming.'

He turned the door handle. 'Patrick will be back in a couple of hours. Try and sleep.'

She nodded.

Fergus opened the door and leaned against it. 'I've left your nightdress in the bathroom. I hope you'll be all right like that.'

Layne looked down at herself, puzzled to see she was in her wrap. When her eyes flew back up towards him, Fergus winked and closed the door.

She fingered the edges of the wrap, sliding them

down to the tie, which she determinedly tightened. Had he really undressed her? She had a horrible feeling it had been while she was dreaming about Lizzie. It did not bear thinking about . . . or even 'bare' thinking about. Well, that was it, wasn't it? No longer did she love him more than anything else in the world. He had abused her while unconscious. Besides, how could he ever find her attractive again, once he had ogled her like this: bedraggled, naked and miserable?

A deep reluctance to ever sleep again took root and Layne kept an eye on the door for as long as she could before the cooling, soporific effect of the pills sent her drifting into a fitful doze.

To her relief, Max was the next person to appear, though he did not stay long, fearful he may become another victim of the virus. He was, however, deeply sympathetic, passed on everyone's wishes for a speedy recovery and handed her a gift from Tim. It was a drawing the boy had done of Layne making a huge, splashing entry into the swimming pool. Layne shook it at Max. 'Tell him I may be ill but my memory's quite unaffected. I have not forgotten!' she warned, thinking to add, 'How's Inge today?'

Max waved a hand. 'Don't ask! What with the damage to her pride and a hangover, she slept in, didn't she? When she finally swanned along, Axel gave her such a bollocking that she stormed off again, leaving Jerry wondering which of the two it would suit his ambitions to pacify. I'm afraid sex came a poor second to career.'

'Inge must feel the world is against her.'

'I don't think Inge has much in the way of sensitivities, Layne. I wouldn't lose any sleep. The main thing is she hasn't caught a chill.' Max's lips curled cruelly. 'God, he's macho that man, isn't he?'

Despite herself, Layne smiled. 'He likes to be in control but I think he's got a soft centre.'

Max moved to the door. 'Oh, don't ruin my illusions. I like my chocolates with nuts in the centre. Now, get some rest and don't worry about a thing.'

Layne felt too weary to worry. She was almost too weak to drag herself to the bathroom and, as soon as she saw her damp nightdress hanging over the shower rail, wished she had not made the effort.

Around five, Patrick returned with some soup in a flask and bread rolls. Layne tried to look grateful. 'Two more tablets this evening,' he ordered, 'then two three times a day until the bottle's finished. Let's take that temperature again.'

'Again? You mean you've taken it once already?'

He nodded, slipping the thermometer beneath her tongue. 'You wouldn't have noticed, Layne.

You were delirious. We got you out of your wet nightwear and slipped that under your arm.'

'Mmmmm!'

Patrick deciphered her concern. 'Oh yes, Fergus helped me. You were thrashing about a bit. He replaced it with the thing you're wearing.'

Layne made a high-pitched noise, shaking her head agitatedly. Patrick readjusted the thermometer's position, smiling at her concern. 'Well, don't blame me! He said he'd seen it all before, anyway.'

Layne kept her exasperation in check long enough for Patrick to remove the obstruction and read her temperature, before finding the energy to thump the bedding and voice a 'humpphhh!'

'I know,' he sympathized. 'There's not much chivalry about these days. Still, give him credit, he spent such a long time with you this afternoon that he was late for a set-up and Axel lost his rag . . . said he'd never work with a star name again.'

'Oh no. Oh Lord!'

'Fergus can take it. It's all hot air, anyway. Now you listen, my girl, although your eyes are looking a bit brighter already, you've a long way to go. Drink plenty of that bottled water and try and get some food down. Is that understood? I think we may have a couple more people going down with this, so I shan't be here to spoon feed you.'

Layne acknowledged his attentions. 'Thanks for what you've done, Patrick.'

'Never mind thanks,' he warned, stroking his beard, 'just take heed.'

When he had gone, she tried to feel hungry and failed, so she drank a glass of water instead and snuggled back down. Her headache, at least, had eased slightly but her limbs still ached and, although a breeze was blowing in from the balcony, it was a hot, airless breeze. It took some time but, at last, Layne slipped into a deep, more restful sleep.

Sometime later the sound of laughter outside roused her a little but she drifted back, happy to give in to her body's demand for rest.

When she did finally clamber up from the depths of sleep and force her eyes open, the room was dark but there was a glow of light from the balcony. She yawned loudly, stretched and began fumbling for the bedside table. To her surprise the light on the balcony moved and behind it she could make out a man's long legs coming toward her.

Fergus had been learning his lines by torchlight and now slid the balcony door open, closing it behind him. Aware she had woken, he stood over her. 'All right to put on a light?'

Still half-asleep, Layne gave a mumbled 'yes' but when the light flooded on, she put up a hand for protection. 'What are you doing here? What time is it?'

He clicked off the torch. 'It's quarter to midnight. Hanna's fast asleep so I thought I'd keep you company while reading through tomorrow's scenes.'

Layne's eyes began to adjust, though she continued to peer at him, puzzling over his presence. 'I didn't hear you come in.'

He stepped forward and lowered himself carefully onto the edge of the bed. 'I'm afraid I didn't knock. You were well away this time.'

Layne began to feel self-aware and raked her fingers back through her hair. 'I must look a terrible sight!'

'I've seen you look better,' he admitted. 'How do you feel?'

She thought for a minute. 'Quite a bit more human, surprisingly.'

'Then I think you should try to eat something.'

She frowned at him. 'Did Patrick send you?'

'No.'

Layne still felt puzzled. 'Well you must go back to Hanna. I'll be all right, Fergus. Really.'

'Let's just eat something first, shall we?' he said, actually sounding concerned.

Layne's features relaxed. 'As in the Royal "We", I suppose?'

He smiled. 'One needs to keep up one's strength.'

He reached for the flask and poured some clear

soup into the cup. It looked harmless enough but her first reaction was to pull away as he offered it. 'At least try,' he insisted.

Layne wrinkled her nose but took the cup gingerly.

'Go on,' he urged.

Taking a deep breath, Layne put her lips to the cup and made the effort to drink. It turned out not to be too bad. Luckily, it did not taste of much. She downed the lot, only to look up and finding him holding out a roll of bread with one hand and removing her cup with the other. He refilled the latter.

'Now hang on,' she complained.

'The tiniest mouthful?' he suggested, reaching out to break off a piece of bread and hold it to her mouth. She gave him the kind of resentful look Hanna employed to make him feel guilty. It never worked then and it didn't seem to work now.

Layne put her lips to the bread and forced it into her mouth. She was immediately confronted by the soup and it soon became obvious that, if Patrick was not going to spoonfeed her, then Fergus was. Halfway through the roll, which she had now commandeered, Layne pointed out, 'I am a big girl, you know.'

'I know,' agreed Fergus amiably enough, though still he stayed to witness the conclusion of the meal.

'There! Are you satisfied now?' demanded Layne.

'Almost. There's just the matter of the two pills you should have taken earlier.' He tipped them from the bottle and handed them to her with a glass of water.

Layne still had her mouth full with one of them when she queried, 'Why are you doing this?'

He shrugged, waiting to remove the glass from her before answering. 'I think perhaps I owe it to you.'

'Owe? Why should you owe me anything?'

'Max came up to me today. He told me he was gay but cheerfully celibate and, though there were times he was tempted, the two of you were "just good friends". I got a bit carried away last night.'

'I'm the one who should be apologizing, Fergus.' Layne risked patting his knee with a grateful hand. 'On top of everything else, I got you into trouble with Axel.'

He covered her hand with his own. 'I've had a number of fleas in the ear today on your account. Still, I told Axel he couldn't throw me off the set and use someone else because, apart from a cast-iron contract, I had it on the good authority of the writer the part was tailor-made for me.'

Embarrassed, Layne tried to pull her hand away, but Fergus held onto it, pressing ahead. 'Axel had to agree that only Fergus Hann, or a clone of Fergus Hann, could portray a fast-living, hard-drinking, sex maniac like Lennox.'

Layne hid her face and slid down the pillow. 'You're trying to drive me to a relapse, that's what this is!'

Fergus leant forward, pulling her hands from her face. 'I'd really like to know more about all this.'

Layne shuffled sideways away from his gaze. 'You used those words about yourself, not me. You drew your own conclusions.'

There was a short silence and her heart sank when she heard him say, 'I hit the nail on the head, though, didn't I?'

Her fingers picked nervously at the corner of the pillow. His voice was persuasive. 'I think you should tell me.'

'I'd like to go to sleep now,' murmured Layne, feigning a yawn and laying her head down. It did not work.

'Look at me,' he insisted. Receiving no response, he slipped a hand beneath her chin and turned her face slowly toward him. 'I said look at me, Layne.' His eyes were examining her features carefully. 'I think you'd feel better if you explained.'

Layne felt like a worm wriggling on a glass slide beneath a magnifying glass. Not content that her naked body was already familiar to him, it seemed he had to lay bare her mind.

'I . . . er . . .' she began.

'Yes?'

Delicately, she removed his hand from her chin and hauled herself up, pushing her hair back over her shoulder as she did so. She could not look into his eyes. 'I . . . always admired your work, Fergus. Not only that, like women everywhere, I was . . . drawn to you. It didn't really matter who you were playing, or how good or bad the film. No one can explain what it is. Certain actors, men or women, possess a magnetism. You know that as well as anyone.'

At this point Layne dared to face him and the enquiry in his expression made it easier for her. 'You did, kind of, obsess me, but I also wanted to write for you. I can't honestly say who came to me first . . . you or Joseph Lennox . . . because you were always in the back of my mind when I was plotting the script. You can't always help the image the media portray, Fergus, but it's there all the same. I'm sure I don't know you at all but your "persona" helped extend my ideas for Lennox. He took on a life of his own yet, all the time, you were there, sort of pushing me on.'

'But you'd no idea I'd be offered the script or accept the part?'

'No! That was the wonderful thing. It came out of the blue. I couldn't believe my luck. I still can't.'

'And the obsession? What happened to that?'

This time it was Layne who did the examining. Her eyes went steadily over his features and when they reached his lips, she smiled, relieved of the deception. 'It's more . . . soft focus . . . but it's still there. Women don't easily discard their dreams but they usually know that is all they are.'

'So, is the real me a disappointment?' He tried to make the question sound casual.

Layne gave a slow shake of the head. 'Never that. Different, naturally. Better, if anything.'

He looked sceptical. 'I can tell you're ill. For once, you're saying all the right things.'

'I don't deserve your attention. I feel bad that I've had so much of it. I feel bad that I shouted at you. Yesterday was so lovely. Now I feel bad that I cried all over you . . .'

'It's a humbling experience, being cried on. It probably did both of us good. You'd been delirious. You said Lizzie's name a few times.'

'Did I?' Layne sighed. 'I remember dreaming about her and then it upset me to think I never really gave myself the chance to grieve for her. It was a case of supporting Mum and Dad in their grief at the end, trying to hold it in. And we did feel some release.' She reached out her hand. 'I am sorry, Fergus. To use you as a repository for repressed feelings. You should go back now.'

He smoothed a thumb back and forth across the

back of her hand and edged forwards. 'You really don't know why I'm here, do you?'

The look of gravity on his face worried her. 'I meant what I said last night,' he explained. 'I want you for yourself . . . not what you call "the sex". I want a serious relationship, Layne, and I want you to consider it carefully.'

She opened her mouth but he put a finger to it. 'Think hard first and get some more sleep.' He got up and dropped a kiss on her forehead, before making for the door. As he reached for the handle, he turned, humour back in play. 'Though I think we should include the sex. It would be a shame to miss out, especially with a body like yours, so keep that in mind, will you?'

Over the next three days, Fergus ensured he spent some time with Layne, checking on her progress, reporting on the shooting, trying out his lines or encouraging her to eat.

She found she had never wanted to sleep so much in her life. In fact the only thing that disturbed her rest was Fergus's request to consider a 'serious relationship' and she was only grateful he had not mentioned the subject again.

Every now and then, Hanna would wave briefly from the doorway, having been warned not to harass the patient under any circumstances. Hanna was not short, it seemed, of volunteers to take her under their wing while Fergus was working.

As Layne's strength returned, she began to grow anxious about her other projects. It was unlikely there would now be much rewriting. Shooting was nearing completion, production was over-budget for Greece and there was still work to be done at the studios in England. Already they had managed four days without any assistance from Layne, apart from the odd suggestion to Fergus when he had passed on queries about how to get round minor difficulties presented by technical or location problems.

While she was sitting on the balcony on the road to recovery, trying to make a few notes and take advantage of a freshening breeze, Layne lowered her pen and forced herself to face the prospect of her response to Fergus and subsequent departure for home. The truth had to be that any relationship was impossible. They surely both knew it. She did not believe either could deny mutual respect and attraction, especially on her side. But how could an ordinary woman conceivably conduct a normal relationship with the fantasy object of a million women's hearts? It was a pipe dream . . . and surely best left that way, no matter how it might hurt right now.

The sooner Layne saw Rowan and got her return flight booked, the better, for the longer she was with Fergus and the more she learned about him, the more painful it would be to leave.

Since that first day of her illness, the only time he had touched her had been when he had helped to wash her hair. She had felt too weak at the knees to attempt it herself but Fergus, tired of hearing the complaint that it looked like rats' tails, had managed to shampoo her tousled locks in the bathroom basin. He'd pronounced her a far easier subject than Hanna, who would just howl at the thought of a hair-washing session. As he had towelled Layne's hair and combed it through, Layne wished she had felt stronger. The whole experience proved so sensual that it could have been the ideal prelude to lovemaking.

Of course she wanted him. She did not know how any woman could not want him . . . and therein lay the problem. How could she hope to compete with those from his past, let alone all the beauty and talent he had yet to meet in his career? Any 'relationship' was doomed from the start.

Layne never knew when to expect him so she was not surprised that Fergus turned up in the late afternoon. He joined her on the balcony and produced a bougainvillaea flower he had nipped off the tree framing one of the villa windows.

'How are we today?' he asked, slipping the flower behind her ear and standing back to view his handiwork.

'We are much improved, thank you.' Giving a

genuine smile of pleasure at seeing him, she reached up to remove the flower, a little embarrassed by this adornment, but he caught her hand.

'No. It's you. You should leave it.'

Layne gave a co-operative shrug but he held onto her hand. 'Can we go inside? I feel like kissing you – and it's a bit public out here,' he reminded her unnecessarily.

The nervous flutter created by his unexpected request had Layne inwardly cursing him for so casually announcing such a personal desire. He didn't wait for her to hesitate.

'Come on,' he said, moving away with a tightening grip on her hand. She threw a backward glance at the balcony as the rest of her followed him in. The words, 'Come here,' were softly spoken but insistent.

Layne allowed herself to obey. His hands were either side her waist, warm and firm. She had to smile. 'What did your last slave die of?'

He thought for a second. She caught a glimpse of humour in the blue eyes, as he suggested, 'Ecstasy?'

'Such . . .' The word 'conceit' was allowed no voice.

His kiss was long and hungry. Like a starving man, he seemed to swallow her in, rendering her breathless and anxious to be consumed. In no time at all, her arms were clinging round his neck, fingers clutching at his hair, curling in and out.

All at once, he scooped her up and laid her on the bed. As he drew away, Layne watched his face through lowered lids. He lifted her neck and fanned her hair out across the pillow, as if preparing her for some ritual.

Content with his handiwork, Fergus's lips moved to the swell of her breasts, kissing their way slowly but determinedly upwards along her throat. They took a diversion at her chin, moving left along her cheek-bone and up to her forehead, so that by the time he arrived at her lips Layne had dug her nails deep into the sheets with anticipation, holding herself in check until the last second.

At long last, possessive lips claimed her mouth and it was as if something inside Layne exploded. She ripped the shirt from his waist, sliding her arms inside and along the length of his warm back, flexing her nails on his flesh. Fergus lifted his face to see the fire of demand in her green eyes. He gave a smile of satisfaction, refusing to be hurried, and kissed her with a depth of feeling that stirred Layne to the pit of her stomach.

To her heartfelt disappointment, she felt his arms leave her and fasten her wayward hands between his fingers. 'You do seem to be feeling better,' came the wry comment.

She tried to pull him back. 'I'm responding to the medicine.'

He twitched his lips and resisted the pressure, pointing out, 'To overdose would be dangerous.'

'You pulled the cork.' She smiled the accusation.

He leant forward, brushing his lips against hers, then whispering so she could feel his hot breath in her ear. 'I'd underestimated the power of the mixture.'

Layne reached up, smoothing his cheek beneath her palm, then trailing a finger down along his jawbone. Fergus caught her hand, studying the pleasure shining in her eyes. 'There's something we have to discuss,' he said.

Layne's heart sank. She drew her hand away regretfully, offering the criticism, 'You have great self-control.'

He smiled indulgently. 'Since your will-power's been run down by illness, someone has to compensate.'

Layne gave in, stroking his arm and admitting, 'I know. I was still on cloud nine. Sorry.'

'I don't want you to be sorry.' He ran the back of his fingers down her cheek, fixing her with serious eyes. 'I want you with me so that we can be as irresponsible as we like. What do you say?'

Layne could not withstand the blaze of hope in those blue eyes and looked away, shuffling herself up the bed until she was almost sitting. She flicked a handful of hair back over her shoulder and opened her mouth, hoping the right words would come out, but Fergus, too, shifted his body, diverting her attention.

'You're going to refuse me, aren't you?'

'Fergus . . .' she pleaded, but he insisted.

'Is it Yes or No?'

Layne shook her head sadly. 'No.' This time, she kept her eyes on his face, though it told her little.

He raised a questioning eyebrow. 'Another man?'

Her feelings screamed at her that she was making the wrong decision, but her head said otherwise and she shook it, attempting to be true to her resolution.

'Any reason?' he urged.

She forced a smile. 'A million!'

'One would do.' He sounded hurt.

Layne gave a huge sigh. 'This isn't easy for me, Fergus. If things were different, there's nothing I'd like better.' He waited for clarification. She managed a short laugh. 'You must see for yourself! Just your being who you are makes it impossible.' Layne slapped her chest. 'I'm . . . only me.'

'You haven't given me a reason I can understand yet,' maintained Fergus.

'All right.' She sat forward determinedly. 'We would both get badly hurt because it simply wouldn't work. You'd be travelling away all the time. Fans would be throwing themselves at you. You'd be making love to half-naked leading ladies. There's no way I could compete and one day, sooner or later, you'd succumb. I would want a man to be faithful, Fergus, and you have far more temptation thrown your way than the average man.'

He looked equally determined. 'The fact that my experiences started young have made me more capable of commitment than your "average man". I wouldn't be asking this, Layne, if I weren't prepared to give a hundred per cent.'

'I'm not saying that isn't your intention.'

'But the flesh is weak . . .?'

'Really, I'm not being cynical. I'm being realistic. And, remember, I have a career too, now. Our jobs are bound to keep us apart.'

Disappointment registered in Fergus's eyes. He got to his feet. Layne guessed what he was thinking. 'I've worked hard for what I've got, Fergus. I can't just throw it away.'

'No one has asked you to throw it away, have they?' He took a turn round the room, shoving his hands deep into his pockets, clearly not expecting a reply. Layne slid her legs off the bed, wanting to say more, but he spoke first. 'It isn't Hanna, is it?'

Amazed he should put Hanna forward as an impediment, Layne caught at his arm, making him turn to look down at her. 'I'm ashamed to say I hadn't even considered Hanna's feelings in the matter,' she replied truthfully.

'Well, I had . . . but it's *your* feelings we're talking about.'

Layne felt nervous bringing up the subject, but it had to be tackled. 'I really don't know enough about you, nor you me. Hanna has a mother, Fergus. I don't know whether or not her mother is your wife but Hanna's surely too young to be the result of your "oat-sowing" days.'

He turned to move away, smoothing a hand down the back of his hair, as if unsure himself. All at once, he looked back over his shoulder, his expression almost accusing. 'She is my wife. Darcey is my wife.'

It was as though he were either challenging her or himself. The knowledge felt like a crushing weight on her chest and she found herself staring at him, hardly able to speak. She muttered, 'Well, there it is . . .'

Suddenly angry with himself, he swung round and lifted Layne to her feet, giving her a shake. 'It's *you* I want.' The blue eyes blazed into hers. 'I never thought I'd be saying this at the age of thirty-eight but I think I'm in love, of all things!'

Layne tried to avoid his eyes but he put a hand either side of her head, holding it firmly. 'Can't you try and be honest?'

She had nowhere to hide. Her voice was small.

'Maybe it's the same for me,' she ventured. 'Maybe I'm still obsessed . . . but . . .'

'No buts.' He emphasized the order by closing his mouth over hers. Only when she pushed against his chest, did he release her.

'That isn't fair!' Layne objected, feeling it vital to get her point across. 'Look, Fergus, we're both old enough to know that "being in love" is just chemistry. It's temporary. It wears off! I wouldn't give us six months!'

'I happen to think chemistry is there for a reason. Besides, aren't you underestimating my ability to keep you "amused"?'

'But what about me?' retorted Layne, trying to ignore the humour in his eyes. 'Compared with half your previous bedfellows, I'm sure I'd be unbelievably dull.'

He gave a suggestive wink. 'I have reason to doubt that.'

Seeing he was not treating the matter with the delicacy it deserved, Layne put her hands on her hips and actually stamped a foot on the floor in frustration. 'Sooner or later you're going to have to take "no" for an answer and the sooner the better. I really do have to get back home and continue with my life.'

His hand moved over his mouth and on down his chin to his neck, which Fergus scratched thoughtfully, before announcing, 'I don't know what I'm going to do about you.'

Layne decided she could no longer cope and slumped down onto the bed. 'I feel tired, Fergus. Do you mind?'

There was a long silence. At last, he ventured, 'Would you mind if Hanna popped in to see you at bedtime? She's been pestering me for days.'

Layne gave a limp nod and forced a smile. 'Of course I wouldn't.' She watched him move to the door, then looked away.

'We haven't finished,' he warned, as a parting shot.

As she heard his footsteps fade, Layne flopped sideways onto her pillow and began to weep quietly. She did not know what was the matter with her. It could only be that the virus had left her physically and emotionally drained.

Though she was pleased to see Hanna properly again a few hours later, Layne found she had to force the cheer in her voice and did not like herself for it. Luckily, Hanna was happy to chatter, though she gave the occasional nervous wriggle. Having been told not to stay too long, she was not quite sure just what 'too long' meant. As it happened, it was Hanna's sudden onset of yawning and drooping eyes that told them both her time was up.

Hanna reached out to hug Layne goodnight and Layne held on, kissing her cheek, and wishing her, 'Sweet dreams, little one.'

The little one withdrew but pointed her finger at the single tear trailing down Layne's cheek. 'You're crying.'

Layne sniffed and rubbed it away, forcing a smile with the explanation, 'Layne's still just a bit poorly. She'll be better tomorrow.' She waved her fingers. 'Night, night, Hanna.'

Hanna was just about to wave a hand in reply when Fergus gave a light knock on the door. His voice called, 'Time's up, Horrible.'

Hanna scampered to the door, opened it and waved back at Layne, recommending, 'Mind the bugs!'

Overhearing the wondering words, 'Laynie's crying!' made Layne feel like throwing the covers over her head. Fergus was out of sight and all she heard him say was, 'Why, what did you do to her?'

Hanna slammed the door shut and Layne heard her giggling as she went down the landing. Fergus did not come back.

CHAPTER 8

The next morning, Layne forced herself out of bed. Sleep had come only after enduring hours of the wheels of her mind grinding interminably round in ever-widening circles. Then she had been swallowed up by gaudy, nightmarish dreams that had dragged her to such depths of sleep that she had had to struggle to resurface. She looked at her watch and, despite all her good intentions to get an early start, found it was already nine-thirty.

She felt slightly more human after showering and dressing in a white, sleeveless top and lemon cotton trousers. Layne was fastening her hair back over her shoulders in a pony-tail when she heard a child's scream from the far end of the landing and the clonk of something hard. She raced out of the room and practically skidded into the doorway of Fergus's bedroom.

Hanna was lying on the floor beneath a fallen chair, howling convulsively. Layne rushed to lift the chair away and dropped to Hanna's level, putting a reassuring hand on her shoulder while she tried to check for damage.

'It's all right now, Hanna. Can you manage to get up?'

Still sobbing, Hanna made an attempt to bend her legs. They seemed to work. She reached up to Layne and Layne lifted her across to the bed, lowering Hanna onto her knee for comfort. Hanna clung onto her for dear life, now sobbing on Layne's shoulder.

After feeling in her pocket, Layne found a hanky and tried to help Hanna dab her tears but the child seemed almost hysterical. Layne knew that she would soon have to find Fergus, even if it meant taking Hanna with her.

'Hush,' she said, stroking Hanna's hair. 'It's all right now. Does anything hurt?' Layne rubbed her knees, trying to distract Hanna from the shock. 'Does this leg hurt?' she asked. In among the crying, there was a just discernible shake of the head. 'What about this one?'

The head shook again. Layne felt relieved. Slowly, the sobs were beginning to subside.

'What about your arms? Do they hurt?'

A tiny voice hiccuped a negative reply to this.

'That's good,' said Layne. 'Do you think, perhaps, we should go and find Daddy?'

There was a tremendous howl that seemed to pierce Layne's eardrum and then Hanna was sobbing again in earnest. Layne jiggled her knees up and down, trying to provide a rocking, comforting motion and urged, 'If you don't hurt, then what is it, sweetheart?' As the tears kept coming, she suggested, 'We could go downstairs and get a drink.'

Hanna smeared her tears with the hanky and looked up at Layne with imploring blue eyes. 'Don't tell Daddy,' she hiccuped.

This took Layne by surprise. 'Why? I think Daddy should know you've had an accident, don't you?'

Hanna shook her head vehemently. Slowly, she lifted a hand and pointed towards the floor. 'Wasn't supposed to touch.' Her face began to crumple again and Layne cast her eyes over the area where Hanna had fallen.

She saw the cause of Hanna's distress lying scattered beneath the window. Shifting Hanna to one side, Layne crossed over to look closer. A coloured gift box lay empty, its lid lying behind the door. A piece of pottery, presumably from inside the box, now lay broken into two halves. Still unsteady, Hanna pointed out, 'It was up there. I fell off the chair.'

Layne glanced up at the wardrobe.

'Daddy said no peeking,' came the statement that explained her anxiety. It was closely followed by a nervous whimper.

Layne fitted the lid back onto the gift box and reached up to place it back on top of the wardrobe. Turning back to the pottery, she picked up the pieces and sat back down next to Hanna, assuring her, 'Don't worry. The important thing is you haven't hurt yourself.' She could see the two halves made up a beautiful porcelain lady.

There was a loud sniff from Hanna. 'It was my birthday present.'

Things were getting worse. There was little point reflecting that such a gift would get broken sooner or later by a child. 'When is your birthday, Hanna?' asked Layne.

'Next week.'

Something made them both jump. Suddenly there were footsteps approaching and the footsteps were recognizable. Layne swiftly shoved the two halves of the ornament behind her back. Hanna began to whimper but Layne hissed, 'I could try and repair it. Don't say anything,' she warned.

The worried look lifted from Hanna's face. Her eyes shone hopefully into Layne's and she put a finger to her lips.

'Breakfast's arrived, Horrible,' announced Fergus, as he rounded the doorway carrying a tray of coffee and rolls, to find Layne and his daughter sitting on his bed, smiling so widely at him that he knew something was up. He saw that there was a damp patch on the shoulder of Layne's shirt and that Hanna was holding her handkerchief. 'What's happened?' he asked.

Layne leapt to her feet, still smiling, which made no sense after the previous evening. She seemed to swing sideways away from him, crossing her hands behind her back. 'Oh, nothing now.' With a shrug of the shoulders, she explained. 'It's just that Hanna . . . bumped her head on the door.'

Fergus looked round for somewhere to put his tray, repeating, 'Bumped her head on the door?'

He ended up putting the tray on the bed and leaning over his daughter to examine her hair, enquiring, 'How did you manage that?'

Having worked her way round to the doorway, Layne said, 'You slipped, didn't you, Hanna?'

Hanna nodded her head beneath her father's hands. 'It was a bit of a shock, I think,' added Layne, 'but she seems to be all right now.'

'Layne's made it better,' declared Hanna.

'That's very kind of Layne.' Fergus was unable to keep the suspicious tone from his voice, as he glanced across at the saint in question, now still cheerfully backing away from his doorway.

Layne gave another emphatic shrug and told them, 'Well, afraid I must rush. I've got to see Rowan. Bye.'

'Bye, Laynie!' called Hanna, smiling sweetly to herself as Layne's footsteps sped away down the landing . . . smiling, that is, until she looked up into her father's knowing eyes.

As soon as Layne had escaped to her room, she rummaged for her bag and stuffed the two halves of the unfortunate china lady into the bottom of it. She had things to do.

It proved to be a hectic day. Instead of coming away from Rowan with a departure date, Layne ended up being asked to concoct a fight between Lennox and his wife over his latest affair. Tim, it seemed, had gone down with a feverish illness that morning, much to his self-disgust, and Patrick had not yet pronounced his diagnosis.

Layne made Max her next port of call. He ushered her in. 'How is he?' asked Layne. 'Can I see him?'

Max held up a hand. 'It wouldn't be wise, Layne. We're not sure if it's the virus yet but if it isn't, it's something you wouldn't want to catch. He's on paracetamol at the moment to help with the temperature and Patrick's coming back in a couple of hours.'

'Well, if he is like me, Max, it's important he sleeps. I've never felt so weary in my life.'

'You certainly look better than when I last saw you. I hear Fergus has been playing Dr Kildare?'

Layne tried to glare at him without humour, but failed. 'Fergus is more of a headache, talking of which, I need help desperately.' She rummaged in her bag and brought out the two halves of the porcelain lady.

'Oh my! What happened to her?'

'It's a long story, Max. Suffice it to say that not just one little girl could get into trouble because of this. How can I get her repaired quickly?'

'Mmm . . . well, it so happens . . .'

Within the next few minutes, Layne had kissed Max soundly on the cheek and was whistling on her way to her sweatbox. She had been relieved of the broken pieces and told that Max had a friend in make-up, who might be able to help. The light mood lasted until she came face to face with her VDU. A fight between Mr and Mrs Lennox, was it? It took Layne a good ten minutes to realize that this was a scene she could actually take pleasure in writing. After witnessing the state of Hanna that morning, it might do Fergus good to experience a bit of fear himself.

When she finally declared herself satisfied, Layne printed up copies and set off to deliver them to Rowan. On her way, she bumped into Jerry and Inge, heads down in frantic conversation. For once, Jerry spoke first, 'Are those for us?' he asked hopefully.

'Yes. I hope it's what you want,' said Layne, handing over the scripts. 'Four copies, is that OK?'

His smile of relief almost rendered him attractive beneath the glasses. He seemed to spend so much of his time looking harassed.

'You haven't let us down yet,' he declared, causing Layne to blink with shock. 'Could we make use of the swimming pool area, do you think?' came the unexpected question.

'I don't see why not,' agreed Layne, glancing at Inge. 'You could make it work.'

Inge snatched a couple of the copies out of Jerry's hand, announcing, 'I'll find Fergus. We'll run it through.'

'I'll come with you,' said Jerry, adding, 'We may need you later, Layne.'

Layne hesitated. 'I'll . . . catch up with you.'

Jerry nodded and Layne headed in the opposite direction, turning briefly to check they had gone. She did not honestly want to be there when Fergus read through his script. She took a detour. A *long* detour to the beach.

It was an ideal day for walking. The sky was overcast, holding the sun's power in check. One half of Layne felt guilty for trying to escape her responsibilities, the other half knew she would be insane not to.

When she reached the beach, she took off her sandals, swinging them between her fingers as she trod her way through the soft sand to the water's edge. Here, Layne rolled up her trouser bottoms and paddled back and forth, glad to feel healthy at last and free of the dreaded virus. She hoped, for Tim's sake, that he had not succumbed.

When the top of her head began to feel hot, she looked up and saw that the sun was winning its fight with the cloud. It was time to turn back.

On the way, Layne knew she should be mulling over what had happened since her arrival in Greece but she was reluctant to do so . . . it was as though her mind wanted to block out anything that disturbed the peace of the moment. She knew that she would miss this place, that she would miss little Hanna, but further than that she was not prepared to go.

It was probably just as well. As she was about to round the corner to the swimming pool, she heard raised voices. The logistics of the spat between Lennox and wife were being argued.

Layne took a deep breath. She wanted nothing more than to turn tail and leave them all to it but it would be an act of cowardice. Instead, she lifted her chin and strode purposefully into the hub of activity.

The first glance she met was that of Fergus, who had just looked up from arguing a point with Inge over the script. He frowned at Layne, looking her up and down, then slowly back up, as if at last

171

recognizing her. Layne suddenly realized that her trouser legs were still rolled up. She tried to rise above the casual picture she presented.

'Here she is now,' pointed out Inge. 'If you're really not happy about it.'

Fergus straightened and came to meet her, waving the script meaningfully. 'You've been busy since I last saw you.'

She aimed at a casual shrug. 'Axel needed to cover Tim's absence. Jerry and Rowan came up with the idea of conflict between husband and wife.' He gave an accusatory smile, totally lacking in humour, concluding, 'And the only thing you had to do was write it?'

Layne tried to keep her features smooth. 'Is there something you're not happy about, Fergus?'

'Motivation for a start,' he complained. 'What's so different about his latest dalliance that drives his wife into a rage after fifteen years?'

'I'd say that's approaching it from the wrong angle,' suggested Layne, straightening her shoulders. 'There's nothing different about his latest fling but there is something different about his wife. It takes place on Greek soil with a girl related to her mother's family. I'd say it's a case of the last straw.'

'Yes,' acknowledged Fergus irritably, 'but it hardly merits her throwing everything but the kitchen sink at him.' Fergus gripped her arm

172

and hissed into her ear, 'Have you forgotten the other night? Let Inge loose with the cutlery and she might just remember I'm not really Joseph Lennox. I could be badly mutilated.'

Layne patted his shoulder heartily. 'You're both professionals,' she reminded him. 'Chin up, Fergus. You can give as good as you get. And if you want her to cut down on the weaponry, have a word with Jerry or Axel. They won't want to lose their leading man.'

'And what about you?' Fergus asked her.

Over Fergus's shoulder, Layne could see a slim, darkly beautiful young woman talking to Rowan and she guessed this was Helena Popadopasomething . . . Lennox's 'latest'. Acting with *her* would surely make up for a few missiles aimed by Inge. She looked back at Fergus through narrowed eyes. Already holding him oddly responsible for Hanna's fall that morning, Layne muttered the words, 'Me? I have something to attend to,' before swirling around on her heel and making off.

She heard his voice irritably call her name but strode steadily on. She would not have liked him to see the slow smile creeping to her lips.

In the event, Layne considered the reason she ultimately missed the filming entirely valid. In a restless sleep, Tim was undergoing a similar, distressing delirium to the one she had experienced. Patrick had pronounced it 'the virus'.

Max allowed her to sit with him while he soothed the boy's brow with a flannel he had soaked in cool water.

'You feel so helpless,' complained Max. 'I wish I could do something for the boy.'

'You are,' Layne assured him. 'Even though I was like this, I knew someone was there, trying to keep me cool, giving me moral support. It is a comfort.'

'Fergus must think something of you, Layne, to have spent all that time with you. Surely by now you've settled your differences. You must see he fancies you?'

Layne sighed heavily. 'What's the point, Max? He's got his life. I've got mine.'

'And ne'er the twain shall meet? Don't be silly. You only live once.'

Layne giggled. 'This is a cliché-ridden piece of dialogue!'

'I don't care,' said Max. 'I'm not averse to a good cliché when it's the truth. We've one life and nobody knows how long that's going to last. Get it lived, girl.'

'As far as Fergus and I are concerned, we might enjoy life for a time but we'd suffer far longer for it afterwards. You reap what you sow.' There was a low groan of discomfort from Tim. 'Tim doesn't go much for the dialogue, either,' decided Layne.

Max smoothed Tim's hair back before damping

his forehead with the cloth. 'I hate to see him like this.'

'It won't be for much longer, I promise. It'll be far worse when he wakes up miserable and you've got to get the pills into him. Look, I'd better go and sneak that figure back before they finish the shooting, Max. You're sure the glue will have set?'

'So Teri said. Just handle it carefully.'

'Bless you, Max. I'll catch up with Teri later, then I'll be back,' she promised.

Max waved the flannel in her direction. 'You're a brick,' he declared.

'You mean pretty thick?' Layne suggested, waving a cheery farewell and heading off back to the villa, taking care not to swing or jolt the precious cargo concealed in the bottom of her bag.

Relieved to reach her room unhindered, Layne took the figure out of her bag to examine it. Teri had done the very best she could, so that from the front it looked almost perfect. As she turned it, a hairline crack appeared, widening slightly, as though a minute chip was still missing.

She sighed heavily. Perhaps it would be wise to make a clean breast of it. Even if Fergus knew nothing about it before Hanna's birthday, he would notice sooner or later. On the other hand, she had promised Hanna, and, as she remembered saying once before, a promise was a promise. And, after all, if Hanna did not mind having an imperfect birthday present, then why should anyone else?

Layne stood still and listened. Shooting was still going on and she even thought she could hear Inge shouting her lines but Layne dare not go to the window in case she was seen. This was her opportunity.

She stole down the landing, feeling deeply guilty. No one was about. Even Hanna was supposed to be in town with the rest of Axel's family. Fergus's door was closed, so she had to turn the handle very slowly and quietly, before peeping in to check all was clear. Behind her, there was no noise from the landing.

Carefully, Layne laid the figure on the bed while she reached up to lift the gift box down. She was glad she was tall enough not to need a chair. After sliding the figure into the box, she replaced the lid and, very gently, eased the box back into position on top of the wardrobe, stepping back to ensure it looked just the same and was not about to topple over.

As she did so, her eye alighted on the brunette pictured in the frame. So Hanna's mother was called Darcey and she was still his wife. That was that then, wasn't it? How could he suggest otherwise? He really had to be a Joseph Lennox character, after all. He would have used Layne and discarded her like an old shoe, for certain. She moved away. The sound of footsteps in the distance made her jump.

Giving a last guilty glance around the room, Layne closed the door quietly and ran back up the landing, swinging herself into her own room and sinking back against her own door with relief. She could hear her heart thumping. It was clear she was not cut out for a life of deception.

The worst of it was, she was going to have to show her face by mingling with the crew for the rest of the set-up, before seeking out Teri to thank her. Layne forced herself to do some deep breathing and, at last, found the courage to return to the fray.

Fergus had survived the experience unscathed, despite the re-enactment of some of his screen-wife's pan-throwing to satisfy the camera. Inge had managed to subdue her personal instincts, having no wish for her image to sink to that of fishwife. Even so, Layne's conscience pricked. At heart, she knew quite as well as Fergus that Mrs Lennox was acting out of character.

It was while Layne was deciding to avoid any filming of Fergus with the beautiful Helena that Rowan approached her. 'You were asking for more definite news, Layne. We'll be wrapping up Greece in three days. Axel and Jerry see no reason why you can't make arrangements for the flight home now. I can ask Ari to find out if there's a single seat going, if you like?'

Layne found herself saying, 'Yes, if you would, Rowan. Thanks.'

'Don't be surprised, though, if Jerry has me on the phone to you every day once we're back in England.'

She forced a smile. 'Well, it won't be quite like Greece, but you've got my number.'

He nodded and moved off, with the assurance, 'I'll get Ari to go into town tomorrow.'

Layne made her way slowly back to her room, as if weighted down by some invisible burden. She had been itching to get back to her work. The opportunity had arrived and now the prospect frightened her.

But why go over it all again? She had to leave, as did they all, and that was that. Layne had given Fergus her decision. Why waste the evening regretting it? Only an hour ago, she had been branding him a two-timer. Now she reminded herself Fergus was probably already taking comfort in the arms of Helena.

Remembering her debt to Teri and that Max was in need of moral support, Layne decided not to brood in her room. She freshened her lipstick, ran a comb through her hair, snatched up her bag and determined to leave her worries behind her.

CHAPTER 9

She awoke early next morning after a deep night's sleep, aided by two small Metaxas from Max's bottle. For the first time in a week her head felt clear and she celebrated by whistling in the shower. After a long soap and rinse, she clambered out, wrapping a towel round her body, and padded across her room to run a comb through her hair.

A movement on the balcony made her gasp and swing quickly round. Fergus was getting up from the seat. The shock made her defensive. 'You could have knocked!'

He looked far from happy and was unmoved by the accusation, simply replying, 'I did.'

His approach seemed threatening and she felt vulnerable in her state of undress. 'What's wrong?'

He shoved his hands into his pockets, as he took another step forward, and his tone was not a little angry. 'I'll tell you what's wrong. What's wrong is I object to someone teaching my daughter to tell lies.'

179

Layne took a step back to protect her bare toes. The thoughts in her mind whirled. Any moment, he looked as if he would take a finger out and wag it at her. 'Tell lies,' repeated Layne, hoping a hopeless hope he did not know what she suspected he knew.

His eyes studied her expression and seemed to find it wanting. 'I've tried to bring Hanna up to have an honest and open relationship with me. Up until now, I thought I'd succeeded.'

Layne took another step back, trying to cover the move by protesting, 'I don't see what this has to do with me.'

He shook his head in disbelief. 'You really are in the wrong profession,' came the conclusion. 'Are you denying that yesterday you told me Hanna had bumped her head on a door?'

'Well . . . no.'

'Which, of course, completely explains the black bruise on her thigh today.'

'What!'

'She's utterly distraught this morning. Didn't you realize you'd burden her with a massive guilty conscience? The truth had to come tumbling out.'

Layne bowed her head. He was right. All that deception and for what?

'I think you owe both of us an apology,' he said coldly.

Layne forced her eyes to meet his. 'Can I see her?'

His eyes were still accusing. 'I think you'd better. I can't do anything with her.'

Her state of undress no longer seemed important. Layne turned, threw back the door and ran down the landing. She could hear Hanna's sobs all the way.

As soon as she appeared in the doorway, Hanna ran into her arms and clung on tight. 'Sorry,' she hiccuped, pushing her face into Layne's stomach, damping her towel even further.

'It's all right, Hanna.' Layne dared not lift the child in case her towel got completely dislodged and fell off. She rubbed Hanna's shoulders and then tried to direct her to the bed, coaxing her. 'Come on, sweetheart, let's look at that bruise.'

Hanna moved but continued to sob on the bed as she leant sideways so that Layne could examine the elongated black blot in question. With one hand, Layne stroked the child's hair, trying not to look over-concerned and trying even harder to pretend Fergus was not leaning in the doorway, watching.

'I've got something good for bruises, Hanna,' announced Layne. 'A bit of arnica cream will have that right in no time. Honestly. I'm just sorry we didn't know about that bruise before.'

Hanna's watery blue eyes looked imploringly up at her. 'Daddy made me tell.'

181

Layne rubbed a hand up her back. 'Of course he did. He was worried. We should have told the truth straightaway, shouldn't we?'

Hanna was still looking up at her, her expression almost desperate, as if she wanted to say something but could not find the words.

Fergus stepped forward and looked down on them as if they were both naughty schoolgirls. 'I can't be expected to let this go unpunished.'

Layne glared at him for even suggesting such a thing. Strangely, Hanna, apart from repeated sniffs, seemed almost resigned. Layne was steadily beginning to think less and less of Fergus Hann. Nor was she persuaded otherwise when he added, 'And since it was Layne's idea to lie, I think Layne should take the rap.'

It was almost laughable. What was he going to do, for heaven's sake! Make her hold out her hand, or confine her to her room?

Fergus had not reckoned that the idea would horrify Hanna, who jumped off the bed and cried up at him, 'No!'

'As for you,' he said. 'Go to your room.'

Hanna's hands flew to her little hips. Now she glared at him. 'No.'

Never having witnessed such rebellion in the family ranks, Fergus's blue eyes glittered a warning at his daughter. All at once, he dropped to a squatting position, on a level with her, and said very quietly, 'Are you going to your room?'

Very slowly, the resolution in the eyes glaring back at him began to crumble. There was no alternative. She turned away from him, pushing her lower lip out and dragging her feet to the doorway. He was still squatting, watching her, when she turned on the last step and mumbled, 'Was my fault, not Laynie's.'

With this, the door banged to and Fergus pushed himself up to full height, sighing with impatience and raking a weary hand through his hair.

Layne had no sympathy whatsoever. She got up and headed for the door. Fergus caught her arm. 'We haven't finished yet.'

Layne tore her arm free, almost spitting her words with venom. 'Well, I have!'

She threw her hair back over her shoulder, clutched her towel close and strode determinedly back to her room, unknowing and uncaring whether Fergus was following. He was.

There was a loud bang as she swung her door shut behind her and it met the flat of Fergus's palm. Layne turned on her heel, so angry she could hardly get the words out. 'I don't want you here.'

She headed for the bathroom but he got there first, folding his arms, equally determined. 'There's some business outstanding.'

Layne's green eyes blazed into his. 'The matter is closed.'

He unfolded his arms and they slid into his pockets. 'Well, far be it from me to differ from Miss High and Mighty but I'm in a mind to reopen it for you.'

Layne stepped back, seeing she was not going to be allowed past, and looked him up and down, concluding, 'You've been watching all the wrong films, Fergus. Now, unless you want an earful of home truths, you had better get out of my way and out of the room.'

He raised that irritating eyebrow. 'Home truths, is it? Well, this will be interesting, coming from someone who wouldn't seem to know the truth if it came up and bit her on the behind. Go ahead,' he invited.

Goaded beyond endurance, Layne gritted her teeth and dared to release one hand from her towel to point an accusing finger at him. 'All right! Number One: It was your fault Hanna fell off the chair.'

He gave a humourless laugh. 'Oh, it was *mine*?'

'She was alone,' stated Layne, not waiting for this criticism to sink in. 'Only an idiot would have put a child's birthday present in full view beyond her reach. It was as if you were wanting her to give in to temptation. Those chairs are heavy, Fergus. It's no joke. It was lying on top of her when I arrived. She could have broken something. She was screaming her head off and you couldn't hear her.'

Fergus looked as if he were about to speak but Layne waded in. 'And you *had* to give her something breakable, of course! If she hadn't broken it then, she would have done some day . . .'

His expression had changed, his eyes narrowing, trying to understand what he had just heard. He used the same quietly ominous tone he had while testing Hanna's will. 'She *broke* it?'

Layne was caught off guard. She thought he knew everything. The reason for Hanna's worried expression slowly dawned on her. She had wanted to tell but could not because of her father's presence. More evenly, Layne was forced to say, 'The chair began to tip. She tried to save herself and dropped the box. And a good thing, too,' added Layne, with fervour.

'So, it's even worse than I thought! She could have been badly hurt!' Fergus reached out a hand to remove Layne from his path. 'I think I'd better have a talk with my daughter, don't you?'

Layne saw no alternative. She caught his outstretched arm and kicked his shin viciously. Air hissed between his teeth. Slowly, he looked up from his leg to her face and it was far from a nice look. He shook his head with repressed anger, 'God damn it, Layne!'

185

To add insult to injury, Layne whacked at his shoulder with the back of her hand, hurling back the words, 'God damn it, *you!* Can't you see that child is already terrified! Why do you suppose we tried to hide it from you? *You're* the reason she was distraught, both yesterday and this morning. She's afraid of you, Fergus, and you're intent on making things worse.'

Layne prodded a finger into his chest. 'This whole mess happened from the best of motives. Hanna wasn't just trying to protect herself. She thought you'd be hurt because your present had been broken. She was prepared to accept a repaired version and never say anything about it.'

The prod in the chest was repeated with more vigour. 'I was trying to protect Hanna from a prospect that terrified her . . . your anger and retribution, which, no doubt, you would term "justice".'

Layne suddenly realized Fergus had hold of the offending finger to prevent further damage. She relaxed and pulled it away from him, using a more gentle tone of voice. 'All this wasn't a huge conspiracy against your child-rearing methods, Fergus. It was an accident that happened. Hanna's more than sorry for anything she did wrong. Forget it.'

His expression was grave. 'And forget that you think I terrify her? That you think I'm irresponsible?'

'I was provoked into anger myself,' she said.

He began to push her out of his way but his eyes were still fixed on her face. 'Forget that you could calm her when I couldn't?' he said quietly, before reaching past her for the door handle.

Layne held him back, careful to keep her voice low and sympathetic. 'It could just simply be that I'm a woman and, sometimes, she needs a mother figure. It's natural.'

Fergus removed her hands. 'But it's a job you don't want.'

A lump came to her throat. She swallowed it back. Clutching her damp towel close, she lifted her chin, reminding him, 'It's a job that isn't vacant.'

Twenty minutes after he had left, Hanna arrived. Layne called from the balcony, where she had been looking out to the horizon, chin on hands, trying to bring calm to agitated emotions.

Hanna ran in, smiling as if nothing at all had happened, making Layne wish all adults could remain childlike.

'How are you now?' asked Layne, holding a hand out to her.

'Better,' declared Hanna, beaming, and pointing downwards. 'Daddy kissed it better.'

Beneath the relief, Layne could not deny a twinge of jealousy. 'That's nice,' she said.

Hanna folded her arms behind her back and swung from side to side. 'I've got to say sorry,' she admitted.

'What for?'

She didn't look too sure but then decided, 'Causing bother, that was it.'

'You only hurt yourself,' Layne told her.

'Daddy didn't smack you then?'

Layne blinked. 'No. Why? Does he smack you?'

'No.' Hanna had second thoughts that made her smile. 'Well, only once when I threw his pants out of the window.' She giggled. 'They fell in the bird bath.'

It was a scene Layne found attractive. She laughed. Then Hanna subjected Layne to her blue gaze and announced, 'I wish Daddy would like you.'

Layne reached an arm round Hanna's waist and drew her near. 'Shall I tell you a secret?'

Hanna nodded enthusiastically. 'I think he does . . . just a little bit.'

She realized Hanna was shaking her head. That conclusion was confirmed with the breathless report, 'Not any more. He said you kicked him, the goddamn interfering, wasp-something witch, but I told him he got crosser than anyone because he gets a blue face.'

Layne couldn't help herself. She kissed Hanna's

cheek and Hanna gave an amazed smile. 'That's when he kissed me better, too!'

'It's that blue face, I expect,' decided Layne, trying to subdue the mixed feelings stirred by his name-calling on the one hand and their common show of affection towards Hanna on the other.

Just as Hanna was about to slide away, Layne caught her hand. 'Hanna, I have to go back home in a day or two. We all do soon. But I promise I won't forget you and I'll send a card for your birthday.'

'Where do you live?' asked Hanna.

'Near to London,' said Layne.

'I'll be going back to Granny's,' volunteered Hanna.

'Where's Granny?'

'By the sea. Umber-land,' said Hanna, adding, 'in the north.' Her face lit up. 'You could come and see us!'

Layne kept the humour in her eyes for the child's sake. 'Maybe.' She managed a wink. 'If Daddy decides, one day, he likes me after all.'

Fergus was conspicuous by his absence most of the day but she almost collided with him when she had her head down checking her air ticket on the way back from Rowan's office.

'Sorry,' she said, self-consciously, stuffing the ticket in her bag. He realized what she was doing.

'You've arranged to go back.' It was a statement rather than a question. 'When?' he asked.

'Tomorrow on the noon flight.'

He looked as gloomy as she felt. 'Look, I . . . I'd like a word. Are you in this evening?'

'I expect so.'

'Can I see you? It's just that it could be late before I'm free.'

Layne nodded. 'That's all right.'

'Good. I'll see you then.'

She envisaged herself nervously kicking her heels until his arrival, having already said good-byes to the other people who mattered to her.

Tim was improving but too groggy to complain when fussed over by Max, who threatened to contact Tim's mother if he threw up Patrick's pills.

Layne swore that giving him the virus was not her idea. She had had a more imaginative repayment in mind for being dunked in the pool and Tim had obviously decided the virus was a safer bet. Tim had found the strength to force a humorous roll of the eyes. At least, she reflected, he was too weak to torture himself over his absence from the filming.

Max had kissed her cheek as she left, reminding her of his earlier words of wisdom. He even threatened to renounce his vow of celibacy if Layne did not 'get on with it soon'.

In the event, she spent the interim searching frantically for her passport. Finally, in desperation, she had turned her newly-packed suitcase upside-down, shaking each piece of clothing and fumbling for the tell-tale feel and shape of the missing item.

Eventually, she discovered it tucked in the pocket of her wrap, of all places. It was while she was smothering the prodigal passport with kisses of relief that there was a sharp tap on the door. It was after nine, but sooner than she expected.

Her hair and clothing already at sixes and sevens, Layne tried to remedy the remaining disarray as Fergus watched, flinging what belongings she had back into the case and clasping the locks with determination. 'Sorry about that,' she said breathlessly, 'I thought I was never going to see my passport again!'

As Layne slid the case from her bed, Fergus took its place. 'Why didn't I think to confiscate your passport?'

'You'll be away yourself in a couple of days, so there wouldn't be much point.'

Fergus reached out and took her hand. He was looking vulnerable but his fingers took a firm grip of her. To her surprise, he said, 'I have an apology to make.'

Layne allowed him to keep hold of her hand,

aware that apologies would not come easily to Fergus.

'I shouldn't have bawled you out over Hanna this morning. It was good of you to see to her and get the figure repaired. I overreacted.' He tugged on her hand and pulled Layne a few inches closer. 'You were right to give me a bollocking. It was well-deserved.'

Layne found herself bowing her own head in humility. Had she really given International Film Megastar, Fergus Hann, a bollocking? How appalling! 'I'm sorry,' she sighed.

She did not have the strength to resist the pressure when he tugged her closer still, reaching his other arm round her waist and drawing her onto his knee. She dared to look into his eyes and saw humour.

'This is my apology,' came the reminder. 'Make the most of it because they don't happen very often.'

Layne forced a smile. 'All right.'

He looked down at her fingers, entrapped in his own. 'You'll have realized that Hanna is my raw nerve. It's over-sensitive. I try to make up for the obvious shortcomings in her upbringing but . . . don't always succeed.'

Layne had to interrupt. 'Hanna seems a perfectly well-balanced child. You've done really well with her.'

192

He looked frankly into the reassuring green eyes. 'That isn't the message I was getting earlier . . .' He leant forward, almost tipping her sideways, and pulled up his trouser leg, to exhibit the bruise on his shin. 'And there's the evidence to prove it.'

He pulled her back towards him, a smile of admiration in his eyes, but Layne did not admire herself. 'I don't usually kick people, Fergus. I just didn't want Hanna getting in any more trouble. It isn't that I think you're a bad father at all. In fact, I think you're very good at it. I was just caught up in the heat of the moment.'

'Well,' he said, reaching a hand up to her hair and smoothing it back over her shoulder, sending alarm signals travelling the length of Layne's body. 'It's kind of you to say so but then I always said you'd make a good nanny, didn't I?'

Layne cocked her head to one side, deliberately acquiring a nanny-look. 'As opposed to a . . . what was it? . . . goddamn, interfering, WASP-something Bitch?'

His hands fell from her but the blue eyes were alight with humour. 'Now I really shall have to concoct a hideous punishment for The Horrible! She can't even get it right. The words I used were "venomous Witch"!'

Layne's eyes narrowed. 'Are you sure?'

His arms returned, encircling her, 'I wouldn't

lie to nanny, would I? I might get my legs smacked.' He smiled, as if he might enjoy it.

'Hanna was afraid you were going to smack mine!'

Fergus picked up one of her hands, smoothing it open, before pressing a kiss into the palm and promising her, 'Oh no. My mind was on higher things.'

He waited for realization to dawn in her widening eyes, then added, 'You have such a pert . . .'

Layne clapped a hand across his mouth, aware he was smiling beneath it, but even more aware of his palm smoothing its way along her leg up to the thigh, where his fingers took a hard grip of her flesh.

Any resolution dissolved away. Slowly, she shifted her imprisoning hand to his jaw, running her thumb back and forth along the line of bone, before passing it gently across his lips, admonishing softly, 'You're the wicked one around here.'

Her caress failed to travel the full distance. The lips parted and her thumb was taken captive between his teeth.

By the time Layne had salvaged her thumb to kiss him, the arm snaking up her back had already disappeared beneath her hair. Fergus tilted her sideways, taking the initiative, kissing her comprehensively. Equally determined, Layne gave as good as she got, driven by some deep-seated need hungrily yawning open inside her.

Aware things were going too far too fast, Fergus laid her gently back on the bed and pulled away. Layne was already reaching across to flip open the first button of his shirt but he caught her wrist before it got there. Kissing her finger, he spoke with gentle humour. 'Hold on now, I came here to apologize and leave you with a farewell kiss.'

Layne did not like the sound of 'farewell'. She rolled closer, freeing her wrist and pressing her palm against the warmth of his chest, admitting, 'I want you, Fergus.'

Appreciation twinkled in his intense eyes and he smoothed his own hand over hers. 'I want you too, beautiful, but I don't intend to consummate this relationship unless you give me some guarantees.'

Layne sighed heavily. 'We've been through all this before. Can't you see my point of view?'

'How about trying to trust me? Give me a six-month probationary period if you like?'

She flopped back hopelessly, reaching a hand into her hair to pull down one of the strands, twiddling it between her fingers, before turning her head to look him in the eye. 'Don't ever think I'm not flattered. I could never, in my wildest dreams, have expected an offer like this and most women would jump at it.' She rolled back towards him, catching his fingers. 'But it *is* a dream, Fergus . . . whereas now . . . is now.'

Layne pulled him down and kissed him. At the

same time, she bent her knee and raked her toe along the side of his leg, upwards to his hip. Her lust for satisfaction was steadily driving out conscience and logic. So what if it made her look like some wanton . . . Well, men liked that, didn't they?

His hand reached out and trapped her ankle, holding it fast. Air hissed between his teeth. 'Have you any idea what you're doing!'

'I think so,' replied the coy voice.

'I'm just beginning to wonder about that. Just how much experience do you have?'

'I don't ask you questions like that,' she complained.

'You don't need to,' he replied brutally, shifting her body so that some inches of safety parted them. 'I'm afraid you're the one that's living in a dreamworld if you think you can have a one-night stand without repercussions . . . mental and emotional, if not physical!'

Layne did not want to hear. She tugged at his arm, trying to hang on to her humour. 'Look, Fergus, you've got me on a plate. I promise there won't be 'repercussions'. Let's just enjoy the moment.'

He looked angry. 'You're a hypocrite, Layne Denham! If I'd said that, you'd be accusing me of just wanting you for the sex, wouldn't you?' He released her ankle in apparent disgust. 'And don't lie to yourself that there won't be repercussions. Hanna is a living contradiction to that piece of self-deception.'

Taken aback, Layne only managed to repeat the name, 'Hanna?' before Fergus slammed a hand down on the bed in frustration and got to his feet. He did not give a backward glance but the words were spat out like a curse. 'You'll be safer at home!'

With that he was gone.

CHAPTER 10

That was the last Layne saw of him. She did not see Hanna again, either. It was as though he had whisked her out of the way, in case she became tainted by this scarlet woman. When Ari ran her to the airport and waved goodbye, Layne's sunglasses had offered welcome concealment, as she joined the long queue for the baggage check.

The rest of the journey was a blank, so empty did she feel inside. And now, six weeks later, she felt just the same, simply going through the motions, living in a twilight world, where nothing seemed real. Practical matters were not difficult. She could unbung the sink, cook, shop, get from A to B and even plot and analyse her work. But her heart was not in it and she knew this lack of reality was reflected in the characters she represented on paper.

John Trevor, her agent, had not failed to notice something was wrong from the two meetings they had held since her return and from samples he saw of her work. It was for this reason he called a third meeting and suggested she take a holiday.

'But I've been away,' protested Layne.

'Hardly a holiday, though, being laid low with a virus. Come on, Layne, admit you're not over it yet. You should see a doctor.'

He recognized the defiance in her eyes. 'Well, if not a doctor, you should take a proper break.'

'John, the deadline's in two months!' she reminded him.

Never one to mince his words, John declared, 'Sod the deadline! You certainly won't make it on this form because of all the rewriting.'

This time humour tinged the resentment in her expression. 'Thank you for your confidence.'

'You're welcome. Now, are you going to get something booked, or do I have to do it for you?'

She sighed heavily. 'It looks as if I have no option.'

He sat back and suggested, 'Why don't you go back up to Skye? You always said you intended to, one day, and it won't be clogged up with tourists this time of year.'

Layne looked at him as if in a dream. 'Skye?'

'The Isle of Skye, remember. Somewhere off the coast of Scotland? Unless it's moved, of course. I suppose it could have gone to the Bahamas for its holidays . . .'

Layne opened her mouth to speak but a horrible

noise came out. It was quite unaccountable and Layne's eyes swam with tears at the shock of it.

'What the ✶✶✶✶ now?' demanded John, appalled.

He came round and sat on the desk, looking down at her. 'You see what I mean, woman!'

A torrent of emotion swallowed her up. All she could manage, with bowed head, was a strangulated, 'Sorry John . . .!'

He waved his handkerchief under her nose but, salvaging what little independence was left to her, Layne fished out her own.

As her body heaved silently, John considered the top of her head, deep in thought. Then, as she seemed to regain some self-control, he cursed himself for not having seen it sooner. 'It's not the bloody virus at all, is it?'

Layne did not answer.

'You met some slimy Greek waiter who promised you some Shirley Valentine Shangri-La. That's it, isn't it?'

He watched carefully as she shook her head, then nodded, then shook her head again. 'I take it from that that I'm warm.'

Layne sniffed loudly, cleared her throat and tried to put on a brave face. 'It's a man,' she confirmed.

'Well, I suppose it could be worse,' he mumbled, before getting dismissively to his feet and returning to his seat. 'Look, Layne, my name isn't Agony Auntie and I've got a bloody awkward client due in two minutes. Take two weeks to sort this mess out and come back in full working order. There's a good girl.'

Layne nodded and got to her feet.

He leant forward, viewing her with a touch of sympathy. 'I don't suppose I get to know who the swine really is?'

Somehow she made it to the door and turned. It was the first time she had said the name aloud since her return. 'Fergus.' A touch of humour came to her blotched and swollen face. 'Fergus sodding, bloody, sodding Hann.' It was the kind of confirmation John would understand.

Once outside the door, there was a sudden explosive shout from the other side. Layne felt a little better and forced her feet down the steps, out into the welcoming embrace of an impersonal London street.

The more she thought of Skye, the better she decided John's idea was. Two months after Lizzie's death, she had stayed there and found it an uplifting, healing experience. And there was certainly a wound that needed healing inside her now. She decided to spend a weekend visiting her parents, who had retired to Shropshire, before making the long drive north.

To people who did not know better, her father

appeared a gentle, absent-minded man, who preferred to spend his time bumbling amiably about the garden. Yet his mind was every bit as acute as it had been in the days when he taught maths and accountancy. He became a freelance financial adviser and, three years before taking early retirement, opened his own business consultancy with a former colleague, who then took over the reins.

It did not seem strange to Layne when, on spying his newly-arrived daughter at the door of his greenhouse, Ray Denham simply said, 'Ah,' picked up a pair of scissors and beckoned her to follow him into the garden, where he cut some sprigs of fresh thyme. 'Give these to your mother before she nags me again, will you?'

Layne sniffed at the scent of the herb. 'Mmmm. That's beautiful.' She looked up to catch him passing judgement on her appearance.

'You look a bit peaky. Been working too hard?'

'Those were my lines!' she complained, leaning forward to kiss his cheek. 'You've been doing too much digging.'

'There's a lot of land.'

'Well, try and leave some of it green,' she suggested.

'You sound like your mother. Take those in to her or I'll never hear the end of it.'

Aware she had been dismissed, Layne turned towards the house.

'You never did answer my question,' he called after her. Layne laughed and waved the thyme at him. She knew it would be her father who would notice any difference in her.

Her mother led far too hectic a life to examine physical appearance. She was always up to her ears in baking or jam-making, or collecting jumble for some cause or other. Layne believed this was why she had dealt with Lizzie so well. Ann Denham was a capable, resourceful woman, who saw life as a personal mountain. It was a matter of strapping on the gear, finding some sturdy footwear and battling through the elements to reach the peak. And she had no intention of coming back down voluntarily. Someone would have to carry her.

As she chopped up the thyme, she told Layne, 'You should have let us know you were coming. The governor from the WOP's giving a talk this evening.'

'WOP?'

'Women's Open Prison. You could have got some ideas, like Lynda La Plante, but the hall's going to be full. They might have a whist drive after . . .'

'Thank heavens it *is* full,' declared Layne. 'You know I can't stand card games. I'll be quite happy here with Dad, so go on and enjoy yourself. Can I peel some potatoes?'

Her mother nodded towards the vegetable rack

and arranged glacé cherries on the trifle while Layne peeled.

'You seem quite in demand now,' came her observation.

'That's a bit of an exaggeration.'

'No, it isn't. You don't have to assume this cloak of false modesty, you know. Once your film's a success, the work will pour in.'

'It isn't my film. It's a team effort.'

'There you go again.'

'It would be nice to see it a success, though,' conceded Layne.

'What was Fergus Hann like?'

'What!' The peeling knife slipped and Layne stabbed herself. 'Damn!'

Ann Denham popped half a glacé cherry in her mouth and looked over her shoulder. 'You've already become blasé about the whole thing, haven't you? Fergus Hann, the filmstar, dearest. The man you wanted to give you children.'

Layne gasped. 'Mum!'

'Well, you said it, not me. Admittedly that was two years ago but, since you haven't had anyone else's children in the meantime, I thought you might have found him worth a mention.'

Despite herself, Layne smiled. 'You haven't changed. You're just as terrible! If you must know, he is quite nice.'

'How boring.'

'I didn't say "boring". I said "nice".'

'Can't you give me more than that? I do have to report to the WF tonight.'

'Not about Fergus Hann. Besides, I thought it was the WOP.'

The trifle was banged emphatically down in the middle of the table. 'The WF is the Women's Fellowship and they all like a bit of gossip!'

Layne turned on the tap and ran the potatoes under the water, before dropping them in the pan.

'He was kind to me when I had the virus,' she admitted.

'Virus? What virus?' Ann Denham looked Layne over closely for the first time since her arrival.

'The virus I caught from his daughter's nanny,' came the explanation.

Her mother's brow was furrowed. 'Daughter's nanny?'

Layne picked up the pan and put it on the hob. 'He has a daughter and his daughter has . . . *had* . . . a nanny. The nanny went down with a virus and I caught it.'

'What were you doing with Fergus Hann's nanny?'

'His daughter's . . .'

'Yes, then, his daughter's nanny?'

'Well, nothing illegal, mother, if that's what you're thinking. I had her room, or she had my room. I can't remember exactly.'

'It sounds very funny to me. You never mentioned it on your postcard.'

'There isn't much room on a postcard. Now what's to do next?'

Mrs Denham was still trying to get her brain round the complications. 'Why would he be kind?'

Layne gave a casual shrug. 'Why wouldn't he? I told you. He's quite nice.'

'No. Why would he be kind to you?'

Her daughter laughed out loud. 'It does seem inconceivable!'

'You know what I mean.'

'Well, why wouldn't he? He's probably kind to everyone. And I did have a virus.'

Layne's mother narrowed her eyes suspiciously. 'Did *he* catch this virus?' she asked.

'What are you suggesting?' Layne prompted her mother.

'I'm just curious,' she explained defensively.

Layne flung a handful of hair back over her shoulder, then brushed her hands together, as if making an end of the matter. 'All right. If you really want some scandal for your WOF, tell them it was love at first sight, we fell straight into bed and now I'm throwing up every morning!'

'You're not pregnant?'

Layne flattened a hand against her stomach and stood sideways. 'Can't you tell?'

'You're having me on!' Despite this dismissal, there was still a sparkle of hope in Ann Denham's eye.

Layne shook her head, sighed, 'I give up!' and left the kitchen.

It was only when her father switched off the nine o'clock news that the topic was raised again.

'Your mother was behaving strangely while she was getting ready to go out.'

Layne was hardly surprised but did not say so. 'In what way?'

'She kept muttering about you and some Angus man and his nanny's daughter. Something like that. Shall I have her put down?'

Layne grinned. 'What would you do without her?'

'Everything I've ever wanted.' He sighed happily.

'You don't mean that.'

'I suppose I'd miss the old steamroller. So are you going to tell your Dad or should he mind his own business?'

There was a huge sigh from Layne as she flopped back in her armchair. 'I don't think you'd want to know.'

'No, but I'd put on a brave face.'

'The trouble is, I don't think I know myself. I'm going up to Skye to sort myself out, Dad.'

'Skye?' His expression brightened. 'I wish I could come with you.'

'You can,' she offered.

The resignation reappeared. 'No, no. It's a pipedream. There's the garden . . . and my wife would miss me desperately. You're quite safe,' he concluded.

Layne got to her feet. 'How about a cup of tea?'

'That's always a good idea,' her father agreed. It was not the only observation he made. 'You've lost too much weight. Your legs look thin. You're not anorexic, are you?'

'Of course not. I had a virus when I was in Greece and it's still hanging about.'

'But the man isn't,' he concluded.

'Dad!' she admonished gently, head cocked to one side, hands on hips.

'I always know I've hit the button when you stand like that. It's this Angus man, then?'

'Fergus Hann, Dad. His name's Fergus and only you would never have heard of him.'

'I doubt that. Is he worthy of my daughter?'

'He's married with a daughter of his own,' confessed Layne.

'Oh.'

Layne sank back onto the arm of a chair. 'I really don't know if his . . . wife is still in the picture. She seems to have nothing to do with her child.'

'Have you asked him?'

208

'Sort of, but I couldn't press it. He's still somehow protective of her.'

'Doesn't sound very hopeful, does it?'

'No,' agreed Layne. 'That's what I thought.'

'But you like him?'

'More than like him,' she admitted. 'But where does that get me?'

'There are times you've been known to demonstrate your mother's brutally practical side,' observed her father. 'Of course I realize he's only a man but he probably has feelings, too. How old's the daughter?'

She smiled to herself. 'Six. She's gorgeous. She's got these great blue eyes. Just your type.'

He scratched his chin thoughtfully. 'A ready-made grandchild would be nice for your mother. She keeps saying she can't wait much longer, as if she has anything to do with it! Baby blue eyes, eh?'

Feeling a bit better for being able to talk about it, Layne managed a wink. 'Just like her father's!'

Ray Denham leant forward in his chair, as though he were going to ask something of great import. 'Layne?'

'Yes?'

'Did I imagine it or did you mention something about a cup of tea?'

Layne jumped to her feet. 'All right. I'm going, I'm going!'

* * *

209

Her departure for Skye was not quite as early as anticipated because Ann Denham kept emerging from the kitchen with home-made bread, cakes and other supplies to keep her daughter from, at least physically, wasting away while on retreat. Layne had assured her they did have shops dotted about Skye but her mother had made snorting references to frozen foods and chocolate bars.

When, at last, Layne got behind the wheel of her car, she was treated to one of her mother's nuggets of worldly wisdom.

'Don't forget,' she warned. 'Kind men don't grow on trees, isn't that so, Dad?'

Ray Denham rubbed his chin thoughtfully, before admitting, 'I haven't seen one yet and I do spend a lot of time out of doors.'

Layne smiled and revved the engine, while her mother dug her father in the ribs with a well-padded elbow.

'I'll keep that in mind,' called Layne through the window and sped off in a cloud of dust.

CHAPTER 11

By the time she arrived in Fort William, Layne wondered why she had allowed herself to be persuaded into attempting the long haul. It was already after five and the accumulated weariness of recent weeks seemed to have caught up with her.

After parking and walking into the centre, she went into the first available eating place. Once a meal and coffee had been ordered, Layne found all she wanted to do was put her head down on the table and sleep.

Although Skye was now no great distance, Layne did consider seeking bed and breakfast overnight, but the food and two cups of strong coffee slowly revived her. By the time she paid the bill, her head was clearer and sufficient energy had returned for Layne to face the remainder of her journey. She made straight for the car, casting only a casual eye over the shop window displays of sporrans, woolly jumpers and models of Nessie.

211

Most of the stores were closing up for the night, anyway.

Once she had made the ferry from Kyle of Lochalsh, Layne began to feel a sense of optimism creeping back into her soul. As they chugged across the water, with Skye clearly defined in her sights, the weight on her shoulders seemed to lighten.

At last, she found herself on the road to Ord. Layne saw the farmer had erected modern sheep pens in one of the fields, but the black-faced sheep and their lambs blundered across the road as obstinately as ever. The leggy black foal with the star on its forehead was missing. By now it would be three years old.

On rounding the familiar tight bend, the land fell away steeply so that, before her, bathed in silver evening light, sprawled the magnificence of the wooded valley, glistening loch and unmistakable serrated ridges of the Black Cuillins outlined against the sky.

Layne slammed on the brakes, reversing into a passing place to drink in the view. The sudden longing for Fergus to share this moment had Layne blinking back sharp, blinding tears that stabbed at her eyes. Shocked, she forced herself to focus instead on the helpless, pleading roots of an upturned tree, wrenched from its base in the steep valley side, a stark mirror to her feelings.

She stayed a long time, watching the changing sky, listening to the chirrups of small birds making ready for the night, until, at length, on noticing the chill air on her cheek, she drove on.

Once at the cottage, Layne unpacked only vital provisions. Her clothing could wait. She poured herself a restorative brandy, then moved over to the long window with its spectacular view across Loch Eishort to the unique backdrop of mountains.

It was then she remembered that complete darkness never came to Skye at that time of year and sleep did so with reluctance.

Overtired from the journey, Layne's first night proved restless and even her eventual fitful, dreaming sleep was intruded into in the early hours by persistently bleating lambs that had lost their mothers.

As one day merged into the next, alienation from everyday life and absorption into things natural calmed Layne's soul. She would climb high above the loch and settle down on a grassy bank to watch the small, blue lobster boat sliding silently through calm, clear waters. As it slowed to offload its cargo of pots, leaving behind a trail of bobbing, orange buoys, she risked reflection on circumstances.

What was she, after all? Just a speck among the dust of humanity. The times she stopped hurting were the times she stopped thinking. Why torture herself? Surely, if she could look forward, never back, she could move on?

On her fourth day, Layne climbed far into the hills, trekking through bog and over slabs of slippery, marble-like rock, higher and higher, until her muscles screamed. But the magnificence of the view more than compensated for the pure physical exhaustion. Both the spectacle and the cool mountain breeze buffeting her insignificant body took Layne's breath away, as fresh air forced its way into her lungs. She felt exhilarated and cleansed.

Some time later she made the descent, half-limping to save her blisters but, instead of collapsing with fatigue on her return, Layne was fired into unpacking her paper and pens and began to write.

For two days, she hardly left the cottage, churning out pages of dialogue with hardly a break but for drinking in the purple beauty of the evening sky or spotting the occasional seal frolicking in the waters of the loch.

By the time Monday arrived, there was precious little left of her mother's home-cooked foods and Layne drove into the nearest village to stock up on provisions.

Arriving back at the cottage, she found a sleek

black car with darkened windows parked on the road outside. There was no sign of an owner and, apart from thinking it hardly fitted in with the surroundings, Layne paid little attention, unloading her shopping and putting it away before returning to her haunt above the loch.

Occasionally, she would see a couple walking with their dog or a family with small children trekking across the white sand of the small bay below her but today she spotted a lone figure. She did not see him at first, for he had perched on a rock, looking out across the loch, as if deep in thought. The blue of his jumper betrayed his presence and, at length, he pushed himself to his feet. He seemed to have lost someone, looking first to his left, then to the right.

She felt sorry for him and scanned either side of the bay for a woman who could be his wife or girlfriend but there was no one. When she tried to find him again and did, Layne felt a stab of guilt for spying, for he was gazing up in her direction. It seemed as if he were looking straight at her.

A wave of familiarity washed over her, sending Layne staggering to her feet. There was a distant shout. Seconds later, her name seemed to echo along the cliff.

There was no point in trying to fool herself. It couldn't be anyone but Fergus. Layne turned and ran.

Without a thought in her head, she stumbled over stones and ran on, arriving breathless just yards from the black car, to see him striding up the road from the bay. He got so far, then stopped still, as if trying to reassure himself of something, but Layne did not wait. She sped off down the road towards him, only stopping to thud happily into his chest.

'Fergus!'

She looked up to see dry amusement lurking in the blue eyes but his arms closed around her and he subjected her to a swift, irascible kiss, before holding her away and studying her face.

It was only now the thought actually occurred to her and she expressed it with surprise and amazement in her voice. 'What are you doing here!'

'Do you mind if we walk?' he said. 'I could do with stretching my legs.'

As the cloud clustered to create a dirty cloak that clung to the steep slopes, they headed over the hill to the next bay. Small birds flew up out of the long grass and chinked in complaint from rocky outcrops. A family of ducks paddled back and forth in the shallows of the loch, dabbling among the weeds. Black and white oyster catchers clucked in alarm at the sight of them, before continuing nervously about their business on the shoreline, examining the gifts of the tide with alert red eye and probing scarlet beak.

They filled their lungs slowly with the clean air

and shared a sense of peace, settling at last on a flat rock, watching a lone seal dip and dive before surfacing to inspect them from a safe distance.

Layne studied his profile and concluded, 'I can't believe you're here. I can't believe it's you.'

Fergus picked up a lump of loose rock, got to his feet and hurled it at the water. It sploshed loudly, sending ripples far and wide. He turned back to her, shoving his hands into his pockets. 'Skye seems to suit you. You look better than I expected.'

'I feel as if I'm in a dream. Better than expected? What do you mean?'

He lowered himself back onto the rock beside her. 'Your agent tried to phone me at the studios. The message wasn't passed on, so he sent a very irate, very public fax that could well have been construed as libellous . . . something about inflicting my well-worn charms on an innocent woman, who happened to be his client. I then phoned him and got an earful, threatening that, if I had got his client pregnant and walked away, then my already questionable character would be shredded for eternity in the tabloids.'

Layne did not know whether to seethe or cover her face in shame. 'Well, John Trevor has just lost himself his client. How dare he?'

Fergus was actually smiling. 'I think he must be in love with you.'

Layne gave a contemptuous laugh. 'You wouldn't say that if you knew him.'

'He left me in no doubt he was jealously guarding your interests and, ultimately, his own. I hear that you have not been able to write since you came back from Greece, that both you and your work are incoherent, *and* he was convinced you weren't eating. It was only when you blurted out my name in an unprecedented eruption of unbridled emotion that he knew where to lay the blame.'

By now, Layne's hands were covering her face.

'I thought I'd better salvage what was left of you before his worst fears were realized, that is . . . no more ten per cent commission,' observed Fergus.

'I don't know what to say! I feel terrible,' concluded Layne. 'That man is infuriating at the best of times, but this! He . . . well, he's just about . . .'

'. . . The best friend you have?' suggested Fergus.

Layne groaned. 'That was *not* what I had in mind!'

'Even so . . .'

'But you should be filming!' she protested.

'We should be but there's a slight hiccup . . . a contractual dispute with the unions has delayed work for several days already.'

'Oh no.' Layne studied Fergus's features, thinking he looked tired. 'You shouldn't have come all this way. I don't even know how you found me. John doesn't know the address.'

'No, but you gave Rowan two contact addresses, one at your flat and the other was your parents'.'

'What? You phoned them?'

He nodded. 'I spoke to your father. He said your mother would know but she wasn't in, so why didn't I travel via them and pick the address up on the way.'

For a second, Layne's mouth gaped open, before articulating, 'What a nerve! I hope you did nothing of the sort!'

'I got the impression that if I wanted to discover your whereabouts, I would have no choice.' He cleared his throat meaningfully. 'John Trevor's isn't the only earful I've had on your account.'

Layne shook her head in disbelief. 'This is appalling. Really awful! I'm so sorry!'

He reached out and took her hands in his. 'You're very lucky to have people who care about you, Miss Denham!'

'Including you?' she ventured.

He squeezed her fingers. 'Including me, yes.'

'Will it help to make up for all the trouble if I give you a hug?' she asked tentatively.

His eyes smiled down into hers. 'It might go some of the way . . .'

Layne slipped her arms round his neck, put her cheek to his and squeezed hard. It felt so good to have him close again, his skin next to hers, the smell of him. His arms tightened around her, locking her in. As she relaxed to nestle her head in the crook of his neck, his lips found hers, teasing and coaxing at first, before reminding her in no uncertain terms what she had been missing for the past two months.

As they made their way back to the cottage, Layne was proud to have Fergus's arm about her shoulders. Just once, they stood aside, allowing an elderly couple to pass by on the path, and, although the pair nodded grateful thanks, no recognition of Fergus registered.

'My father must be right,' remarked Layne, as they moved on.

'About what?'

'About him not being the only one who has never heard of Fergus Hann!'

'It's clearly time you wrote me a screenplay to fix me firmly in the hearts of senior citizens.'

Layne chuckled. 'Can I help it if these fast-living, boozing, womanizing parts fit you like a glove?'

He gave her a sideways glance. 'You may regret you said that when we get you back home, madam.'

Layne stopped and regarded him with a gleam of humour. 'And what makes you think you'll be allowed in, sir?'

Fergus stopped, too. He reached out with one hand and tucked some stray strands of her hair behind Layne's ear. Thus diverted, she did not see his other hand stretching to pluck the keys from the pocket of her jeans. He gave a slow, equally diverting smile, and bent towards her, almost whispering, 'I didn't think you were that much of an exhibitionist.'

'I don't know what you . . .' She felt a tug at her pocket and suddenly her keys were being jangled in front of her nose. 'Fergus Hann!'

But he was away before his name was out. Layne dropped the hands she was about to fold across her chest and chased after him. She arrived a matter of seconds after he had got the right key in the lock.

'I hope you haven't got a man tucked away in here,' he warned. It didn't seem a bad idea.

'Yes!' she said, catching her breath. 'I have. A man,' she confirmed.

Fergus turned, a sceptical smile on his lips. 'Who is he?'

Layne had to think fast. 'The . . . warden.'

'The warden?' He was far from impressed with her lack of imagination. 'What warden?'

The lock clicked back and the door swung open. 'National Trust,' improvised Layne, adding, 'Of course!' for effect.

Fergus now stood dangling the keys above her head. 'And what would a National Trust warden be doing inside your holiday home, pray?'

Layne reached up to snatch them but was too slow. 'Looking for the rare Skye spider,' she declared. 'He's very good-looking. You'll recognize him by the binoculars.'

He shook his head. 'C minus for effort. Go and write "Must try harder" fifty times.'

'You go first,' she suggested brightly, feeling she still had some control, but without warning, Fergus dropped down and caught Layne round the back of her legs, hoisting her over his shoulder.

'Put me down, Fergus,' she hissed, acutely embarrassed, but she was bundled inside regardless, while he kicked the door shut with the back of his heel.

'Where's the bedroom?' he demanded.

'I'm not telling you!'

'Well, I could drop you on the floor, but the bed would be a lot less painful.'

There was some truth in this, she realized quickly. 'Second on the right,' she admitted reluctantly.

'Right.'

'And hurry. All the blood's running to my head.'

Layne landed smack on her back in the middle of the bed and bounced. 'If you've broken my springs, Fergus Hann, I'll . . .'

He had straightened up and seemed to tower

over her in the restricted space of the room. 'You'll what?'

She changed tack, leaning forward on her elbows. 'Don't ever do that again! I am not a sack of potatoes. I've told you before that you watch all the wrong films.'

He dropped to a squatting position in front of her. 'Well, here's another challenge for you . . . to write a love story for the politically-correct hero and heroine without sending the audience to sleep.'

Layne eyed him suspiciously but conceded, 'I'll put it on my list. Now, if you'll excuse me . . .'

He shook his head. 'Not just yet.'

'Why?'

'This is real life. It's much more entertaining. I haven't finished with you.'

She looked him hard in the eye. Fergus may have been a big man but she was far from frightened of him. 'Oh yes you have,' she advised, sliding off the bed and reaching for the door handle.

Strong fingers, hooked into the waistband of her jeans, spun her round, as Fergus rose to his feet and pushed the door shut with his other hand.

Layne lifted her chin. 'Now what do you intend to do?'

'To do what I came for. To find out what's going on.'

'Nothing is going on. You can see for yourself. No National Trust wardens, nothing.'

'Very funny.'

She glared up at him, trapped, and backed up against the door though his hand was still preventing her exit. 'Please may I leave the room, sir?' she ventured.

'If and when you give me satisfactory answers to my questions.'

He took Layne by the shoulders and sat her down on the bed, returning to lean back against the door himself. 'Why haven't the words been flowing?'

Layne was happy to contradict him. 'They are now. I've written reams.' She jumped to her feet. 'I'll show you . . .'

Fergus took hold of her and sat her firmly back down.

'Stop manhandling me,' she growled ominously.

He ploughed on regardless. 'You know very well I'm referring to John Trevor's complaint that you've been neither use nor ornament since you got back from Greece.'

'That's just . . .'

Fergus jabbed a finger in her direction. 'And I don't want to hear you saying that's just John being John!'

She tossed her hair angrily back over her shoulder. 'I had a virus, remember. It took a long time to get it out of my system, that's all.'

Fergus rubbed a hand across his forehead, muttering, 'Of course, the virus. How convenient.'

Layne smacked her hands down on the duvet, making it billow around her. 'It was not convenient at all. It was very unpleasant, as you well know!'

He took a couple of steps forward. 'And is the virus out of your system now?' She stared sullenly at the knees of his trousers. 'I said,' he repeated the words quietly and deliberately, 'Is the virus out of your system now?'

She continued to stare at his knees as she spoke. 'You've seen for yourself that I'm not going down the drain. I've already told you I'm writing again.'

Layne could have cursed when he resumed the squatting position in front of her, forcing her to look at his face and enabling himself to examine her features carefully. 'Did you blurt the name Fergus Hann out at John in this eruption of unbridled emotion because of the virus, too?'

Her heart wanted to say, 'Of course not, you bloody fool but you know that already, don't you,' whereas the words she spoke were ruled by her head. 'I was trying to stop him going on at me, that's all. I . . . said the first name that came into my head.'

Layne had kept her lashes lowered but when she heard his groan of impatience, she looked up sharply. 'So you're saying,' he concluded, 'that I've had a completely wasted journey?'

The words took any bravado out of her sails. 'I don't know.'

'Of course you damn well know,' he muttered getting to his feet, turning his back and shoving an irritated hand through his hair.

All at once, he rounded on her, more angry than she had ever seen him. 'For God's sake, Layne, stop playing games! If Hanna and I are prepared to admit there was this gaping black hole in our lives after you'd left, I think the least you could offer is a bit of honesty.'

Layne searched his face, trying to digest this revelation. It would have been all too easy to allow it to sway her resolve. Slowly, she got to her feet. 'If I've hurt anyone, then it's been unintentional. And, yes, all right, I know how it feels to have that gaping black hole in my life. I desperately wanted you and you weren't there. But I don't fool myself, Fergus. That's how it would always be . . . a future of disappointment and hurt. I've spent the last week screwing down the cover on that black hole and I'm not about to lift the lid off now. Can't you understand that?'

On the contrary, the blue eyes were glacial through lack of comprehension. 'It's the same line you were taking when you left but you still suffered weeks of hell. If you weren't so damn stubborn and let things take their natural course, you could be nicely surprised. Don't be so selfish. Let people in.'

Layne bristled at the criticism. 'I seem to remember being quite prepared to let things take their natural course before I left but that was considered selfish, too. It's a no-win situation.'

She pushed past him to the door, only to be told, 'Your six weeks would have been more hellish if I'd obliged, believe it or not.'

'I don't!' Layne turned the handle, only to have Fergus click the door shut again. 'Let go,' she warned.

'Layne . . .'

'Fergus, are you going to let go of this door?'

'No.'

He should have seen it coming but he did not. Layne kicked him in the shin and wrenched the door open as he doubled up. The fact that she felt immediate remorse did nothing to help. Fergus sucked in his breath. 'God dammit, woman!'

By now, Layne was on the far side of the door but was riveted by the awfulness of her action. There was more disbelief than anger in his eyes. 'That's the second time you've done that!'

'I'm sorry.'

Fergus gave his shin an angry rub, then straightened up and met the apologetic green eyes with a challenge. 'Come back here.'

She did not move but gave a slight shake of the head.

He crooked his index finger. 'Are you coming here, or do I have to come and get you?'

Layne straightened her shoulders, admitting frankly, 'I don't like the way this dialogue's going.'

'We can always scrub the dialogue, Layne.'

She did not like the sound of that either. Accepting the inevitable, she came towards him. 'Just as long as you remember I *am* sorry.'

Fergus took her gently by the arm, drawing her in through the doorway. Layne waited, hands clenched behind her. He ran the back of his hand along her cheek, then trailed a finger to her chin and down the length of her neck. When it reached the top button of her shirt, it slowly retraced its path. 'Turn around,' he said.

She hesitated, searching his features for some betrayal of intention. He was acting well. They revealed nothing. 'Go on.'

Layne spun on her heel. Whatever he chose to do, she knew in her heart she trusted him. All the same, she took a deep breath to calm herself.

Fergus stroked her hair towards him, gathering it together. She felt her head being tugged sideways and realized he was winding her hair around his fist. A thrill of anticipation rippled the length of her body, then she shuddered as his lips burned into the flesh beneath her ear, then kissed their way along her jaw to the corner of her mouth. His free hand slipped inside her waistband, freeing her shirt, working its way slowly upwards, flipping open every button as it went.

At last he folded back the loosened shirt, baring one shoulder. Unable to move because of the tight grip on her hair, she was about to moan his name when he spoke softly. 'You're really sorry, aren't you, Layne?'

'Yes.' It came out as a sigh.

'Then say after me, "I promise".' His lips were close to her ear.

'I promise,' she managed breathlessly.

'Never ever . . .'

'Never ever.'

Fergus kissed her neck before continuing, 'To kick Fergus in any bodily region . . .'

She dared to smile to herself. 'To kick Fergus in any bodily region.'

'On any occasion whatsoever . . .'

This time, he kissed her shoulder as she spoke, making her voice shake. 'On . . . any occasion whatsoever.'

'No matter how much he deserves it.'

'No matter how much he deserves it.'

His lips were close to her ear again. 'On pain of . . .' They played with her earlobe. Layne screwed up her eyes, forcing down the threatening eruption of raw want. He whispered again, 'On pain of appropriate punishment.'

With the slow release of her hair, Layne began to turn her head. She felt naked, as though he had stripped away every last piece of clothing and liberated her. He was close behind, his arms closing round her waist, drawing her back against him.

As he lowered his head into the crook of her neck, Layne kissed his ear and whispered suggestively, 'You mean on pain of corrective, corporal chastisement?'

'Whatever the lady prefers.'

She glimpsed humour in the blue eyes, just before his mouth found hers. Warm hands slid round to lift and squeeze her breasts, while Layne's arms snaked upwards, linking behind his neck, enabling him further, so anxious she was to give everything she had to offer.

As the kiss went on, her breasts swelled, their tips stiffening in his palms. She wanted to turn but he held her fast, smoothing a hand down inside the waistband of her jeans to press hard against the flat of her stomach. Layne gave a sharp intake of breath. He seemed intent on driving her to distraction. The hand slid back up and now he did spin her round. She landed against his chest and found him smiling down at her, like a cat that had very definitely got the cream.

'I really don't think it's struck you yet, you blonde and beautiful, green-eyed witch, that I love you.'

Her body swollen with desire, Layne found it impossible to accept that he had, indeed, confessed love. She had one thing on her mind, sensation . . . She heard herself say, 'You don't mean that, Fergus.'

The smile had gone but he still *looked* as though he loved her. 'Don't tell me what I mean! I know what I mean and, unlike some people, I'm not afraid to admit it.'

'It just isn't possible.'

She was giving her head a shake when her feet lifted off the floor and she was kissed in a way that told her it was more than possible. As he lowered her, he enquired, 'Why not?'

Layne knew any reason she gave would be shot down in flames; not that she was exactly in a reasoning frame of mind.

He gave a shrug. 'There you are then. All that's left is for you to love me.'

She gave a huge sigh. 'A second ago we were making love. Why can't that be enough?'

'It doesn't need to be enough, when there's more,' he said quietly.

Reluctantly, her arms slid from his shoulders. 'I don't understand, Fergus.'

'It seems to me you're inexperienced in the ways of the world.'

231

'I am not a virgin!' she snapped.

'Neither am I. You see how little *that* means.'

Layne pulled completely away and began to fasten up her shirt. Fergus watched, a limited amount of sympathy in his eyes. 'Who is he?'

Layne subjected him to a green glare. Unable to help herself, she demanded, 'Who is your wife?'

It obviously hurt him less than she expected. He remained calm, collected and said, 'Is that supposed to be *touché*?'

She was unable to keep the humour out of her expression. 'Yes, it is,' she admitted, tucking her shirt back into her waistband.

He reached out and took her hand. 'I don't intend keeping you in the dark and I will explain, I promise, but let's see what you've got to eat first. I'm hungry.'

On their way to the kitchen, Fergus got distracted by the view. 'You've found a glorious spot. I came to Skye camping with my brother when I was in my teens. The weather was so bad I never came back. You're really out on a limb here at Ord too.'

'That's what I like about it,' smiled Layne. 'I didn't know you had a brother.'

He half-turned. 'I'm boringly normal, really. My mother's a Scot. My father was a Tynesider . . . and I have an older sister and brother.'

'So your father, is he . . .?'

'Died eight years ago.'

'I see,' said Layne. 'And . . . how is Hanna?'

'She's fine. Back at school, staying with Mother . . .'

'In Umberland. In the north?' suggested Layne.

Fergus smiled, visibly relaxing. 'That's about it.' He approached and put an arm round her shoulder. 'Come on, I'll make you some pasta.'

'I haven't got any,' she admitted.

'Don't tell me you live on rabbit food? No wonder you're so thin.'

'I am *not* thin!' she said crossly.

'You've definitely lost weight. You're not anorexic, are you?' There was genuine concern in his voice.

Layne shrugged him off. 'You're as bad as my father.'

'He noticed, too, did he? I quite took to the old stick.'

'He is *not* an old stick!'

Fergus dived into the fridge and waved a couple of tomatoes at her. 'But your mother. Oh dear, your mother!'

'What is wrong with my mother, pray?' Layne could no longer maintain her straight face.

'It doesn't look as if I have to tell you.' He kicked the door shut and put down the tomatoes. 'Suffice it to say, I shouldn't want to risk mugging her on a dark night.'

She picked the first cookery utensil she came to from the row of hooks on the wall and waved it at him. 'I'd advise you to get on with what you're doing.'

Fergus came towards her. 'Or you'll give me a thorough mashing?'

Layne tried to examine the utensil's suitability as a weapon but he removed it from her hand, saying teasingly, 'You know, it's a well-known fact that wives get more like their mothers as they age.'

The humour drained from her as his words sank in. Unable to look him in the eye, she recommended, 'Then, let that be a lesson to you.' Then she turned aside pretending to search frantically for something in a cupboard, feeling suddenly out of her depth.

It was not until they had eaten and were drinking a glass of red wine, looking out at the ever-changing sky above the loch, that Fergus opened up on the subject of his wife. It was as if he were talking to himself. 'I didn't know Darcey was an alcoholic when I met her in the States. You probably got the message that Hanna was the result of total irresponsibility by the pair of us. I was looking for female comfort when a relationship didn't work out and, looking back, I see Darcey had her sights set on money.'

He smoothed the handle of an unused knife between finger and thumb. 'I have been learning a slow, painful lesson with Darcey ever since. The last thing she wanted was a child. If it hadn't been for a mutual friend, I doubt I'd ever have known about Hanna's existence. It took a lot to persuade Darcey to endure the pregnancy. When she suggested financial inducements might carry the most weight, I began to see what I was dealing with.'

Layne stared at him, unable to stop herself from voicing her feelings. 'That's appalling!'

Fergus allowed Layne some sympathy but kept the condemnation for himself. 'What was more appalling was that I married her, fooling myself into thinking Hanna's arrival would change things. Darcey did seem taken with her at first but it proved to be the interest of a child with a new toy. Like the marriage, Hanna was one of her stepping stones in her pursuit of new experiences. After the first month, I had to work in the Far East and employed a nanny to care for Hanna until I could get back. By the time I did, Darcey was not only heavily back into the alcohol but, without my knowing, had moved onto soft drugs. Unwittingly, I'd been financing her habit.'

He hesitated, then looked Layne in the eye. 'Darcey started off as a spoilt little rich girl, who was given so much at the start of her life, she really had nothing to strive for. If you're handed everything on a plate, you don't get much pleasure from the little things in life, so where do you look for excitement? Men? Anything that's out of the ordinary, risky or dangerous? In no time you're in a downhill spiral. You may think I can be hard on Hanna but I'll do my utmost to prevent any child of mine going down Darcey's road.'

Layne shook her head, insisting, 'I don't think you're hard on Hanna, Fergus.'

He held up his glass and peered through the red liquid as though into the mists of time. 'Shortly after my return, Darcey did a disappearing act and I had no option but to bring Hanna back home to England, where I had work and could spend some time with her. I employed help but my mother gradually took Hanna under her wing. As you've seen, when work allows, I whisk The Horrible off with me to give Mother breathing space.'

'So has Hanna met her mother since she was a baby?' enquired Layne.

He put the glass down. 'No. Eighteen months later, Darcey resurfaced, needing money. When I met her again, she'd already moved on to heroin and was so sick I got her straight into one of the best clinics in the States. I can't tell you how many times she's been in and out of there since. To answer your question more fully, although I once wanted to take Hanna out there to meet her biological mother, I had to seriously rethink that one. You can hardly tell a child her mother doesn't want her, nor that her mother is out of her head on drugs.'

'So what *can* you say?' What did you say?'

'That, although her mother knew her as a baby, she fell ill and died months later? Does that sound callous?'

Layne shook her head slowly. 'Not in the circumstances, I suppose.'

'You're faced with a limited number of options but you have to think of Hanna. If I'd said Darcey died in childbirth, Hanna might have subconsciously blamed herself at some stage. I considered saying her mother had married again but that could have laid down trouble for the future.'

'What, though, if Darcey ever changes her mind? Wants to see her daughter? It could put your own relationship with Hanna at terrible risk.'

'I'd have to accept it, explain the circumstances and lay myself at my daughter's mercy, wouldn't I? I simply don't see it as a possibility any more. But the mess was of my own making and I'd have to take the consequences.'

'You still blame yourself, don't you?'

'We have to live with our mistakes.'

It was not said in any self-pitying way but Layne felt the need to reach across to him. 'Hanna's growing up beautifully. It wasn't all a mistake.'

She smiled encouragingly. 'Where would we be without her?'

He turned her hand over in his, then subjected her to the most disturbing examination of her features yet. 'And then you wonder what it is about you I love! Look, I can't offer you conventional marriage, Layne . . .'

She knew her expression looked tortured and could do nothing to stop it.

'. . . But I want you to consider seriously. I love you and I want you to be a real mother to Hanna. I know it's a lot to ask but if you turn me down, make it a damn good reason . . . none of this nonsense about your career or my career or my past, or fellow actresses.'

'They sound good enough reasons to me,' Layne managed to point out gently.

'They're not,' he said simply. 'I want you to spend what's left of your time on Skye thinking very hard about this.'

'Fergus, I came away to write . . . to get away from mental turmoil!'

'You came away to put your head in the sand. This is real life,' he reminded her.

'It's not that I'm not grateful. I really am,' she assured him.

Fergus pushed his plate away and got up. 'There's nothing to be "grateful" for. You either love somebody or you don't. It should be as simple as that.'

'Then,' she said miserably, 'maybe I don't.'

'Maybe you choose not to see it when it's staring you in the face?'

She scowled up at him. 'I wonder if you would ever take "no" for an answer?'

'A solid reason, Layne. That's all I ask. Otherwise you could find keeping that head in the sand gets more uncomfortable every day.'

Layne began collecting the plates and banging them together, only for Fergus to make the observation, 'You haven't told me about him yet.'

'Who?'

'Your lover.'

'Ha!' exclaimed Layne at this inappropriate description.

'Not very good, then,' came the conclusion.

Layne gave a wry smile. 'In fairness, he wasn't the only one.'

'Not the only lover?'

'You know very well what I mean. Not the only one who wasn't any good.'

'Wasn't *any* good? He's getting worse.'

'Don't, Fergus. It wasn't funny.'

'That's a shame. A bit of humour can often salvage disastrous lovemaking.'

'You obviously know more about that than I do,' she accused.

'Ouch! I'm sorry, you were saying . . .'

Layne put the plates down and tidied a handful

of hair behind one ear. 'If you must know I got to what is now regarded as the ancient age of twenty-two with my virginity weighing like a millstone round my neck. It seemed important at the time to lose it and get on with my life, so I . . . propositioned a close friend. It was a mindless thing to do. He was willing but there was really no sexual attraction between us.' She sighed heavily. 'We had a couple of drinks. Then he just, sort of, crawled on top of me and performed the function, roughly, crudely and without feeling.'

'What an appalling waste!'

'As soon as he'd gone I was sick in the loo.'

'He was no friend then. You were practically raped.'

'The friendship ended but I can't claim rape. I co-operated.' She gave a cynical smile. 'I lost the millstone. Went straight out and bought a chastity belt!'

'How long ago was that?'

'Six years.'

'If only I'd known you then . . .'

She grinned. 'I could have had five children by now . . .'

'So much for the chastity belt!'

She picked up a fork and pointed it at him, admitting, 'One thing about you, Fergus, is you do know how to turn a girl on. Mind you . . .'

Layne had second thoughts and returned to clearing the dishes.

'Mind you, what?' enquired Fergus.

'Nothing.'

'Tell me,' he insisted.

Layne sighed. 'Well, I must admit that until you told me the full story just now, I did wonder why you kept backing off. You know,' she teased, 'whether there was something I ought to know about . . .'

Fergus rubbed his chin thoughtfully, then came back to face her across the table. 'I think you know, Layne Denham, that questioning a man's capabilities in that area could incite him to prove otherwise.'

She cocked her head to one side, assuring him, 'It was just a joke, Fergus. I've no doubt you're more than capable.'

He came round the table and placed his hands at her waist. 'Have you any idea what it's like dealing with a sexual time-bomb that's liable to explode any minute? You've been ticking away for six years now. I'm just waiting for the permanent green light to perform a controlled explosion.' He put his lips to her ear. 'I'm really looking forward to detonating you!'

The plates rattled in her hands. 'Behave, Fergus, or I'll drop the dishes!'

He drew back and remarked, 'That seems to

have brought a glow to your cheeks.'

A twinkling gleam in her eye betrayed her sense of humour. 'You should write your own material. You obviously have a vivid imagination. Now, are you going to wash up or am I?'

Fergus stood back and waved her past. 'You are. I think this is a job for the little woman.'

She knew it was meant to be a joke but turned slowly to glare threateningly over her shoulder. He shook his head. 'Ah-ah. You promised. No subjecting Fergus's bodily regions to assault, remember?'

'No kicking, only,' advised Layne. 'This leaves many other means of inflicting pain at my disposal.'

He grinned. 'Just get on with the washing-up, witch!'

When Layne emerged from the kitchen, she found Fergus lying on the floor alongside the television set. As he rolled over, her heart sank. He was holding up one of the videos she had brought with her.

'You see,' he announced, 'we do have a problem. To a greater or lesser degree I appear to have roles in each of the films you have here.'

She aimed at a casual shrug. 'Well, can I help it if you're ubiquitous?'

He collected them up, got to his feet and walked slowly towards her, shaking his head. 'No. Sorry. I wouldn't let you into the local amateur dramatic society with that audition piece, luvvie.' He moved on past.

'Where are you going?'

'I'm going to lock these in my car. They're confiscated.'

'Those are my videos. Bring them back here!' she ordered.

'All right.' He returned to the open window and held one up. His picture was on the front cover. He pointed to it. 'See this. This is not me.' Fergus threw the video out of the window. He held up another. 'This isn't me, either, nor this, nor this.'

One by one, Fergus tossed the films out and Layne watched, open-mouthed, as they bounced on the grassy bank. He came back and stood in front of her, pointing at his chest. 'On the other hand, this is me, Layne. I'm not Joseph Lennox or any of those fictional characters. I act for a living just like the plumber plumbs and the builder builds. There's nothing romantic about it.'

Out of a combination of embarrassment and infuriation, Layne promptly smacked his face. In fact, she so enjoyed seeing the surprise register, she aimed for his other cheek, too. He caught her wrist in mid flight. 'You're out of your league, nanny. I play dirty and below the belt. I'm simply saying that *you're* the one who watches all the wrong films around here.'

Layne felt herself shaking. She could hardly get the words out. 'Don't flatter yourself that I've spent every waking moment on Skye glued to videos of the great acting icon! I brought those for a rainy day, which, so far, I have not had. I've had them years . . . long before I met you . . .'

'You're either not hearing me or you refuse to hear me,' he interrupted her.

But she confirmed his criticism by ploughing on. 'To someone who's had to struggle to make a living, those things cost money. We can't all afford to smash up our old possessions and buy new!'

Fergus swore under his breath and began to reach for his wallet. Although he was merely teasing, Layne did not consider it a tactful move. She turned on her heel and stormed out of the cottage.

He watched through the window as she lovingly gathered up the films, some of which had spilled out of their cases. She was about to straighten up when, all at once, she seemed to crumple. Layne sank down in the grass and sobbed.

It slowly dawned on Fergus that all he had done was uncover the tip of the iceberg. He was no Freud. He saw there was little more he could do. Only Layne could sort herself out. Reluctantly, he took a blank sheet off the top of Layne's pile of papers and wrote down a telephone number with the words: 'Let me know if you change your mind.'

CHAPTER 12

Layne could hardly believe it when she saw the black car had gone. She rushed indoors to check every room. At last, she noticed the paper with unusual handwriting next to the scripts on the table. She picked it up.

Her hand shook as she read the brusque instruction. There was no name. No 'love from Fergus'. She realized she did not even know his handwriting, had never seen it before. It was unlike the man . . . or, at least, the man she thought she knew.

A lump came to her throat. It grew increasingly painful to swallow. With the paper still in her hand, Layne lowered herself into an armchair and stared out at the sky. For a long, long time, she sat there, vacant and motionless, limbs refusing to move.

As clouds scudded overhead, tears began to slide the length of numb cheeks. They dripped, unhindered, into space, blending the colours of the sunset to one russet blur. Emotion oozed painlessly from some well within until it bled dry.

When the desire for conscious thought returned to her, Layne felt suspended, like some fossil, gripped in the claws of time. But she saw with new clarity and perspective. Her greatest fear confronted her, issuing her with a challenge. That fear was dependence.

Fergus was right. She had not been honest with him because, until now, she had not known the truth. Only now was she able to relive Lizzie's total dependence on others to wash, toilet, feed and entertain her . . . from the simple things everyone took for granted, like cleaning the teeth or blowing a nose to the vital ones of medication, physiotherapy, even love. She had been dependent on all the love of her family to get her through each day. Yet Layne was not even sure if Lizzie had been able to love for herself. She could laugh, yes, and she knew what she wanted. She could be wilful.

Layne recognized that Lizzie was tough and, through necessity, endured the one thing she, herself, dreaded. Since the loss of her sister, Layne prized her independence above everything. Now Fergus was asking her to place himself and Hanna at the top of her 'most-valued' list and let that independence slide.

It was good to share things. It was good to love and be loved. But was it enough? He saw it as selfishness on her part but didn't she have the right to weigh her own needs? It was not as if they could marry. The objections she had already raised were still valid. Maybe Fergus was the one who was not facing reality.

There was, of course, the other side of the coin. Layne knew if she did not meet this situation head-on, then it could arise again. Was she really telling herself she never wanted to experience a full loving relationship or have children? And if she was not, then how could she turn down Fergus in favour of some other, subsequent man? Even Layne knew that was unthinkable.

At length, deciding she would never sleep unless she got some air in her lungs, Layne pulled on her jacket and left the cottage, taking the road down to the bay. All was quiet in the darkening dusk except for the gentle lapping of waves at the shoreline. Layne had not thought to change her shoes and the damp sand soon penetrated the canvas layer about her feet.

Halfway across, feeling chilled by the night air, Layne lowered herself onto one of the rock fingers thrusting out toward the loch and realized she had, at last, assumed a calm objectivity about her circumstances. She could no longer tell herself there was a choice.

She was not, in any case, allowed to contemplate for long, for there was a brief but needle-like stab at her cheek, swiftly followed by another and another.

The sudden realization that she was being attacked by the notorious Scottish midges had her on her feet and hurrying back along the shore, wafting her hands ineffectually at the invisible assailants as she went. In her haste back up the road with her head down, she did not notice the figure heading in her direction.

Fergus had to call out to gain her attention. 'Layne!'

He, too, was slapping at his face. 'For Pete's sake, hurry and get the door open.'

She had no time to query his arrival beneath the onslaught of multiple stabbings, but fished for her keys and held them up. He snatched them and rushed back to open up the cottage.

They both breathed with relief on slamming the door on the bloodthirsty hordes. 'Swines!' swore Fergus, slapping his forehead.

Layne rushed into the bathroom and returned with some spirit and cotton wool. 'Come here,' she ordered, pulling away his hand and dabbing the already reddening areas of skin. 'I thought it was too early for them. It must be this fine weather.' She stood back a second. 'What are you doing here, anyway? I thought you'd left the island.'

He waited patiently while she attended to him.

'My conscience got the better of me. I headed for the ferry, stopped to make some phone calls, then changed my mind and drove down to the south. I did a lot of thinking. Here, let me.'

Fergus took the bottle and cotton wool and applied the spirit to Layne's face. 'I'm glad I came back,' he concluded. 'You look as if you've been crying ever since I left.'

She smiled, admitting, 'Pretty much.'

'You'll need to replenish your liquids!' he teased affectionately. 'Shall I get us a drink?'

'That would be nice. I'll just get out of these wet shoes.'

'Why don't you take a shower? It'll relax you.'

'All right,' she agreed. 'I won't be long.'

'Take all the time you want.'

Layne gave him a long look and sighed contentedly to herself.

'What does that mean?' he enquired, a spark of humour lighting his eyes.

'I'll tell you later,' she promised.

By the time Layne had slipped off her clothes and pulled on a towelling robe, Fergus had run the water to the right temperature. He waved her into the bathroom as he left, bowing his head. 'Your servant, ma'am.'

Her eyes shone into his. 'Why thank you, kind sir.'

Fergus closed the door and went rummaging through the kitchen cupboards.

On her way out of the shower, Layne noticed him sprawled on the settee with a glass in his hand, reading a woman's magazine, and took a few steps into the room to tell him, 'There's enough hot water if you want one, too, Fergus.'

He looked up and decided she looked pinker and less weary. 'I might take you up on that later.' Getting to his feet, he threw the magazine aside, inviting her, 'Come and have that drink. G & T all right?'

She nodded. 'Lovely.'

He brought her glass in from the kitchen and handed it to her, commenting, 'You seem well supplied in the refreshment department.'

Layne took a sip of the gin and tonic with ice and lemon. 'Mmmmm,' she said appreciatively, 'there are some priorities I do get right. If the weather had been poor, I'd have needed some consolation.'

'Come and sit down,' he recommended.

She looked down at herself. 'I ought to change.'

'It's nearly bedtime. Hardly worth it,' came the response. He took her hand. 'Come on.'

Layne allowed him to draw her onto the settee next to him. She felt at peace. He could even have been her husband. She was surprised to hear him say, 'I'm sorry I upset you.'

Layne put her drink on the table and looked him squarely in the face. 'It wasn't you, Fergus.'

He took a mouthful of his gin and declared, 'You gave me the impression it was.'

'I know. It was easier to take it out on you. I've had some time to think since then and I was wrong. I am sorry.'

His expression was not without sympathy. 'Did you come to any conclusions?'

'More than I ever could have hoped.' She reached for her drink. 'Do you want to know what they are?'

He watched the level of liquid drop rapidly down her glass and relieved her of it, putting it aside. 'Tell me before the edges get fuzzy.'

'Number One,' she began, 'I'd managed to fool myself I was self-sufficient. I'm nothing of the sort. I have this need to be an island and, as the saying goes, no man is! I've been slow to realize that simply by having someone dependent on you makes you, in turn, dependent in some way.'

Fergus waited for her to continue, his expression inscrutable.

'Number Two, unless I want to become a nun, I'd be seriously off my head to lose you.' Layne put a hand on his knee and fingered the denim of his jeans as she went on. 'Therefore, Number Three follows that I should, at the very least, accept your suggestion of a six-month probationary period . . . that is, on both sides.'

'Any more?'

'Only a confession that, for some time now, I've known I must be the luckiest woman on earth and not admitted it to you.'

Fergus caught hold of her hand. 'Stop mincing words, and give it to me straight. I can take it.'

Layne smiled into the blue eyes. 'I love you,' she said, then, supposing she could sense some scepticism on his part, she threw her arms round his neck. 'Honestly! What more can I say?'

He shook his head. 'I'd prefer you didn't. I'm having a job enough digesting that little lot!'

'Then how about this?' She kissed him hard and he let her, before drawing her arms down from his shoulders.

He spoke softly, 'I've been thinking, too.'

'Yes?'

He reached out and handed Layne her glass. 'You may need this. I don't think you're going to like me once I've said it.'

'Why?' she said, not believing him.

'I think you need a breathing space.'

'A breathing space?'

As if emphasizing the fact, he got up. 'A bit of time apart to get used to the idea.'

Layne was still too suffused with warmth and love to be daunted, so it was with affection she enquired, 'Are you getting cold feet?'

He shook his head slowly, then bent his knees to squat in front of her. 'You, my lady, are still very vulnerable. I've never known a woman cry so much.'

She blinked. 'I never used to!'

He gave a reluctant smile. 'I realize it's my fault, putting all this pressure on you. I feel as if I've trodden in a termites' nest.'

'Thank you very much!' Layne hung on to her sense of humour. 'You have a lovely turn of phrase.'

He shrugged. 'Well, I mean it when I say you need time . . . to come to terms with changes you're apprehensive about.'

'It sounds as if you want space as well, Fergus,' suggested Layne.

He took her hands. 'What I want is for us to start right. How long do you need to finish your commission?'

'The deadline's in six weeks or so, though I expect, if they take it on, I'll be involved long after that.'

He nodded, adding, 'I don't know how long filming will last. I spoke to Jerry today and it looks as if the dispute could be solved in the next couple of days. Shall we give it three months?' Layne stared at him, not quite speechless.

'Three months!' Her tone was incredulous.

'I can prepare the ground with Hanna. Perhaps, by then, we'll have free time to spend together?'

'But three months!' repeated Layne. She could already feel the ripples disturbing her newly-discovered peace of mind.

He shifted to sit alongside her. 'It really isn't that long. We're both busy.'

Then reality hit her. This time, Layne got to her feet and flung her hands in the air. 'You've gone off me. As soon as I say I love you, you go off me!'

'Don't be so melodramatic.'

'Well, *you'd* know all about that, wouldn't you?' came the retort. Fergus simply smiled appreciation. 'I can't believe this,' she persisted, 'You're blowing hot and cold. I don't know where I am!'

He got up and placed his hands on her shoulders, contradicting her. 'Hot, Layne. I've been blowing hot . . . and only hot, ever since we met.'

He pulled her closer, stroking the hair back across her shoulders. Layne held the two halves of her robe tightly together. Her eyes held a challenge. 'I hope you're not going to try and start something you don't intend to finish.'

For long seconds, his eyes fenced with hers, until at last he let his hands drop. 'I think I'll take that shower,' he said. 'I'll fetch my bag from the car.'

Layne watched him pick up his keys and leave

the room. She sank down on the arm of a chair, finished her drink and saw she had been right about one thing. If you didn't allow yourself to become dependent, you didn't get half so disappointed.

Restless now, she got to her feet and paced back and forth from the kitchen to the sitting room. She heard the front door close, then the running of the shower. If he was serious about this 'three month breathing space', then there really was a matter that required dealing with.

Layne made for the bathroom. Turning the handle slowly, she gently edged the door open. With his back to her and the water running, he heard nothing.

Layne inspected his rear view with interest. She was not disappointed. Nor was she as he turned sideways, allowing the spray to rinse off the layer of soap. Layne was smiling with self-satisfaction when she caught his eye.

'What the . . .!' Fergus reached to turn off the spray.

Boldly, she looked him up and down and declared, 'Well, I've seen it all now, darling.' She winked. 'And it seems pretty good to me.'

He snatched at a towel and rubbed it down his chest as he climbed from the bath, fastening it round his waist as he drew level, demanding, 'Just what do you think you're up to?'

Layne sprawled back against the door, draping one arm above her head in exaggeratedly relaxed fashion. 'I no longer feel at a disadvantage. We're at least even in one respect.' A finger hovered in the general direction of his towel. 'You know,' she decided cheerfully, 'I could write a Kiss and Tell now, couldn't I? I could describe the famous Fergus Hann down to the very last millimetre . . .'

Fergus was catching on. 'Centimetre, I hope . . .'

Layne smiled. 'Very last inch even. We'll allow you that. I could reveal all your secrets and make a fortune. No longer would I have to scale the typeface with meaningful prose . . .'

His hands were on his hips and he looked fleetingly indulgent. 'What is this all about, Layne, because, as you see, I should like to get dry?'

She reached out for the towel, volunteering, 'Let me help you.'

He stepped quickly back. 'If you're not going to make any sense, then I think you should leave.'

Layne pulled at the tie of her robe and shrugged it off, letting it fall. 'Does *this* make any sense?'

His eyes travelled from her feet slowly and critically upwards until they finally met the challenge in hers. 'Put it away,' he recommended.

The green eyes smiled back at his towel. 'But you're pleased to see me, I can tell.'

He grinned. 'You really are asking for it, aren't you?'

'I don't think I could put it any plainer,' she agreed.

'Then I suggest, *darling* – ' he lifted her robe and arranged it loosely around her shoulders – 'that you wait for me in your room.'

Layne smiled to herself and reached for the door. 'Oh,' said Fergus. 'Put a few sexy things on. I like to undress my women first.'

Far from keen on the possessive plural reference to 'my women', Layne did not look back. On the other hand, she felt ridiculously pleased with herself. She had acted in a manner quite alien to her usual self and enjoyed it. Of course, it could have been the gin talking. It seemed to have gone straight to her head.

Layne wondered why one drink had given her confidence such a huge boost, then she realized Fergus had probably been over-generous. Well, if he had hoped to lift her spirits, he had succeeded. It also occurred to her that all this was on an empty stomach. Neither he nor she had eaten for hours.

As she rootled through her suitcase to find something remotely sexy, Layne considered whether it was such a good thing to make love on an empty stomach. Hers always made terrible groaning or pathetic whining noises. Still, if they were enjoying themselves enough, they ought not to notice.

It soon became apparent that she had brought nothing to Skye that came close to sexy. She had been prepared for practicalities like cold and rain. He would hardly find her sexy in nothing but walking boots and an umbrella, unless he was terminally kinky.

Layne sighed and sank down on the bed. She suddenly felt dog tired. She had lost interest in the sexy clothing. It had been a long, mentally exhausting day and the bed was soft and inviting. He would have to make do with her body alone.

She shrugged off her robe, slid between the sheets and snuggled her head into the pillow. Bliss. Layne closed her eyes.

She did not hear Fergus softly calling her name, nor notice when the light went out. Neither did she smell the appetising aroma emanating from the kitchen, as Fergus cooked himself an omelette.

Layne was awoken next morning by a metallic-sounding noise outside her window. She peered through the curtains to witness a ram butting its reflection in her car door with tightly curled horns.

It took no notice of the banging on the window, so Layne was forced to throw on some clothes, rush out and confront it in person. The ram glanced from ranting human to reflection and back again. Layne saw that it was grumpily contemplating its options and made its mind up for it. She picked up a stick, waved it threateningly and the ram lolloped away on a disgruntled baa.

Only on her way back to the door did it strike her that there was no black car. Sudden memories of the night before came spilling into her head. She went slowly along the hall and turned back into her bedroom. The clock said seven forty-five.

Layne pulled the curtains right back and dropped onto the edge of the bed. What a complete fool she had been . . . and what an opportunity she had missed. She hardly dared imagine what he thought of her now.

It was only when she was examining her features in the mirror with utter contempt that the folded piece of paper caught her eye. Her name was written across the front in capitals. She picked it up, sank back on the bed and opened it with a sense of dread.

It read:

Darling,
How I hate to leave you after spending the most memorable night of my life. You took me to heights of passion surpassing ecstasy . . . so many times. I didn't know I had it in me and you certainly didn't know you had it in you. I can't wait for three months to pass, so that I can

possess your welcoming body again and again. At least I have that lovebite on my left buttock to remember you by.

By the way, I didn't mean you to think we should have no contact in all that time. We can phone and feel free to fax me as often as you like.

Meantime, I do recommend you keep off the booze, unless you're hoping for the part of the bag lady in my next film. Take care of yourself. (I thought you would like something to remember me by, so I left the dirty frying pan in the sink.)

I love you, Laynie
F.

P.S. Do you really think I'd make a writer? I'm sure I have the imagination.

Layne flopped back on the bed and slapped the letter over the smile on her face. The man was completely mad. She kissed the paper and sprawled ecstatically. It had taken all this time to sink in. She really was in love and, at long last, she was beginning to enjoy it.

For the next three days, Layne had a spring in her step and a blossoming of new ideas in her head. Even though the weather turned to cloud and rain, she whistled and hummed and wrote. And on no occasion did she attempt to salvage or play any of her videos. Nothing could dampen her spirits.

CHAPTER 13

In the end, Layne left Skye before her two weeks were up, eager to present John with the fruits of her labours.

He was surprised when she rang to say, 'I've got something for you, John. When can I come round?'

'Eleven thirty, Wednesday,' he suggested, adding, 'Just as long your "something" doesn't consist of three heavies armed with baseball bats.'

Keeping him guessing, she had simply said, 'I'll see you then.'

He was deeply embarrassed, therefore, when Layne staggered through his door, armed with a huge bouquet of flowers and one completed commission. More embarrassed still, when she kissed him soundly on the cheek, announcing, 'I was all for sacking you until someone showed me the error of my ways. Now,' she told him, dropping the bouquet on his desk, 'get those in water. I'm taking you out for lunch.'

'Oh no, you're . . .'

'No arguments!' ordered Layne. 'If you choose to stick your nose in where it's not wanted, then you must take the consequences . . . flowers and all!'

He got reluctantly to his feet, grumbling, 'What the hell am I supposed to do with those things?'

She shrugged, suggesting, 'Give them to your girlfriend of the moment if you don't want beauty and fragrance in your own life, John.'

He grasped hold of them and opened the side door to his secretary's office. Looking and sounding very awkward, he told her, 'Stick these in the sink for me will you, Lorrie?'

'With water,' Layne reminded him.

'Of course with water,' grizzled John.

Once relieved of his embarrassment, he looked more amenable.

'Right,' said Layne. 'Where's the nearest hamburger-and-chip joint?'

'I knew this was a bad idea,' he said, turning to lead the way.

On the way out to the street, Layne stopped him and pointed at the narrow steps. 'How do you ever hope to get your bathchair up here, John? Have it widened and put in a ramp or something?'

He studied her face and sighed heavily. 'I made a terrible mistake, didn't I? I preferred your blue period.'

She shook her head. 'The blue period was hardly productive. Now you may get a lot of earache but at least you can start rubbing your hands again. Come on, Scrooge, and don't forget to do something about those steps. None of us stays young and sprightly forever!'

John was not the only one on the receiving end of Layne's restored humour. She sent Fergus a fax via John that read, 'I thought it was the right buttock.'

Eventually the reply: 'No. It was the wrong one,' was read out to her over the phone by Lorrie.

When John intercepted her reply of: 'It looked like the right one in the mirror', Layne found herself banned from the use of his fax.

She began to write letters instead. Stupid letters. The kind of letters that were always unearthed for Kiss and Tell Tales to demonstrate beyond a doubt that the writer was deranged or past hope. Layne even wrote 'I love you' so many times in one of them that she came to the same conclusion herself and tore it up.

When she had heard nothing for two weeks, Layne phoned the studios. Fergus was not available, so, in the end, she asked for Max. He could not be found, so she left a message and Max phoned her back the same evening. After exchanging pleasantries and discussing the topic of Tim's improved health, Max remarked, 'News has it that you took my advice, Layne. I'm green with envy.'

'Well don't be just yet,' she advised. 'Fergus thinks we need three months apart . . . breathing space for me was his excuse.'

'Well, far be it from me to appear tactless, but I'm hardly surprised. We're surrounded by a bevy of female beauties at the moment . . . or, more accurately, Fergus is. When you wrote that script, you offered him a veritable candy box of licentious goodies.'

'Max . . . I'm supposed to trust him!' She bit her lip but had to ask, 'Is he behaving himself?'

'Off set, I think he is . . . but then dear old Lennox is having so much fun on camera that . . .'

'All right, I get the picture! Don't tell me any more.'

'Even young Tim is having his eyes opened. I can't tear him away.'

'Yes, Max. I said *all right*!'

'Sorry, dear. Can't you get over to see us for yourself?'

'I probably could. I'm waiting for some comeback on the work I've submitted . . . but I don't want Fergus to think I'm spying on him. I'd be falling at the first hurdle, wouldn't I?'

'I suppose so. Don't you want him to know you phoned?'

'Oh yes, Max. The least he can do is ring me. Will you ask him?'

'It'll be my pleasure. I'll waltz up to him on set, if you like, and tell him the love of his life demands his attention. How about that?'

Layne smiled to herself. 'It sounds perfect, Max. I'll be eternally grateful.'

'For you, dear, anything.'

It was close to midnight when the phone rang and Layne heard the humour in Fergus's voice. 'Is that the love of my life speaking?'

'As a matter of fact it is,' confirmed Layne, a smug smile on her lips at the sound of his voice. 'I was just about to fall into bed.'

'With or without clothes?' he enquired.

'Emphatically *with*. I'm wearing three pairs of socks, two flannelette nighties and a chastity belt,' declared Layne.

'You really know how to turn a man on, don't you?'

'It sounds as if you don't need me to do that, Fergus.'

'Do I detect a certain peevishness in your voice?'

Layne wound the telephone cord slowly round her fingers. 'Max did just happen to mention you were making the most of your lovemaking scenes.'

'That's Max for you. Not that I wanted to let

you down. You know you like me to act my socks off.'

She could almost hear him smile. 'Socks, yes. It's the rest I'm worried about.'

'Well, you needn't be. You should know by now that performing with strange women in front of hordes of technicians complaining about the angles is far from erotic,' he assured her.

'I suppose it depends on your exhibitionist tendencies,' remarked Layne sceptically.

'I'd prefer to have done the job with you. You haven't got an Equity card, I suppose? Are you any good at faking?'

'At what!'

'*Faking*, woman!'

'I'm not expecting to have to!' retorted Layne. 'I'm expecting to reach those heights . . . what was it . . . beyond ecstasy?'

'I'm not sure I'm *that* good,' he said, laughing.

'I shall demand no less,' she assured him.

'I feel tired already,' complained Fergus. 'Now did you want me for something in particular, or can I retire . . .'

'Don't tell me!' interrupted Layne. 'You have a hard morning ahead of you.'

'You said it.'

Layne sighed heavily. 'I miss you, Fergus.'

'And so you should.'

'How's Hanna?'

'Just as horrible as ever.'

'I suppose I'd better let you go.' She sighed again.

He mimicked her, sighing. 'I suppose you had.'

'All right, then!'

His voice became gently sympathetic. 'Sleep well, beautiful.'

She felt soothed. 'You, too. Night, night.'

'Night, Laynie.'

The dialling tone purred in her ears. She wished she had said she loved him but it didn't matter. He knew. She snuggled down in the bed and fell asleep trying to match up the features of his face in her mind's eye.

Two days later, John phoned to say he had heard very encouraging noises about the work she had submitted and that he would let her know when a meeting could be set up. In the meantime, he urged her to press on with her other projects. Layne knew as well as John did that if the film became even a moderate success any ideas she had would be viewed with interest by the 'right people'. The more polished they were, the more chance she stood of acceptance.

The encouragement was a boost to her ambitions and yet she also felt curiously deflated. She wanted to celebrate her minor triumph with the one person who was not there.

There was nothing for it but to get her head

down and work, putting any Fergus-related distractions aside. She was surprised to find this easier than expected, for Layne still had confidence in him and felt secure in the knowledge he was not too far away if she really needed him.

When, at last, Layne got swept up in a series of meetings over her commission work, she invested in an answerphone. It would give Fergus no excuse to say he had rung and received no reply.

She arrived home one evening to find a brief message from him demanding, 'Why have the love letters stopped coming? Has the adoration worn off already? The lovebite has.' The message ended with irritation. 'What on earth made you resort to one of these infernal machines, Layne?'

Quietly pleased to have rattled him, Layne immediately got down to writing a letter. She studiously avoided all mention of love, keeping the tone brusque with career news until the very last paragraph, which informed him: 'When my three month sentence is up, I look forward to re-establishing that lovebite. I think that this time however, you should have a matching pair, giving no cause for dispute over the relevant bodypart. I'm now off to have my teeth sharpened. Love, Layne.

P.S. I should write more often if you bombarded me with sickening tokens of love.'

Three days later, she answered a ring at the doorbell to be greeted with an arrangement of yellow roses in a basket. The card read: 'Are yellow roses sickening enough? F.'

When she wrote back this time, her style reverted to the original one of wild infatuation and the lighter mood lasted for days, even though that one flower delivery was the only 'bombardment' she received. She was easily pleased.

At her next meeting with her agent, she was surprised to find John enquiring about her relationship with Fergus.

'Well, I can't exactly call it a relationship at the moment,' she told him. 'We're too busy. But I am hoping to resume where we left off when the film wraps up.'

'How long is it since you last heard from him?'

Layne totted up and forced down her surprise at having to announce, 'About three weeks, I suppose.'

John sat back in his chair and stared hard at her. 'What?' she demanded. He said nothing. Layne leant forward. 'John, you're the one who's always telling me you're no agony aunt. So long as I produce the work, you're not interested, remember.'

He rubbed his chin and sighed. 'Don't worry. I'm not exactly happy about it.'

'Happy about what?'

269

'Being asked to test the water.'

Layne sat back and folded her arms. 'John Trevor, just what are you rambling on about?'

He was looking at the desk, not Layne. 'I wouldn't do it, if it weren't for the fact that the fellow has influence.'

She jumped to her feet. 'If anybody else talks round and round an issue without coming to a point, you give them a great flea in the ear.'

'I know, I know,' he agreed. 'All right. Sit down and I'll explain.'

Reluctantly, Layne lowered herself back into her seat. 'What then?'

'Ian Thornton took me out to lunch yesterday.'

'Ian Thornton?'

'You do remember who he is?'

Irritated, Layne snapped, 'Yes, of course I know who he is. He's the script editor dealing with my series. He's attended all of the meetings. He looks about twenty and wears dark-rimmed glasses. Why wouldn't I know who he is?'

'You're not making this easy for me, Layne,' warned John.

'Should I?' she queried, surprised.

John pushed himself to his feet. 'I wish you would, damn it. I soon found out he wasn't discussing work, he was discussing you. He's interested in you, Layne, but doesn't want to tread on any toes. I . . . offered to . . .'

Layne glowered at him. 'Test the water, I think, is how you put it?'

'Well . . .'

'You know what the situation is. To some extent, you brought it about, for goodness' sake! Why not tell him flat?'

'Look, Layne, under normal circumstances I would. But, as I said, the man is not without influence . . .'

'The pound signs in your eyes are betraying you, John,' observed Layne cynically.

He did not allow himself to be diverted. 'And, after all, we are talking about Fergus Hann, here.'

Her eyes narrowed. 'What's that supposed to mean?'

'If you'd try and be realistic for a minute, you'd know what I mean. Hann is one of the top ten male box office draws. He's ten years your senior . . . and to be brutal, Layne, he does have a wife and child.'

Once again, she got to her feet and looked him in the eye. 'I am fully aware of that. He is also the man who drove all the way up to Skye to assure himself I wasn't pining away and to convince me he loved me, despite the libellous vitriol you faxed him.'

'Look at you both now, though,' he pointed out. 'Be honest and admit it's cooling off.'

Layne glared at him. 'I'll do nothing of the sort.

It's as "hot" as it ever was,' she snorted. 'Not that it has anything to do with you or Ian flaming Thornton!'

John bumbled back to thump into his chair. 'He's a good bloke. He likes you, that's all. You could let him buy you lunch. It wouldn't do any harm.'

'If Ian Thornton wants to talk script details, editing or future projects, he can buy me lunch. Anything else, he can forget it, good "bloke" or not. You can tell him from me that if he broaches any other subject, I'll send the advance back and tout my series elsewhere.'

'That's not possible. It wouldn't be legal anyway,' John reminded her.

'I'm not sure if I care! Just make sure he gets the message!' Layne slammed the door on her way out and muttered under her breath all the way down into the street. He had done nothing about those damn steps yet.

She was still slamming things around when she arrived inside her flat, aware, despite her bluster, that John had exposed a raw nerve. Fergus had not replied to her last letter either by hand, telephone or flower. Layne had responded in kind, i.e. done nothing. Well, now it was no longer a matter of private pride. John had made it public. She looked at one of the yellow roses she had kept, its petals now dry, brown and drooping, and hoped it did not symbolize the state of their relationship.

Layne picked up the phone and dialled the studios. Fergus was not available, nor was Max, nor was Rowan. Two days after leaving a message for Fergus or Max to ring her, she had still heard nothing. She had a feeling she could not shake off. Something was badly amiss.

With a sick feeling in her stomach, she rang again, only to be told the unit were on location. It took some time before anyone could tell her exactly where. When they did, she had to look Hengistbury Head up in her road atlas. It certainly was not one of the locations she had used in the screenplay, though this was no particular surprise in itself.

Within fifteen minutes, Layne was throwing her shoulder bag into the car and setting off for Dorset. With no idea what she would find when she got there, at least she felt she was doing something.

On the way, the heavens opened and her wipers struggled with the sheer volume of water splattering against her windscreen. The traffic on the motorway slowed to a crawl, except for occasional suicidal maniacs, who sped blindly on in the outside lane. Layne fully expected her hopes to be washed away, too. Filming would have had to be suspended and she had no idea where the cast and crew were staying.

By the time she reached the A31, carving its way through the New Forest landscape, a miraculous change occurred. The rain stopped and shafts of sunlight lasered their way through the great slate slab of sky, painting the scene with a dramatic brilliance. Layne gasped at its beauty and her spirits lifted.

She took a few wrong turnings after leaving the dual carriageway but stopped to check the map and got herself back on course. As she parked her car on the roadside, at last, she soon saw that work had not been affected. The equipment and motley group of figures at the top of the hill meant that Hengistbury Head had escaped the downpour.

By now, the sun had become fiery, dissipating the cloud. She climbed the grass slope to the top. Halfway up, warmed by both sun and her efforts, Layne had to pull off her jumper and tie it about her waist.

Rowan turned sharply at her approach, afraid some member of the public would go blundering into shot. It took him a moment to recognize her but then he waved a hand and smiled briefly before turning back to the job in hand.

A group of actors of about Tim's age were standing around the young star in his wheelchair, waiting for the call for action. Layne immediately recognized the scene they were to about to shoot.

She sidled up to Rowan and whispered, 'Where's Max?'

He pointed back down the hill. 'In the trailer. Hay fever . . .' was as far as he got before 'action' was called.

Layne watched a while as the boys jostled and threatened Lennox's son but something went wrong and they cut the take. She backed off a few yards, then turned and hurried down the hill.

Max's location was in no doubt. She could hear the sneezing a quarter of a mile up the road. When Layne reached the door, she gave a loud knock and peered inside. 'Max?'

'Who's that?'

Layne went right in, closing the door behind her. 'It's me. Layne.'

Max had his head buried in a handkerchief but slowly emerged. He looked surprised and not a little sheepish. 'What are you doing here?'

'I wrote the thing,' she reminded him.

'It's good to see you. Don't look at me like that, Layne. The pollen always has this effect.'

'You know very well why I'm looking at you like this. You didn't ring me back.'

He blew his nose loudly before admitting, 'No.'

Layne began to search in her bag. 'I think I've got some anti-histamine.'

Max shook his head miserably. 'It's not worth it. It always just knocks me out.'

'No. These ones are non-drowsy. You only have to take half of one to notice a difference. Are you on anything else?'

'No.'

'Try one, then. Is there a kettle in here? I could murder some tea myself.'

'Over there.' Max indicated the far end of the trailer.

Layne filled the kettle and switched it on, before coming back to stand over him. 'Why didn't you phone?'

'Oh, you know; busy, Layne. Tim can be a real little Hitler when he wants.'

She gave a humourless smile. 'Come on. You can do better than that, Max.'

'I'm sorry,' he said.

Layne sat down opposite him. 'Where's Fergus?'

Max looked more miserable than ever. 'I don't know.'

She studied his face, then got up and went back to attend to the rumbling kettle. 'Teabags?' she enquired.

'To the left, behind the mugs. There's a carton of milk, too.'

When Layne returned with the two mugs, she handed Max one with half the anti-histamine tablet. 'Try that and see if it helps.'

'Thanks, dear.' He tried to look grateful, despite his sorry state.

She resumed her seat. 'I think you do know and, for some reason, you're not telling me. Why haven't I heard from Fergus? Where is he?'

Max waved the steam off his mug, then put it down to cool. 'I've had my orders. Not that I do know, really.'

She sat back. 'What on earth is that supposed to mean? Had your orders?'

'All of us.'

Layne stared at him with a total lack of comprehension and he took sympathy. 'Fergus said if you were to phone, not to tell you anything . . .'

'Anything about what, for goodness' sake?'

'Well.' He shrugged. 'That he had gone, I suppose.'

'Gone where?' Layne could hear but not suppress the panic in her voice.

Max risked swallowing the tablet with a sip of tea. 'Look, we're not supposed to know.'

'But you do.'

'Not really.' He saw Layne lean forward and felt a sense of impending doom. She caught his arm.

'Max, I'm really worried. Not knowing what is going on is driving me frantic. Can the truth be worse?'

He gave a loud sigh. 'I don't know, love.'

A thought occurred to her. 'Is it Hanna?'

The way he said, 'I don't think so,' rang warning bells.

Layne sat back. 'Max, if you don't tell me something, I'm going to find someone who will. I mean, what's happening to the film schedule with him not here?'

Max took two strengthening mouthfuls of the tea, then banged the mug back down. 'All I know – ' he declared – 'and Fergus will have my guts for hanging rope. All I know is that he had a call one minute and was packing his bags the next. Someone said he'd flown to the States.'

Layne hardly dared repeat it. 'The States?'

'You see,' complained Max. 'You'd have been better not to know all along!'

'When did he leave?'

'About two weeks ago.'

She clapped a hand to her face. 'Oh, God, Max. What's happening?'

This time Max reached across and patted her reassuringly. 'It'll be all right.'

'But that's just it. I've got this awful feeling inside that something's badly wrong.'

Max sat back and tried to sound authoritative. 'This is only the second hurdle, isn't it? Well, don't send it crashing down, girl.'

'But why hasn't he phoned me? Why "give orders" to keep me in the dark?'

'He'll have a reason, I'm certain of it. You have to trust him.'

'I'm going home,' decided Layne, all at once.

'But you've only just come,' protested Max weakly.

'I must go back in case he rings.'

'Layne, don't go driving all that way in this state. You need to rest and eat, at least.'

'I'll call at a pub on the way.'

'What about the others? You haven't seen Tim.'

Layne managed a smile. 'I have, in the distance. I think he was just about to go over the edge.'

Max tossed off his tea. 'Oh Lord, I'd better get back up there.'

'At least you've stopped sneezing.'

'So I . . .'

There was a thump and Rowan burst through the door, breathless. 'Ah! . . .'

Max jumped up in horror. 'It's Tim! He's gone over, hasn't he?'

Rowan shook his head. 'No. I wanted Layne. We're going to need you. We've got no option but to tell you Fergus is away and the longer he's off, the deeper the hole we're in. Can you help us to write round him?'

Layne looked thunderous . . . not because of Rowan's request but because of the reason for it. Fergus did not have the courtesy to inform her either of his departure or his destination but she was now expected to put in additional work on his behalf. She could not deny her assistance but her feelings towards Fergus were cooling rapidly in response to the rage inside her.

Only a matter of days later, she was at the studios, having forced herself to do what was asked of her. Once Layne got her teeth into altering a script to suit new requirements, she would usually begin to enjoy playing with the logistics and characters' actions but, when the central figure was missing and had to be cut, she found things very different. In this case it made a farce of her work.

She was also aware of murmurings in the background. The confirmation of her relationship with Fergus had become common knowledge as a result of her own infatuation. Of course people would have laughed when they noticed her letters or passed on messages. Now they had even more reason to laugh. She felt badly embarrassed.

Jerry, she guessed, knew more than he would say about Fergus. For one thing, he had demonstrated uncharacteristic patience over the matter of his missing star, and with Layne's efforts to fill the gap. It seemed to be Axel's temper that had badly frayed and Jerry spent much of his time trying to soothe the feelings of those on the receiving end.

In the end, however, it was Layne's own temper that got the better of her. She finished her work, having agreed with Rowan to return home the following morning. After having a relaxing drink in the lounge bar of the hotel used by cast and crew, Layne arrived in her room, relieved the deed was done but still suffering from a sense of self-betrayal.

No sooner had she slung off her shoes and flopped back on the bed than the phone rang. When she answered it, she was surprised to hear Jerry, sounding unusually pleased. 'You're not going to believe this,' he said. 'Fergus has just called from the airport.'

Layne was speechless. She held the receiver away and stared at it. Jerry carried on talking. 'We won't have to make all those changes. That should make life easier for everyone.'

'I see,' managed Layne, not trusting herself to give voice to her feelings, which were far from pleasant.

'I know he'll want to see you, so I thought I'd let you know straightaway.'

'Thank you, Jerry. Thank you very much,' said Layne through gritted teeth. She hardly waited for him to acknowledge this before clicking the receiver firmly into place.

How much time did she have? Layne sped into the bathroom and knocked all her toiletries off the shelf into a bag, which she then threw into her suitcase, along with anything else she had lined up on the dressing and bedside tables. She pulled her clothes out of the wardrobe, sending the hangers clinking together, spinning wildly. Luckily, Layne never used the drawers, so she stuffed all she had retrieved into her suitcase, made for the door and ran out into the corridor.

Avoiding the lift and manoeuvring her case round one corner of the stairs, she bumped into Max coming up. 'Don't ask,' she warned, keeping going. 'Just don't ask!'

'I don't need to. I've been told he's on his way back.' Max called down the stairs after her. 'You won't solve anything that way!'

The worst part was the wait at reception. It wasn't that she had to pay the bill for the room but her departure was unexpected and the cost of a few extra phone calls and snacks had to be calculated. At long last Layne handed over the money and ran off without the receipt.

She was just about to swing out of the foyer when the locks on her case, half-fastened in haste, clicked open, spilling clothing onto the forecourt. A couple of the crew, on their way in, came hurrying over to help her pack but Layne said she could manage. She was still on her knees trying to secure both locks when a cab drew up.

Not daring to look, Layne grabbed the case and tried to stuff it under her arm as she made for the side car park. She heard her name called in a voice that made her stomach lurch but refused to look back, putting on speed.

Layne heard his footsteps gaining behind her but managed to get the boot of her car open and throw in her case. She slammed the lid down and hurried to get the key in her door lock. By now, he was alongside her.

'Layne, stop!'

She dared to turn slowly, trying to summon all her self-possession. Had it not been for her seething anger, the sight that met Layne could easily have dissolved any determination she felt. He looked almost ill. Tired, certainly, but more than that. There was a haunted look in his eyes she had never seen before and did not dare to think what it might signify. His voice pleaded, 'Layne, I need to talk to you!'

She found it difficult to keep her voice level. 'You've had time enough to talk to me. Our three months is up.'

Layne turned and yanked her door open. He caught hold of it as she swung her legs in.

'Please, Layne. This is important.'

'Well this is important, too,' she said, the green eyes ice cold. 'We're finished. It's over.'

He looked stunned, loosening his grip on the door.

Layne took advantage of it. 'Goodbye, Fergus.'

The door slammed to, narrowly missing him and Layne sped away with a squeal of tyres. Fergus watched her go, then, as if in a dream, turned to find a handful of cast and crew gathered outside the foyer, glued to the drama. He put his head down and strode back, charging through the middle of them and into reception without a word.

CHAPTER 14

Layne drove too fast the first half of the way, forcing herself to shut all thought and feeling from her mind, concentrating only on putting distance between them. But every now and then, she would see his shocked face flash before her, and the image threatened to crack her resolution.

Once back in the safety of her flat, she reassured herself. Although Layne had not expected to say those particular words in that particular way, she recognized it was for the best. She had been right first time: all that had happened was that her prediction had been realized.

Fergus left a message on her answerphone every night for three nights. They started with, 'Layne, please ring me at the hotel. I want to explain,' followed by, 'I need to speak to you, Layne. Will you *please* phone?' Finally, 'You know that I can't get away to see you. This is the last time I'm asking.'

Every attempt he made to contact her loosened a

brick in the protective wall Layne had built around herself, but still she held firm. There was some small satisfaction in turning the tables. It would give him an idea how she had felt all that time when he had been out of contact with her.

One week ran into another and before she knew it three weeks had passed. She tried to work on changes to the television series but found concentration difficult. At the end of the third week, Rowan phoned her, catching her as she replaced the receiver after ringing John. 'Layne, we need you here. Can you get over as soon as possible?'

Layne was horrified. She wriggled. 'That's going to be very difficult, Rowan. Couldn't you manage without me?'

'I wouldn't ask if it weren't really important. Please, Layne?'

'Well . . . I can't leave before the morning.'

'If you could be in Jerry's office by eleven thirty tomorrow, we'd really appreciate it.'

Layne heard alarm bells. 'What's all this about, Rowan?'

'Not over the phone, Layne. We'll see you in the morning. And thanks.'

She dropped the receiver quickly, relieved to get rid of it. All the strength seemed to seep from her body. It did not take Sherlock Holmes to guess there was more to this request than script changes. She wished she had stood firm and turned him down flat but she was supposed to behave professionally and, besides, there was an edge of real concern to his voice that had her genuinely worried.

It now became more difficult than ever to concentrate on the job in hand. Layne left the work and went to pack some things, forcing herself to face the probability she was to see Fergus again. It frightened her. She knew she did not trust herself. After she had packed, Layne began to pace the floor. Whatever it was that had gone wrong worried her, so that she became more and more anxious to know the worst.

In the end, she could bear it no longer. After several attempts, she managed to get hold of Rowan again. 'I've had second thoughts, Rowan,' she told him. 'I've decided to travel up this evening. Can someone book me a room?'

'Of course. If it isn't too late maybe we can get together before morning. Can you let me know when you've arrived?'

'All right, Rowan.'

Her driving was very different from the time she had sped away from Fergus. She travelled slowly, with apprehension gathering in her heart.

The finger on the clock in reception sprung from nine thirty-nine to nine forty, as Layne did her best to slip quietly into the hotel. She waited anxiously for attention, keeping her head down, not wanting to be noticed by residents drifting in and out of the foyer.

After registering, Layne took hold of her key and asked for Rowan's room number. The young man checked. 'His room is twenty-seven but he's out at the moment.'

'Could you put a note in his pigeon hole to say I've arrived, please?' asked Layne.

'Of course.'

'Thanks. Goodnight.'

Layne glanced nervously round, picked up her bag and wondered whether to risk the lift. She was on the second floor. Deciding that she could bump into Fergus just as easily on the stairs, she pressed the button.

It was a relief to find the lift empty and even more of a relief to swing through the door marked forty-three and into her room, without having seen anyone she knew.

After throwing her bags on the bed, she turned to the kettle to make herself a reviving cup of coffee. To take her mind off her nerves, she switched the television on without sound.

It was after ten when there was a knock on her door. Layne felt almost sorry as she had at last begun to unwind. She braced herself to answer it.

Rowan had Jerry with him. 'Hello, Layne.'

She held the door back. 'You'd both better come in. Would you like coffee?'

They shook their heads. 'Well, have a seat,' she recommended, turning off the television and settling herself on the edge of the bed.

Both men lowered themselves into the two armchairs. Pushing his glasses back up his nose, Jerry leant forward. 'It's good of you to come at short notice, Layne.'

Trying to keep the desperation out of her voice, she asked, 'What is it? What's wrong?'

'We need your help and it isn't with the script,' said Rowan.

'Yet!' added Jerry. He looked nervous himself but ploughed in. 'This is difficult, Layne, because we're not sure how things stand between you and Fergus any more . . . but we had nowhere else to go. Things haven't been good since he got back from the States.'

'Not good? How?'

'What Jerry means,' chipped in Rowan, 'is that Fergus hasn't been good since he got back. He hasn't been himself. It's affecting his work.'

Layne began to speak but Jerry waved a hand. 'We're not supposed to be telling you this. He had wanted to tell you himself but . . .'

'Go on,' urged Layne, knowing only too well she was responsible.

'Darcey, his wife, took an overdose. That's

why Fergus had to go to the States. They worked hard to revive her but by the time he got there, she'd died. He had to arrange for her funeral. He stayed in the States to see her buried,' explained Jerry. Trying hard not to witness the pain imprinting itself on Layne's face, Jerry employed his back-to-business tone of voice. 'Axel has tried but he's not the most patient of men. As you know, it's a low budget but we're well over. If Fergus can't deliver the goods, we shall either have to threaten to cut his fee or cut the part. I can imagine how you would feel about writing Lennox off in a car crash . . . but we have to get round this somehow.'

Doing her utmost to sound business-like herself and quelling the inner horror she felt, Layne asked, 'Are you saying Fergus is ill . . . or too upset to work? What exactly?'

'Burning the candle,' concluded Rowan. 'Late nights, carousing with the lads, late mornings. When he does a scene, it's clear his heart isn't in it. All the other actors are twitching.'

Layne spoke in a hushed voice, 'God, what have I done?' She put up a shaking hand to still her trembling mouth.

Jerry and Rowan looked from one to the other, then Rowan got to his feet. 'We're sorry to have been the ones to tell you.'

Tears welled in her eyes but her hand fell away.

'It's my fault.' If only she had allowed Fergus to explain his absence.

Jerry got up, too. 'It isn't your fault Darcey died, Layne. I'd guess Fergus is simply fighting grief and losing. Your blaming yourself won't help anyone. I know you're shocked but, to be blunt, we need action . . . now.'

Layne was forced to appreciate this film jargon with a wry smile. Rowan joined in, with a sympathetic smile of his own. 'It's a wonder he hasn't told you to get in there and kick ass!'

All at once, he dropped onto the bed next to her and put a galvanizing arm round her shoulder. 'Think about having to change the ending, Layne. It's the last thing anyone wants. Fergus needs your strength to pull him out of this. Dissolving in tears isn't the answer.'

'Will you help?' asked Jerry.

Layne took a huge deep breath and stiffened her shoulders. 'I won't change the end for anybody,' she reassured him.

Rowan slapped her on the back. 'Attagirl.'

'What's his room number?' asked Layne.

'He's on the first floor. Thirty-three,' said Jerry.

'But,' warned Rowan, 'if he's living down to his reputation, he'll be in the bar by now.'

'Hell,' complained Layne, determination sagging at the thought of a public confrontation. 'How do I get him out of there?'

'You wouldn't need to give me much encouragement,' winked Rowan.

Layne gave a sceptical smile but got to her feet. 'Wish me luck, boys. I'm going to need it.'

To her surprise, they both kissed her on the cheek as they filtered through the door, then Rowan turned back with one last thought. 'Oh . . . and he used to ring Hanna every day. Doesn't any more.'

'What!' snapped Layne.

'It's upset his mother. She's given switchboard earache twice this week.'

Disgust was written all over Layne's face. Satisfied that this last piece of information had clinched it, Rowan and Jerry strode off down the corridor, both looking considerably more relaxed than they had when they had first arrived.

Layne clicked the door to behind them. Her head was so full of these latest revelations, she had no idea how to react. But the disgust she felt for herself and the pity she felt for Fergus would have to be subdued in deference to the practicalities. Even the financial and editorial difficulties of the film took second place, in Layne's mind, to the news that the fool was neglecting his daughter.

She opened her bag and prepared for war. When Layne had finished applying her make-up, she still found herself battling with self-loathing. To have to think about the way she dressed, when she knew

292

that Hanna had lost her mother and Fergus his wife, made her feel sick at heart. She grasped at a crumb of humour when the line came to her: 'It's a dirty job but someone has to do it.' But the humour soon faded: she would be treading on eggshells.

Time was slipping away and there was work to be done. Layne straightened her skirt, pulled her hair free of the collar of a silk blouse that matched the colour of her eyes and headed into action.

There were two circles of drinkers seated, laughing and talking around tables in the lounge bar, but Fergus had his long legs wrapped around a stool, talking to the barman. Alongside him was a blonde in a minute skirt, who looked no more than seventeen. Layne had been prepared for 'carousing with the lads' but not for this.

She hesitated on the threshold, then realized she had caught someone's eye. Max tried to stand, about to call her name, but Layne waved an impatient hand and put a finger to her lips. He looked towards Fergus, nodded and sank back into his seat.

There was no alternative now. She took a few steps further into the room. It seemed news travelled fast. A slow hush descended. Lifting her chin, Layne made her way to the bar. The wide shoulders that had been uncharacteristically stooping, began to lift and turn, as Fergus sensed the change of atmosphere.

The face that met hers, decided Layne, was not that of Fergus but of a bristled Joseph Lennox. As she drew level, he pushed himself to his feet, eyes narrowed.

'You wanted to talk,' she said quietly.

There was a silence before he enquired, 'What brings you *now*?'

She tried to meet the suspicion frowning down on her with courage. 'Circumstances,' she answered flatly. 'Can we go somewhere private?'

He looked at her long and hard.

'Please?' she said.

Fergus turned back to the barman and fished in his pocket for change. 'Another spritzer for Chloe,' he ordered.

Layne bit on her composure and waited. As Fergus moved away, she caught the glare from the young blonde full in the face, and managed to react with a relaxed smile of sympathy she did not feel.

Deeply aware their exit was being watched as closely as any of Fergus's acting scenes, Layne followed him out. It was the first time she felt any power from being the centre of attention and she did not want to disappoint. Layne crossed her fingers behind her back for all of them to see, as the pair stepped out into the hallway. The murmuring began before they were out of earshot.

He walked rudely through a group of businessmen, who had just emerged from the dining room, apparently unconscious of the looks he provoked, while Layne skirted round them, catching him up at the bottom of the stairs. They reached the first landing without speaking and Layne looked over the rail into a sea of knowing, upturned faces.

Fergus's question distracted her. 'Do I assume you're staying here or are you just passing through?'

'I'm staying,' said Layne.

'Your room or mine then?'

The blue eyes were cool, reminding her painfully of how she must have hurt him.

'Yours,' she said.

He got out his key and showed her into room thirty-three. She saw that where she had a kettle with tea and coffee bags, Fergus had a row of bottles. He went straight to them and poured himself a whisky, before picking up a gin bottle and saying, 'This is your tipple, I seem to remember.'

Not for the first time that night did Layne experience shame. She felt spots of heat warming her cheeks but knew the dirty part had only just started. 'I'm not drinking tonight, Fergus. Do you think you should?'

He gave a humourless smile. 'It hardly matters to you, surely. We're finished, remember.' He took a swig of the whisky and retreated to an armchair, stretching out his legs and inviting her, 'It won't harm you to have a seat, though.'

Layne perched herself carefully on the edge of a chair.

'So then?' he asked. 'What are these "circumstances" that bring you here, after all this time?'

'I wanted to hear what you had to say.'

He leant suddenly forward, holding his glass out in front of him. 'Really! Well, I'm sorry to disappoint you, Layne, but I seem to have forgotten what it was.' He shrugged. 'Such a long time ago.'

When she did not speak, he urged her, 'Try again.'

Layne swallowed, her resolve already severely damaged. 'The film is suffering, Fergus. If you carry on like this, we shall have to make ruinous cuts.'

'Ah.' He sat back, satisfied. 'You're worried about the damage to your "baby".'

The insult hurt but she came back at him, 'Aren't you?'

He stared into the bottom of his drink. 'Maybe I no longer have the interest that I had. You'll know how that feels.'

Layne got up. 'Fergus, if I hurt you . . . and I know I did, then I'm sorry. It was inexcusable and I don't expect you to forgive me for it. But for heaven's sake, don't take it out on everyone else. It isn't just my "baby" but your own reputation you're damaging. Remember other people have put money, time and hard work into this film. If you let them down, they all lose out. You must know that.'

Fergus tossed off the whisky and brushed past her on his way for a refill. She caught his arm. 'Please stop this.'

'You haven't forgotten how to nanny, then.' He removed the offending arm and banged the glass down, before turning on her. 'But you're still having trouble with honesty, aren't you, Layne? Hmmm? Are you quite sure you didn't come running back because someone told you there was a wedding ring going spare?'

She slapped his face with all the force in her body and, for once, felt no remorse, despite the fact he staggered sideways and dropped onto the bed. Layne spat out the words, 'I wouldn't marry you if you were . . .'

He gave a bitter laugh, 'Steady, Layne, your dialogue's slipping.'

She looked down on the sorry sight of Fergus, nursing his stubbled cheek with his hand and told him, 'You *are* that irresponsible father, after all. The character of Joseph Lennox has eaten into you. You're no longer acting, Fergus.'

Layne left him and went back to her room. It had not turned out at all as she had hoped, nor had she been able to say what she felt in her heart, but she recognized that he was probably beyond reason. The only thing she had managed to do was shake him, of which she was far from proud.

Layne did not expect to sleep that night but she went through the motions of showering and changing into her nightshift. At length she lay on the bed with the remote control on mute, flashing back and forth through the television channels, trying to balance the day's revelations with her emotions. In the end, Layne could stand the frantic screen images no longer and switched them off, wishing she could do the same with the state of her mind.

Sinking back against the pillows, she considered the nanny label he persisted in applying to her. She often found it difficult not to speak her mind and could be a bit bossy, she conceded. No doubt it was all part of the need for self-sufficiency but it was only ever meant for the best. Cruel to be kind, wasn't that it? Still, the last thing she had intended that night was to be cruel. She could still feel the sting in her hand. Layne knew she had hit Fergus too hard.

At long last, thinking she might doze off, Layne looked at her alarm clock and saw it read ten to midnight. She was reaching out to switch off the bedside light when there was a light knock on her door. Layne hesitated, not wanting to believe it.

Maybe it had been for next door. Then she heard his voice.

'Layne.'

The knock came again.

Layne scrambled to pull her wrap from the doorhook, slipping into it and tying it tight, before turning the handle and peeping through the gap.

'Can I come in?' he said.

As she allowed the door to drift back, Layne thought she must be seeing a different person. He still looked weary, yes, but the stubble had gone. It looked as if Fergus, too, had showered and changed his clothes.

Lowering himself onto the bed, he watched her close the door. 'I've come to apologize,' he said.

Layne hardly dared look at him. All the old desire was seeping treacherously back into her veins.

She contradicted him. 'No. I should be the one to apologize. I'm sorry I hit you.'

He gave a reluctant smile and rubbed a hand along his jaw, acknowledging, 'You're getting better at it.'

She tried to smile back but it would not work.

He leant forward and reached for her hands, drawing her towards him. 'I asked for it,' he told her. Fergus pulled her closer so that she was standing between his knees. His next words were plainspoken and unaccusing and they hurt. 'I needed you, Layne, and you weren't there.'

Layne released a hand from his grip, touching his affected cheek. Trying to keep her voice level, she assured him, 'I'm here now.'

For a time, his eyes searched hers, then his hands went to her hips, bringing her closer, so that he could lean his face against the comforting warmth of her stomach.

Layne clutched him to her, stroking his hair repeatedly, glad to have him back. 'I'm sorry about your wife, Fergus. I'm sorry about it all. I should have come but I felt shut out. I was in the dark. It sounds pathetic now but my pride was hurt. Everyone seemed to know more than I did.'

She felt his voice vibrate against her. 'I handled it pretty badly, didn't I?'

Layne looked lovingly down on his head and curled his hair between her fingers. 'That makes two of us.'

His hands dropped to grip the backs of her thighs, rasping his thumbnails against her flesh. Fergus leant back to witness her reaction. Layne was doing her best to stem the sudden flood of lust pumping its way through her body.

He smiled contentedly. 'It's nice to be home,' he said, his arms snaking up, unhindered, to squeeze the nakedness beneath her shift, forcing her

300

forwards, so that Layne had to steady herself against his shoulders . . .

'Fergus!' she warned.

He lay back and pulled her down on top of him. 'Let me make love to you, Laynie?'

She felt dizzied by the encouragement shining in the blue eyes and, before she could answer, a hand in her hair was guiding her head, bringing her mouth down onto his.

They kissed as though they had been starved of kissing for a year, exchanging sympathy and comfort rather than passion.

When, at last, Layne lifted herself to draw breath, she was the one to comment. 'As someone once said, it wouldn't be wise.'

He rolled her off him, propping himself on one elbow and tidying the skewed collar of her wrap. 'Could I make much more of a fool of myself?'

She gave a wide smile and nodded.

'You *are* a witch,' he concluded.

Layne caught the hand at her wrap. 'If you're a good boy until the filming's over,' she promised, 'I'll be happy to oblige then.'

He gave her a knowing look. 'Best behaviour, eh? Dangling the carrot.'

Her green eyes held a twinkle. 'If you care to put it that way,' she conceded.

After a few seconds' consideration, Fergus forced himself back into his sitting position at the edge of the bed. Straightening her clothing, Layne sat up on her knees and slid her arms about his shoulders. 'I'd still like you to stay the night,' she offered.

He gave her a sideways look. 'What? Spend the night trying to resist you?'

Layne nodded. 'You've had no problem resisting me so far.'

'That is far from the truth.'

'Please, Fergus. I'd like . . . just to have you here. We get so little time . . .'

He scratched his chin, as if he had an irritable itch. Layne decided to play dirty and slid her arms round his neck, resting her head on his broad shoulders. 'Please . . .'

Sighing heavily, Fergus detached her arms and leant forward to take off his shoes. Layne flopped happily back against the pillows, then frowned. 'Don't you want to fetch anything from your room?'

Over his shoulder, Fergus looked her up and down with resignation. 'Not if I'm resisting you all night.'

The comment led her to scowl to herself. Pulling the sheet up over her legs, she tried to enquire nonchalantly, 'Did you resist Chloe?'

He turned and leant an arm across her body. 'What do you think?'

Layne studied him sadly, concluding, 'I think

she could turn a man's head, especially if she had the hots for him.'

'What an appalling expression.'

'It's not the expression I'm worried about.'

Fergus gave a slight shake of the head. 'No, my dear witch, I do not go in for child abuse.'

Layne put on a pout. 'You bought her spritzers.'

'Is that a crime?' He raised his eyebrows at her.

'Yes,' decided Layne.

He smiled a heart-melting smile, then began to undo his shirt buttons.

'May I?' offered Layne.

'No,' he said firmly, suggesting, 'You could make me a cup of tea, get me back on the path to sobriety and decency.'

The request went over her head. Layne was examining all his facial features in detail. 'God,' she declared, 'I love you so much I could burst.'

Fergus looked at her quizzically, then pushed some stray strands of her hair back over her shoulder, promising, 'I haven't even started on you, yet.'

How she wanted to be started on!

'Tea?' Fergus reminded her, getting up and making for the bathroom. He turned in the door-way. 'And you'd better get some underwear on. I'm retaining mine for decency's sake.'

Layne had a cup of tea ready for him when he returned and plumped up his pillows as he slid his long, bare legs into her bed. She settled on one elbow, watching him drink. Eventually, he put the cup down and complained, 'Stop acting like a Fergus Fan Fanatic.'

She shook her head, correcting him, 'Fergus Hann Fanatic.'

'Well, stop acting like one.'

The green eyes shone hopelessly up at him. 'Can I help it if I'm obsessed?'

Resigned, he turned out the light and slipped an arm round her shoulders, drawing her head onto his chest. Layne encircled his body, hugging it, luxuriating in this new kind of intimacy. His hand was stroking her arm, up and down, up and down, and Layne shifted her head, pressing a kiss onto his bare skin.

Very slowly, he turned towards her, finding her lips and kissing Layne with what she felt to be exquisite tenderness. At last, he concluded, 'This is going to be very difficult.'

'It must be a new experience for you,' supposed Layne aloud.

'Can we change the subject?' he suggested.

There was a long, long silence, until Layne ventured, 'Will you tell me what happened, or is it too painful?'

'It wasn't very pleasant but then nothing involving Darcey ever was.'

Layne was surprised at the matter-of-factness.

'You can't be bitter now that she's died, surely?'

'Don't worry. The bitterness is for me, not Darcey. She obviously couldn't help what she was.'

'Didn't you ever love Darcey? You married her.'

'It was all for Hanna. There was no love. Darcey was very sexy and a skilled manipulator with men: when she was coherent, that is. I hoped we could achieve a united front for Hanna's sake but, as you know, I soon learnt otherwise.'

Still trying to shrug off the feeling of inadequacy aroused by the news that Darcey was very sexy, Layne asked, 'Do you think she meant to take her own life?'

'Yes and no. She knew she was killing herself and that the "lows" were getting lower. Maybe she thought death was the only new experience left, but I suspect that that particular overdose was simply because her brain wasn't functioning rationally any more.'

Layne pushed herself up, trying to look down on Fergus in the dark. 'I'm sorry I wasn't there for you, Fergus. It was utterly selfish of me. I behaved so badly. I'm ashamed to think about it.'

He reached a hand up to her cheek. 'So long as you promise never to run off like that again, I forgive you.'

'I don't think I deserve forgiveness.'

He shifted towards her, raking his fingers through her hair. 'What *do* you deserve?'

Layne circled a finger in his chest hairs. 'Who am I to say?'

'I thought you'd like some input. I haven't heard that promise yet.'

She leant a chin on his shoulder, trying to make out his eyes. 'I promise,' she said, 'never ever to run off and leave you again.'

He brought her closer. 'That's all right, then. We'll keep the punishment sweet.'

Layne was subjected to a prolonged kiss, following which she felt his hand, smoothing its way down her body, wandering in the direction of areas she believed to be banned for the night.

'Fergus . . . we agreed,' she reminded him on a whisper.

He whispered back. 'Trust me.'

'Fergus!'

'Hmmmm?'

'What are you doing?'

'Hush.'

'Oh God.'

'Is that nice?'

'It's . . . mmmmmm . . . wonderful!'

'Mmmmmm.'

'No. No, don't.'

'Yes.'

'Oh God.'

'I prefer "Fergus".'

'Oh God! I love you.'

'Is that God or me?'

'You! Both!'

'I can live with that.'

'Aaaa! This is wicked.'

'I don't think so.'

'I daren't ask where you learnt it.'

'Women's magazines.'

'No, don't make me laugh! Do that again.'

'This?'

'No. That!'

'I might have guessed it wouldn't be long before nanny made an entrance.'

'Don't call me that. Ohhhhhh!'

'I think nanny should be made to take her own medicine now and again, don't you, Laynie?'

'Oooonly if it's like this . . .'

'Like this?'

'Fergus, no more, please . . .'

'No more what?'

'Ohhhhhh noooooohh! Oh God, God, God!'

'I hadn't finished.'

'I can't believe you did that!'

'I can't believe you did, either.'

'Mmmmmmmm. What can I do for you?'

'Unless you want quads, nothing whatsoever . . . at all!'

'You're so very unselfish . . .'

'Your time will come, my love.'

'I think it already did.'

Layne was deep in sleep when a knock came on the door later that morning. Fergus scowled at the clock, threw a sheet over Layne and forced his legs out of bed to answer it.

Rowan and Max were standing in the doorway. Their eyes went from Fergus to the sleeping Layne, then back again. Rowan shook his head. 'Frying pan into the fire, Fergus,' he observed, adding, 'Axel's given you ten minutes, no longer.'

Fergus swore under his breath, caught up the clothes he had thrown on a chair and disappeared in the bathroom.

'I'll catch you up,' said Max to Rowan, seating himself on the edge of the bed and studying the bliss imprinted on Layne's features. 'You did it, then,' he told her quietly.

She did not stir until Fergus burst out of the bathroom, clothing askew, and stopped briefly to kiss Layne's hair on his way out.

'Break a leg,' Max called after him, waiting for Layne to reach consciousness. She awoke fully to Max's comment, 'Well, well!'

A self-satisfied smile curled her lips. 'What are you doing here?'

'Taking the whip to Fergus,' he told her, adding, 'I wish,' on a sigh.

Layne rolled over and threw her arms above her head.

'It looks as if you've had a good time,' remarked Max, deliberately peevish.

She smiled at him. 'I have. I have.'

'Bitch!' declared Max sympathetically.

'This is not what you think, Max.'

'Well, now I really have heard it all! You spent the night with him, didn't you?'

'It was . . . special,' she concluded.

He got to his feet. 'I don't want to know. I'm green with envy. He even stopped to kiss you goodbye and you didn't notice.'

She rolled onto her side. 'Did he? Isn't he wonderful?'

'You make me sick,' he declared. 'The pair of you do.'

Layne waved a hand at him. 'I hope you're going to run along, Max. I want to be left alone with my dreams.'

'Very well then, lady.' Max hovered in the doorway. 'I don't doubt they're X certificate.'

'You don't doubt right,' agreed Layne, giving him a final wave before sinking her nose into her pillow. She chuckled to herself. Things were going uphill again . . . and uphill very fast. When she got back to town, she was going to buy herself a dozen sets of flimsy underwear as a gift to Fergus when filming was over.

Later on in the day, Layne hung around in the background while Axel did several takes of a scene between Lennox and Dale. Things looked hopeful and she had this confirmed as Max was wheeling Tim away for a coffee break. Tim put his thumb in the air.

'Things are looking up,' he declared. 'He was crap all last week. Sorry we can't stop. Only fifteen minutes and I've forgotten your lines.'

Layne laughed, then went up to Rowan and said quietly in his ear, 'You see the sacrifices I make for the sake of this film?'

He grinned. 'We're thankful for any improvement, Layne . . . but 'sacrifices'? . . . my eye! You didn't see your face when we gave Fergus his wake-up call this morning.'

'Did it show?' she smiled, unperturbed.

'Is Joseph Lennox a pain in the backside?' came the response.

She felt a hand on her shoulder and turned to find Fergus standing behind her.

'Ah,' he said to Rowan, 'let me introduce my lover.'

'Fergus!' complained Layne, in embarrassment.

Rowan shook his head, concluding, 'He's going to be more insufferable than ever, now.'

Layne watched him go, then turned on Fergus. 'You didn't have to say that.'

Aware people were watching, he kissed her

briefly on the lips. 'Yes I did. I'm marking my territory.'

'What an unsavoury way of putting it. I'm no one's territory but my own, Fergus Hann.'

'You are now.' He took hold of her hand and tugged, so that she was forced to follow.

'Where are we going?' she demanded.

'I've got ten free minutes.' He led her down a corridor.

'That doesn't answer my question.'

They came to a door marked 'Private' and Fergus pushed her inside. 'Here,' he said, lifting her arms and putting them round his neck.

'You're mad,' she concluded with a touch of humour.

'Mad in love,' he confirmed, fixing his eyes on her lips.

'Fergus?'

'Yes?'

She gave in. 'Come here.'

He kissed her hard, then backed her against the wall and kissed her again. 'I don't think I can wait until the job's finished,' he said.

Layne tried to keep her composure, despite a thumping heart. 'It's just as well I'm going home tomorrow, then, isn't it?'

He drew her arms slowly down and regarded her critically. 'Are you running out on me again?'

'I promised, didn't I?'

'You certainly did.'

'Well, then. I'm just taking temptation out of your way, aren't I?'

'That had better be all.'

'Fergus, look at us both, hiding in a cubby-hole for a quick snog. We're acting like teenagers. We're too old for that . . .' She had second thoughts and the green eyes twinkled up at him. 'Well, *you* are, anyway.'

He brought her closer. 'I'm not averse to spanking the odd witch.'

Layne replaced her arms about his neck. 'Fergus,' she warned, 'You're turning me on.'

He shook his head, lips curving. 'I'm not talking about titillation. I'm talking about pain, Layne.'

Their bout of frenzied kissing was interrupted by the door flying back, followed by two of the technicians carrying in a table.

Layne's hysterical laughter was muffled by Fergus's hand. 'Come on,' he said loudly. 'It looks as if we'll have to find somewhere else to make love.'

The intruders stared after them as Fergus hauled Layne out of the room. When they both clearly heard the words echo down the corridor, 'I thought they'd have been glad of a table,' she knew the sooner she got back home, the better it would be for their sanity.

* * *

That night, Layne was packing up when Fergus phoned to invite her to his room for a gin and tonic.

'I don't know if that's a good idea, Fergus.'

'We can both make it mineral water, if you like.'

'I wasn't really meaning the alcohol.'

'If you think I'm letting you get away with a goodnight phone call, you can think again.'

'All right, Mr Masterful, I'm on my way.'

'That's better, slave.'

When she arrived, he held back the door only to have a finger wag at him. 'Your trouble, Mr Hann, is that you don't seem to know what you want, a slave, a witch or a nanny.'

He put an arm round her shoulder and drew her inside, before looking her up and down. 'I don't see why we can't get you an outfit for all three.'

She stared at him, then laughed. 'You're a hopeless case. Where's that gin? I need it, after all.'

'Coming up,' he said.

Layne cleared her throat before venturing to ask him. 'Have you phoned Hanna today?'

He gave her a knowing look. 'As a matter of fact, I did phone, but The Horrible had gone to a party, so she can't be missing her father *that* much.'

Layne took the glass proffered. 'That's all right, then.'

He came back with a glass and a small bottle of mineral water for himself. Looking from one to the other, he assured her, 'You see, I am reforming, Miss.' He kissed the tip of her nose. 'Albeit slowly.'

'Tim certainly seems happier. He says you're on form again.'

'I know you're trying to protect my delicate feelings, Layne, but when a young Thespian actually wheels off set in a tantrum, declaring you 'crap', you can hardly sink much lower.'

Layne put a hand up to conceal the smile on her lips, and Fergus looked at her affectionately before admitting, 'I'm actually beginning to feel some sympathy for Lennox.'

'Max, more like,' observed Layne.

'Possibly,' allowed Fergus.

Layne lowered herself onto the edge of his bed. 'You don't exactly like Max, do you?'

He waved his glass in the air. 'It's nothing personal. He's just not my type.'

'Not straight, you mean?' She smirked at him over the top of her glass.

'Why should it matter to you what I think?'

'I'm just curious. You must spend quite a lot of your time feeling uncomfortable, if it bothers you.'

'It may surprise you to know I don't spend a lot of my time thinking about people's sexuality.'

'When you get to know him, you'll find Max is a very kind man,' pointed out Layne.

By now, Fergus was adding a touch of whisky to

his water. 'Man being the operative word,' he commented.

'You see,' declared Layne. 'You couldn't resist that! What is a man? He's just a person.'

He came and stood over her. 'What is all this, anyway?'

'I just think Max put it rather well when he said Tim hadn't realized that acting was camping it up with the best of them.'

Fergus removed her gin and put both glasses aside, before joining Layne on the bed. 'You're calling me a hypocrite.'

Layne patted his knee and smiled. 'No, my love. I'm merely suggesting you're already in touch with your feminine side and don't know it.'

Not without humour, he studied her face. 'I do now you've told me. It leaves us with a problem, though.'

'What's that?'

'Which side is which? For lovemaking purposes.'

Layne assured him, 'I don't care, as long as it's you.'

'I think my left profile is the more feminine, don't you? Something about the eyelashes . . .'

Layne nudged him. 'Why don't you just shut up and get on with it?'

'Well, if you put it that way . . .'

He rolled Layne sideways, smiling into her eyes

before taking confident possession of her mouth. Having decided he had asserted sufficient masculine authority, Fergus fell back and put his hands behind his head. She read the humour in his voice.

'You see, Laynie, Max wouldn't worry me at all if he didn't ogle me with those big brown eyes. He makes me feel I'm depriving him. It can be very unsettling.'

Leaning over, Layne reassured him. 'He's celibate, silly. He told you so himself.'

Fergus winked at her. 'I think he might just make an exception in my case.'

She grinned down at him. 'Oh, such conceit!'

'Come here, wench and reassure me that I'm still attractive to *women*.'

Layne stroked his face before kissing him comprehensively but it was not long before she forced herself to withdraw. 'It's time I went,' she said.

Wearily, he pushed his hands through his hair. 'I hate to agree with you but I've got some lines to learn.'

'I never imagined I'd be longing for an end to the shooting,' said Layne.

'That shows you're a novice.'

'You will keep in touch, won't you?'

Fergus picked up her hand and kissed the palm. 'Provided you throw that dratted answerphone out of the window.'

'For you, anything,' she agreed.

He smiled. 'That's what I like to hear.'

'That's because you're a power freak.'

'Are we talking the masculine or feminine side?' he teased her.

'Freaks have no gender,' decided Layne, getting to her feet. Fergus followed suit.

It was beginning to hit her that she would be leaving him in the morning. Seeing the reluctance in her eyes, he took her in his arms, hugging her to his chest.

'I don't want to go,' she admitted glumly, though glad of the comforting feel of his warm shirt against her cheek.

He kissed the top of her head. 'I don't want you to go.'

'I love you, Fergus.'

His blue eyes blazed down into hers. 'I love you, too.' He cupped her chin in one hand and kissed her gently. 'Be good.'

A little of her humour returned as she looked up at him and fingered a button on his shirt. 'You're the one on your best behaviour. Just remember that.'

'Yes, nanny.'

She glared at him. 'Don't!'

'No, nanny.'

Forcing herself to pull away from him, she reached for the door, warning, 'I'll attend to you much later.'

Leaning in the doorway, he watched her go. 'I shall savour every second,' he called down the corridor.

Layne threw him a brief, threatening look, shook her blonde hair back over her shoulders and disappeared from view.

CHAPTER 15

Fergus's early start meant they had agreed not to see each other in the morning and after a restless night Layne was quite relieved to climb into her car and set off home, without the upset of more farewells.

She wished desperately for some normality, for them to have time enough together for their relationship to develop more naturally, and although after two weeks apart, they had exchanged a lot of phone calls, it was never the same. She could not see how he was looking or feeling and sometimes the crackle of unfulfilled need on the line silenced the conversation altogether, until one or other of them opened up.

Layne resumed her occasional script meetings and was surprised when Ian Thornton came up to her at the first of these to offer an apology.

'John put me wise,' he said. 'I'm sorry if I caused you any embarrassment, Layne. I didn't want to tread on any toes.' His mention of it succeeded in embarrassing her but she could see he was sincere and tried to make it easier for him.

'I suspect John might have misled you. He's not the most tactful person to use as an intermediary, I'm afraid and I wasn't at my best that day.'

Ian reached into his pocket. 'Look, by way of an apology to you and your . . . partner, I've got two tickets for *Richard III* at the Barbican in ten days' time. Would you like them?'

'It's really kind of you, Ian, but Fergus won't be able to . . . get away. I appreciate the offer, though.'

'Well, there'll still be one going spare if you change your mind.' He gave a shy smile and pushed his glasses back along the bridge of his nose. 'I'd be happy to take you but I doubt if I could convince you there'd be no strings attached.'

Layne smiled reassuringly back. 'Under those circumstances, I can't say I'm not tempted. Perhaps I could let you know, Ian.'

'We're scheduled to meet before then, anyway,' he acknowledged, before changing the subject. 'You are happy about today's script changes, are you? No problems?'

She saw how much more confident he was on home territory. 'I wouldn't say no problems but I can see the reasons for them. I'll just have to get my head down. See you next time, Ian, and . . . thanks for the offer.'

When Fergus phoned late the following night, Layne asked him light-heartedly, 'How would you feel if I went out with another man?'

'What other man is this?'

'My script editor. He offered us both tickets for the RSC.'

'What are they doing?'

'*Richard III.*'

'Are you desperate to see *Richard III*?'

'I'd like to,' confirmed Layne. 'I've only seen one other performance since I did it for A level. But I can't see you getting by unnoticed in the Barbican crowds, even if you could get away.'

'It's not unknown. When is this?'

'A week on Friday.'

'Doesn't look promising, then, does it?'

'No. I didn't think so.'

'So, your "script editor" has offered to take you, has he?'

'Yes.' Sensing the cynicism in his voice, Layne assured Fergus, 'He doesn't have any ulterior motives, if that's what you're thinking.'

'How do you know?'

'I just do. He's OK.'

'I can't say I'm happy about it. You're blonde, beautiful and sex-starved.'

'Fergus!'

'Deny it.'

'I'm not beautiful,' she grumbled.

'You are to me and, most likely, to Mr Script Editor.'

'Are you saying I can't go?' she accused.

'Would I dare?'

'I mean, I needn't have asked. I could have just gone,' pointed out Layne.

'All I said was I'm not happy about it.'

'I have done self-defence, you know,' she declared.

'What sort of self-defence?'

'The usual sort. Finger-jabbing in the throat or eyes. A kick in the . . .'

She could hear the smile in his voice, as he interjected with 'Shins?'

'That is below the belt.'

'I can testify to that.'

'So, even if he were on the pull,' persisted Layne, 'I could defend myself.'

'You might not want to,' he suggested. 'Attack is the only way to activate a defence mechanism.'

'Fergus, what are you on about?'

'You might let a man in, thinking he's safe . . . a colleague, a friend, someone to confide in. By the time he's breeched your defences, it's too late . . . you didn't know attack was on his mind.'

'You don't trust me. That's what it is,' came her complaint.

'I don't trust rivals in love. I'd be a fool if I did.'

Layne gave a harsh laugh. 'Your imagination is running away with you. This is not a hot date, Fergus. I won't be sitting in the back row of the picture house.' She made a sudden decision. 'I'm going to see Richard III whatever you say.'

'In that case, I don't know why you asked my opinion.'

'Neither do I!'

Disgruntled with herself as much as with Fergus and not knowing the reason, Layne thought about slamming down the receiver but she heard his voice, gentle and insistent at the same time. 'Is it a crime to care what you do, Laynie?'

'I suppose not,' she said ungraciously, then, hearing herself, sighed heavily. 'I'm sorry, I don't know what's the matter with me.'

'I do and that's what's worrying me. The question really is, would you go out with this fellow if we were living together at your flat?'

'Of course not!'

'So what you seem to be saying is our relationship's on hold because there are a few miles between us.'

'I don't mean to.'

'Think about it, Layne. You decide and let me know.'

'I don't need to think about it. The only person I want to go out with . . . and preferably stay in with, is you, Fergus. I love you and I miss you,' she said miserably.

'It won't be long now,' he assured her. 'After thirty years together, you'll look back on this as the best time of your life . . . freedom before the chains of responsibility started dragging you down.'

There was a long silence. Fergus shook his receiver. 'Are you there, Laynie?'

'You're either a cock-eyed optimist or a terrible fraud,' she concluded.

'I think the word is "committed".'

'Don't you think it sounds a bit irrevocable? Like a life sentence?'

'There's not much point otherwise. You obviously haven't got used to the idea yet.'

Layne wriggled her finger through the coils of the telephone wire. 'I need some practice, that's all.'

'A few weeks from now, and you'll be getting all the practice you want.'

With this reassurance and anxious to quash his suggestion that she would cheat because he was too far away to do anything about it, Layne did not take Ian up on his offer. As it happened, John came round to see her on that Friday evening instead. He had been out of the office with flu the first half of the week and then unable to see her because of his backlog of appointments.

On arrival, he tossed the first three chapters of her unfinished novel onto an armchair.

'You didn't like it,' she concluded.

'I need to see more before I start sounding out publishers. I'm not saying it's not promising and the plot's as original as you get. It would just be nice to know it would sell.'

'We'd all be rich if we knew that magic formula,' agreed Layne, checking the papers by her computer. 'I could let you have the next five chapters, if you like.'

'Fine. I'll take them back with me,' he offered, dropping into a seat.

'You'll have a drink?'

'Just a small whisky, Layne.'

'You look as though you need it. You went back to work too soon.'

'I couldn't leave Lorrie on her own any longer. I put too much pressure on her as it is.'

Layne handed him the whisky and took a seat opposite him, sipping her own white wine. 'You know, I wondered whether you and Lorrie would ever get together. She's an attractive, available lady.'

John peered at her over the whisky. 'I don't need a matchmaker. Besides, Lorrie knows me too well. You work with someone, you see all their worst faults. It's already like a marriage, but without any of the compensations.'

'I should have thought it was a good basis for a relationship . . . knowing it can't get worse.'

'I hardly think you're in a position to lecture,' he pointed out. 'The muddle you're in.'

Layne took offence. 'I'm not in a muddle,' she retorted emphatically.

'You could have fooled me. If you thought so much of superman, you'd have found reasons to base yourself at the studios. I'd have thought you'd want to watch him at work.'

'You've a short memory, John. Look what you've just been saying about people who work together.'

'Hardly the same thing, as you well know.'

Layne sighed and put down her glass. 'You want to know the god-honest truth?'

He gave a shrug of indifference.

She smiled, 'We can't keep our hands off each other.'

'I don't think I did want to know that,' he complained.

'We can't trust each other not to do something stupid,' she went on. 'It's like being a demented teenager. Being apart is hell but we need to keep things cool until filming's over.'

John tossed off his whisky and subjected her to a brooding stare. 'Are you sure this "thing" isn't one-sided, Layne? I find it hard to believe the much-used, worldly-wise Fergus Hann has any need to act like a demented teenager.'

'I'll choose to ignore the "much-used" *and* the suggestion he couldn't possibly fancy someone like me. People do fall in love, you know . . . even filmstars. He thinks he wants a steady relationship.' Layne retrieved her drink. 'I can't be sure that, when he's had his wicked way, it won't all change. You may yet be proved right.'

John actually gave a belly-laugh and sat forward. 'You're not telling me you haven't actually consummated this "relationship", because I don't believe it!'

'We haven't! Not everyone has the morals of a rabbit, even in this day and age.'

'Dammit, Layne, you brought me flowers from Skye! Are you seriously telling me this was on the meagre basis of your hero proclaiming eternal love?'

'Yes!'

'Well, I've heard everything now. Thanks for the entertainment but you're either a poor, deluded woman or, if you'll excuse the word, a 'consummate' liar.'

Had it been anyone other than John Trevor, Layne would have felt deeply insulted, but she often found his tactlessness strangely endearing. She found all she could do was smile and shrug. 'Then, take pity on me, for I'm a poor, deluded woman.'

He shook his head. 'I can't cope with this. Hand

me the TV script. Give me something I can cope with.'

Layne grinned and it was not long before they were deep in discussion about the detail of problems she was experiencing with her work.

In the middle of it, Layne got up to answer a loud knocking on her door.

'Who the hell's that?' grumbled John.

'I've no idea.' She opened the door cautiously, only to have her expression change to one of joy. Fergus was standing there, bag in hand.

'Fergus!'

'Can I come in?'

He stopped in the doorway to brush her lips with a hello kiss but, on turning into the room, caught sight of the stranger sitting at Layne's table, surrounded by papers.

'Go in, go in,' urged Layne happily, taking his bag from him.

He looked back down at her, concern in his eyes. 'I thought we'd agreed.'

'What?'

Assuming she was putting on an act of dimness, Fergus turned on John, who was getting to his feet. 'So this is Mr Script Editor, is it?'

Comprehension dawning, Layne intervened quickly. 'Oh, no, Fergus. This is John Trevor, my agent.'

John held out his hand, his words belying the

expression on his face. 'Pleased to meet you.'

Fergus ignored the hand. 'Ah. Mr Ten Per Cent.'

'Fergus!' warned Layne, emphasizing, 'John has very kindly been going over some work with me.'

'Very kind, I'm sure.' Suspicion underlined Fergus's words.

'It looks as if I'd better be going,' sighed John, giving Layne a look that clearly meant 'you're wrong in your head to touch this man with a bargepole'.

Fergus held up a hand. 'No. Why don't I go? It was thoughtless of me to arrive unannounced. I should have realized Layne would have other plans.'

Unimpressed, John pushed past him, telling Fergus, 'Unlike you, *Mister* Superstar, I haven't come here to fill my client's head with wild promises. Layne isn't my type. She's too blunt and too bloody awkward . . . once you get to know her. So watch your step.'

'Thank you, John,' acknowledged Layne wryly. At least she was able to appreciate the way he was handling the situation.

She took a deep breath and glared at Fergus. 'Now, I suggest you two take a long look at each other. For reasons I can't understand, I think a lot of the pair of you and, if either of you want anything to do with me, you're going to have to get on.'

Neither man made a move but each looked at her, instead. She folded her arms and continued, first looking Fergus severely in the eye. 'You, Fergus, cast your mind back. If I'd wanted John in my bed, I'd hardly have gone driving up to Skye, would I? I do know you believe John wants to fleece me financially, whereas I believe he earns his percentage.'

She turned her attention to John who, after his initial bluster, was looking awkward. 'You, John, believe that Fergus is an egotistic bedhopper and can't understand why he hasn't got me into bed yet.'

Fergus contradicted her. 'I have.'

Her eyes flew to him. His expression had changed to one of reluctant humour.

'I thought so,' said John with satisfaction.

Layne felt warmth in her cheeks. Dropping her arms, she blinked at John, finding that he was now viewing Fergus in a new light. He offered his hand to Fergus once more and Fergus took it.

'Her performance was very convincing,' John assured him. 'Maybe you two have something in common, after all.'

'Goodnight, John,' snapped Layne.

John smiled smugly at Fergus from the doorway. 'It's a pity she found your own performance so forgettable. Perhaps you should jog her memory?' he suggested.

Layne scowled at the closing door before turning to find Fergus looking at her with warped amusement.

He shook his head. 'Why, oh why do women like to air their love lives in public?'

This comment, combined with the way he had behaved on arrival, infuriated her. She spat the words, 'Don't speak to me!' whirled on her heel, made for the bedroom and slammed the door.

It burst open behind her. She rounded on Fergus. 'Get out!'

'No way,' he said. They stared at each other, both equally determined.

'I'm warning you,' growled Layne.

Fergus subjected her face to careful scrutiny, then threw down a challenge. 'You're not thinking of subjecting me to physical violence, I hope?'

The blue eyes reflected a small triumph on being informed levelly, 'I'm simply asking you to leave.'

He corrected her. 'Telling me, in fact. But I'm not going anywhere.'

His hands went to his shirt. He wrenched it out of his trousers and flipped open the buttons from bottom to top, before unfastening the cuffs. Fergus tore the shirt off, rolling it up in a ball and flinging it aside, before moving on to undo his wristwatch.

Like a rabbit, frozen in the headlamps of a car,

Layne stared at his naked chest. The words wailed out. 'What are you doing?'

His response was firm. 'I'm not waiting any longer.'

Layne shook her head. 'Oh no, Fergus.'

'Oh yes,' he said, coming closer.

She cast a frantic look up at him, claiming, 'I'm not ready . . .'

'I'm ready enough for both of us,' Fergus assured her. He reached into his trouser pocket, withdrew something that Layne at first thought was a box of matches, and tossed it onto the bed, announcing plainly, 'I called for them on the way.'

She looked from the packet back to Fergus, protesting, 'I'm still angry with you, for heaven's sake!'

He gave a slow smile and her resolution began to crumble. 'The angrier, the better,' came the encouragement. 'Here.'

She felt his hand slip into her hair, cushioning her head, bringing her into him. Looking as if he were about to kiss her, Fergus bent his head and nuzzled her neck instead, making his way slowly to her ear. Hot breath issued a challenge she could not have failed to accept. 'Show me what you can do, witch!'

Spurred on by mounting desire, the 'witch' in her turned her mouth hungrily to his. Fergus allowed Layne to punish him with kisses while he wrestled to strip her. In less than two minutes, every item of her clothing lay strewn across the floor.

With a breathtaking sense of liberation and exhilaration, Layne clung to his body, and he lifted her, kissing her breasts, before lowering her onto the bed.

Impatiently, she watched him remove the rest of his clothes, punching the duvet and urging him, 'Come on. Be quick!'

'I thought you weren't ready.'

'I am now.'

'There,' he said. 'Are you still ready?'

'Oh my God!'

'Not him again.' Fergus joined her on the bed.

'My God, Fergus.'

'That's better. Come here.'

'I'm not as ready as I was.'

'You will be. Your skin's like silk.'

'Forget the dialogue, Fergus . . .'

'Yes, nanny.'

'And don't . . .!'

Two hours later, Layne stirred in his arms and sighed dreamily. 'It'll all go downhill from now on.'

He opened one eye to look at her. 'This is when the hard part starts.'

She smiled suggestively at him but he ignored it. 'Bed was the easy part,' pointed out Fergus. 'It's the commitment that's hard.'

Rolling away from him, Layne declared, 'You'll go off me now, anyway. Men do, once they've had their way.'

He pulled her back. 'Oh no, I'm expecting to get a few more miles out of you yet. After all, I've put a lot into this relationship.'

She grinned. 'You can say that again.'

Fergus propped himself up on his elbow and smoothed Layne's hair back over her shoulder before leaning across to kiss her. 'You realize,' he said softly, drawing back, 'that naughty nannies will be strictly disciplined.'

She sat up and tapped him on the nose. 'Only if the excitement flags . . . and there's not much chance of that yet.' Layne reached for him, drawing his head between her breasts and kissing his hair. 'I love you, you beautiful man, and I want you.'

Fergus lifted his head. His expression was a cross between ecstasy and resignation. 'Again?'

'Yes, please.'

He planted a kiss in her navel and told her, 'I knew a younger woman would wear me out.'

Rolling into his body, Layne assured him, 'You'll die happy, though, won't you?'

In the early hours of the morning, Layne awoke to find Fergus missing from the bed. She found him in the kitchen, cooking an omelette.

'Is that all you ever eat?' she enquired from the doorway.

'I was going to ask you the same question after looking in your fridge. Want to share some?'

'Mmmmmm.' Layne helped herself to a fork and waited at the table.

He gave her a knowing look, as he tipped it out on the plate. 'No wonder you've worked up an appetite. Salt and pepper?' he asked.

'Just pepper.'

Fergus watched her help herself, then sprinkled his side of the omelette with both. 'There's something obscene about all this,' he concluded.

Green eyes flashed up at him in surprise.

'I mean,' he explained, 'not knowing how you like your food. Apart from Shakespeare, I haven't a clue about your taste in theatre, cinema or music. I know the most intimate details about you but I don't know you at all.'

She jabbed her fork in his direction. 'You're getting cold feet already.'

'You have no faith, do you? You know very well what I mean.'

Layne wriggled in her seat as she tried to spear an elusive piece of omelette. 'Well . . . sort of . . .'

'Sort of?'

'You tend to forget,' she said warily, 'that I already knew a lot about you before we ever met.'

He corrected her. 'Thought you knew, surely?'

Layne waved the speared egg at him, 'No. *Knew*. I mean . . . such as your liking for the Russian composers, Pinter and Bennett.'

He smiled. 'Never heard of them.'

She ignored the comment and went on, 'French films, French actresses, Piaf, Miles Davis, Italian food. You even like ballet but you don't dance. You don't like Shakespeare . . . especially Richard III . . .'

Fergus put his fork down and rested his chin in his hands. It disconcerted her. 'Carry on.'

'Well, then, what else?' Layne thought to herself, then carried on eating as she talked. 'You think astrology is bunk, you believe in God but don't practise any particular religion, you had your first kiss when you were eight . . . a late starter . . . from a girl named Lisa Carrington. When you were seventeen someone broke your nose in a rugby match . . .'

He frowned at her. 'You didn't get all of this from the tabloids.'

'I've done some research in my time. A Fergus Hann Fanatic will do all she can!'

Fergus returned to the omelette to find it gone. He gave a reluctant smile and sat back. 'What were you researching me for? Joseph Lennox?'

She shook her head and dropped her fork. 'I fancied you. You know I had an obsession.'

'Had?'

'Have. More than ever now.'

He leant his elbows on the table and searched her face, deciding, 'Well, what do I know about you? You can be over-sentimental . . .'

Layne complained. 'This from a man who likes Russian composers?'

'You're overbearing, like your mother, and your father probably spoilt you like most fathers do with their daughters . . .'

Her mouth opened to protest but he went on: 'You're quick to misjudge and voice the opinion aloud. You have violent tendencies that need controlling and, after six years of celibacy, you act like a hellcat in bed . . .' Fergus shrugged. 'Apart from that, what do I know?'

Seeing she looked highly dissatisfied with this summary, he enquired, 'What's wrong?'

'I am not over-sentimental!'

He grinned, then added, 'Oh, I forgot.'

'What?'

'You'd eat a starving man's food.'

Layne looked down. 'Oh, I am sorry, Fergus.'

He got to his feet. 'You see, over-sentimental. Come on, back to bed.'

Layne let him take her hand but grumbled, 'I wish you weren't going back tomorrow.'

'I'm not.'

She stopped to look up at him in disbelief. 'You're not?'

'Didn't I tell you? Shooting of "The Thorn Field" halted at ten past three today. I left the party just as things were hotting up. Rowan wanted to invite you but I took the liberty of telling him we wanted to celebrate privately.'

Layne gasped. 'It's all done! Wrapped?'

'As far as the actors are concerned, yes, apart from voiceovers.'

She jumped up at him in delight, throwing her arms round his neck and legs round his body, so that Fergus had to take her weight, his hands providing a seat for her bottom.

'Did I mention over-excitable?' he complained.

'Why didn't you tell me sooner?'

'I doubt if I had chance.'

Layne went slightly limp in his arms. 'So what happens now?'

The blue eyes allowed her a little sympathy. 'Well, I suppose we could do it on the kitchen table.'

'You *know* what I mean.'

'If you wouldn't mind taking the weight off my feet, I'll come to bed and tell you.'

'Sorry.' She released her grip and he lowered her to the ground.

'Just so long as you reduce your omelette consumption,' he advised her. 'Come on.'

Layne reacted with mixed feelings to the news that he was taking her up to Northumberland and had booked a hotel on the way up for two nights. 'But my work! John . . .'

'Bugger John,' said Fergus.

The thought made her giggle but she managed to recompose herself. 'You made him go off without my novel tonight,' she declared.

'You've written a novel?'

Layne nodded, then shook her head. 'Well, a few chapters.'

'Can I read it?'

'Not until John's hacked his way through the deadwood and it's completely finished.'

'Tell me about it.'

'Not now, Fergus. Stop changing the subject.'

'You did that. You said he'd gone without your novel.'

'Yes. He's going to read some more chapters.'

'We can drop them off before we leave.'

'It's Saturday. He won't be there.'

'Well, he must have a letterbox, woman!'

'Don't call me *woman*! You know, you should have asked me, not simply assumed I'd come.'

Fergus brushed Layne's hair back from her face. 'Are we having our first post-coital row?'

Layne traced a finger down the middle of his chest. 'No, but you still think you're John Wayne. You can't throw me over your saddle and ride off into the sunset, Fergus. We're fast approaching the millenium.'

He looked disappointed. 'Then you'll have to write me a western, so that I can indulge all my fantasies.'

She fell back. 'No, siree. I'm not providing you with an excuse to break in beautiful young fillies. I've made that mistake once too often.'

Fergus leant over her. 'So are you coming or aren't you?'

She slid her hands round his neck and gave him an inviting smile. 'That rather depends on you, doesn't it, my love?'

Layne recognized the gleam of promise in his eye as Fergus edged closer and told her, 'I guarantee you'll be coming.'

CHAPTER 16

It was ten-thirty before they arrived outside John's office. Fergus slewed his car across a double yellow line, already irritated that Layne had delayed their departure by insisting on going through her papers and bringing work away with her.

Layne ran through the door at street level with her latest chapters beneath her arm and up the steps, aware of Fergus's impatience to get away. John's letter box turned out to be narrow and well sprung. She doubled up the partial manuscript and squeezed and squeezed until it finally fed through. Relieved to hear it drop into the wire basket on the other side, she turned to set off.

A blast on the horn from Fergus had her dashing down the steps but, in her haste, Layne's foot skidded and, unable to stop herself, she fell down the last five or six steps, landing heavily. While she hitched herself into a sitting position, trying to overcome the shock, Layne heard a second impatient burst of car horn. She swore under her breath and tried to straighten up but there was pain in her ankle and Layne was afraid to put her weight on it. When the horn blared out again, she felt like bursting into tears of frustration.

Again Layne tried to let the affected foot take her weight but it screamed its objections and she decided the only way she could get to the outer door was to hop. It was then that the door burst open and Fergus appeared, looking like a thunder cloud. His expression soon changed, for she proceeded to burst into tears at the sight of him.

'What the . . . ? What on earth have you been doing?'

'It's your fault,' she sniffed miserably. 'Blasting your damn horn like some . . . delinquent tearaway! I fell down the stairs.'

He came forward to give her support, reminding her of something she no longer wished to know: 'I'm on a double yellow . . .'

'Why don't you . . . bugger off, then!' she recommended, on a sob.

Fergus, who had bent down to examine the foot she persisted in holding off the ground, smiled to himself, before asking, 'Do you think you've broken it?'

She shook her head. 'It twisted under me as I fell. I think it's just a bad sprain.'

'Are you sure, because we can check at the hospital?'

The thought horrified her. 'No, no. Just help me to the car, Fergus. I'm a bit shaken, that's all.'

He allowed her to rest most of her weight on his arm, so that she could hop out to the car without falling over. It was clear as they approached the rear of the well-built lady traffic warden that she was about to write Fergus a ticket.

'Excuse me!' called Fergus, fishing out his car keys and holding them up. The traffic warden turned. 'I wonder if you'd be kind enough to open the door for this lady. She's fallen and hurt herself. I think I'd better get her to hospital.'

Layne saw recognition dawn in the warden's eyes. They seemed to mist over. Layne felt sick.

'I'm sorry about parking like this,' Fergus said simply.

The warden's eyes smiled. 'You *are* Fergus Hann, aren't you?'

He looked surprised she would know. 'Yes, I am.'

The warden glanced briefly at Layne before opening the passenger door. 'Well, in view of the circumstances, I think we can overlook the offence.'

Fergus ignored the scowl on Layne's face as he bundled her inside the car. When he drew back to his full height, he turned the full power of his smile

on this benefactor. 'What's your name?' he enquired.

She looked pleased. 'Marion.'

'Can I borrow your pen?' Fergus took her
clipboard in his hands and wrote, 'You're an
angel, Marion, love Fergus Hann'.

Marion took the clipboard back and read the
message, by which time Fergus was at the driver's
door. She looked up as though heaven's gates were
opening. Fergus blew her a kiss and climbed in.

'That was close,' he hissed, looking round to
find Layne pretending to poke a finger down her
throat. Fergus grinned. 'Some people have it,
some people don't,' he told her.

As the car squealed away, she decided, 'I don't
think I'll be able to cope with this relationship. I'll
become neurotic if you're doing that every five
minutes.'

'We have more than enough trouble with that
ankle already. Are you sure you don't want to have
it checked over?'

'No, I don't. I'll tell you one thing, though, I'm
going to be suing John Trevor. It's not as if I
haven't warned him. We'll call at a chemist for
some bandage and some of that spray they use on
footballers. When we get to the hotel, we'll soak it
in water.'

'Is this the Royal "We"?'

'No,' Layne admitted boldly. 'It's the Royal *you*,

actually. In the meantime, burn some rubber, driver!'

He gave a sideways look of affectionate resignation. 'I can guess what your last slave died of!'

Layne found it a long, uncomfortable drive. Even though they put the seat back and cushioned her ankle from the ground with soft clothing, Fergus's car was far from a roomy, family estate. The sun had become hot through the glass, aggravating the swelling, and her ankle throbbed painfully. By the time they made their first stop at a country pub, she was feeling depressed.

'Would you just bring me something to eat in the car, Fergus? I don't want to make an entrance like this. I doubt I can even hop now.'

'I'll carry you in,' he offered.

'You will not. I'd feel a complete idiot.'

'Suit yourself. I'll bring you a bottle out. What do you want to drink?'

'Just an orange juice, please.'

She could not see his expression because he was wearing sunglasses but felt soothed when he leant over and kissed her cheek, assuring her, 'I won't be long.'

But the thinking time did little to lift her spirits. It should have been the happiest period of her life. The man of her dreams had made the most glorious love to her, patiently and impatiently, determined to send her to the outer limits of an ecstasy she never imagined attainable. Now, he was not only whisking her away with him, but taking her into the fold of his family.

She was even beginning to enjoy her career and the people she met through it. Yet this cloud of depression had gathered over her. It wasn't simply the pain in her ankle or any sense of anti-climax.

Fergus was probably right. She didn't have the faith . . . and she didn't have the faith because it still seemed unreal, as if she were in the picture, too, and when filming was over, it was simply a matter of putting on her coat and walking, not into the sunset, but into the cool, grey rain of everyday reality.

Not only that, but here she was, the first day after their bodily union, incapacitated and totally reliant on the man. How could he fail to weary of her in the coming days?

The spectacle of Marion, the traffic warden, loomed. How many other women were going to dissolve into syrupy pools at his feet while she looked on, helpless? Fergus would tell her he had heard it all before but Layne seriously doubted she could cope and, no matter how much love he declared, that would not alter.

Why couldn't she have settled for a man of lesser attraction but with quiet reserve and hidden depths?

Layne saw Fergus emerge from the side door of the pub with a tray of food and drink and knew immediately why. She loved him so much that she felt as if she were about to plummet over the highest bend of the latest ride at Blackpool funfair. Now that she had him, it was fear of losing him that haunted her.

At his approach, she struggled to open her door and stand on her good leg. Fergus put the tray down on the roof of the car and helped her to get upright with the door for support. 'And where's Long Layne Silver off to?' he asked.

'Nowhere,' she said. Layne pointed towards her trousered behind. 'Fergus, I want you to kick me really hard . . . right in the seat of the pants.'

'What?'

'Go on.'

'Are you raving, woman?'

'No. I've never been more sane. Will you, please?'

Fergus lifted his drink off the tray and leant back against the car, informing her, 'No I will not. Are you trying to get me arrested or something? You can't even balance on one leg. Imagine where you'd be if I kicked you.'

'I don't care.'

'Well, I do. If you're feeling the need for sado-masochism, at least wait till I've got you in private.'

Still disgruntled, Layne hopped backwards and slumped sideways onto her seat. He handed her a plate of sandwiches, then squatted down, removing his sunglasses to examine her more clearly. 'Do you mind if I ask what all this is about?'

She bit carelessly into a wedge of sandwich and swallowed without chewing, waving the rest of it at him. 'Is this real?' she demanded. 'Are you real? Because you need to convince me. I don't honestly believe it.'

Fergus got up and lifted the tray from the roof, passing her the orange juice, before climbing in behind the wheel to eat his food. 'I'd have thought,' he said, 'that just trying to stand on that foot would be enough to convince you.'

She shuffled round to face him. 'No. It just adds to the illusion. I never get sprained ankles.'

'Maybe not, but just look around you.' Fergus pointed through the windscreen. 'The Dog and Duck pub, the bald-headed, moustachioed, menopausal male in the shorts, socks and sandals, that urchin picking his nose . . . and the ubiquitous woman who looks as if her pregnancy will end any second on the car park tarmac. Isn't that real enough for you?'

Layne was not convinced. 'They're just extras, aren't they? . . . saying rhubarb, rhubarb.'

He turned back to her. 'Why are you determined to hold the dream? It's not all this, me and the outer world, that aren't real. It's you, Layne. You're hanging onto it and you can just as easily let go.'

'I'm not so sure,' she said miserably.

'Just give us time, that's all,' he assured her.

'Fergus?'

'What?'

'I think you'll have to help me find the toilet.'

He grinned. 'You see. How real can you get?'

The hotel was on the outskirts of York and Fergus was known there for often stopping to break his journeys from the south to Northumberland. The staff were not only curious to see the woman accompanying him, but surprised that he carried her in, despite her own vehement protestations that she could hobble perfectly well.

After the bags had been brought up to the room and there was no immediate likelihood of interruption, Layne scolded him, 'You needn't have done that! I feel such a fool.'

'Think of it as my symbolically carrying you over the threshold,' suggested Fergus, plugging in the kettle.

He turned to look down on her, shoved his hands into his pockets and said, 'There won't be much point in staying the extra night. You can't get about.' He dropped to sit next to her on the bed. 'What say we press on up tomorrow? It's not so far. I'll phone Mother.'

'I'm sorry. I've spoilt it for us, haven't I?'

'I thought it was John's fault for having steps and my fault for blasting the horn.'

'Well . . .' Layne gave him a reluctant smile. 'I always blame someone else when disaster strikes,' she confessed.

'I wouldn't have chosen to do this to you, you know,' he assured her.

Layne looked sadly at the bed. 'I shan't be much use in this, shall I?'

He stroked her hair, then drew her head onto his shoulder. 'Perhaps we'll find a way to improvise?'

'I think I'll have a bath, Fergus, if that's all right.'

Getting up to attend to the kettle, Fergus offered, 'I'll run you one, then I'll order a meal brought up.'

Layne flopped back on the bed, ignoring the objection from her ankle and announced, 'I really am in seventh heaven, aren't I?'

'A Yorkshireman would say so,' agreed Fergus.

When Fergus had run the bath, Layne hobbled into the bathroom for the first time and called out to him, 'Have you seen the size of this room? It's like a barn . . . and look at the bath!' She got out a bottle of bath foam and trickled it into the water.

He called back: 'That's why I like the place. The baths are the old-fashioned type you can stretch out in without your toes disappearing up taps.'

Layne lowered herself carefully onto the edge and swished the foam about in her fingers, before fishing a green sponge, in the shape of a demented frog, out of her bag. She dunked it in the water and squished it between her fingers until it oozed foam.

Satisfied at last, she was about to loosen her wrap when she noticed Fergus standing in the doorway. He was stark naked.

'What on earth are you doing?'

'I'm having a bath.'

'I said first,' she pointed out firmly.

'No need,' he said. 'I'm coming in with you.'

'You are not. I want it all to myself.'

Warily, she watched him approach. 'You can't manage on your own. How are you going to get in and out?'

'Well, I can just put my leg over the edge and, sort of, let myself go . . .'

'And damage some other essential part of your body, while you flood the bathroom?'

He began to reach for her wrap, then noticed the three inch depth of froth on the surface. 'What on earth have you done to it?' He smeared some of the froth over one hand in disgust.

'I like to smell nice.'

'Nice?' he complained. 'You'll smell like a Turkish tart and, more to the point, so will I.'

'Well, push off then,' she recommended.

Fergus slapped the handful of froth over her

nose and, ignoring her snort of indignation, reached for the tie of her wrap and pulled.

Layne watched the sides fall apart and looked him severely in the eye. 'You realize all you need is a bunch of grapes for this to reach the height of decadence, don't you?'

He smiled. 'There are worse things than bathing together. Yorkshire does have a water shortage, remember?'

He felt the water temperature, climbed in and sank down, trying to ignore the fizzing foam and, worse still, the vile sponge frog bobbing in its bubbles. 'Now turn your back to me,' he told Layne.

Resigned, she did as she was told. He slipped the wrap from her shoulders and she shrugged her arms out of the sleeves, before casting it away.

He slid his hands beneath her arms and recommended, 'Lie back and let yourself go. I've got hold of you. You can't hurt yourself.'

'Don't let my head go under,' she warned.

'I won't, silly, just slip in gently. Try not to create a tidal wave.'

'I'm not a hippopotamus,' she grumbled. 'Ouch. That handle's cold.'

Fergus eased her in and folded his arms round her as she slipped into his lap. 'There. That's nice, isn't it,' he said softly, sweeping Layne's hair away from her neck and pressing a kiss beneath her ear.

She gave him a sideways glance and a satisfied smile. 'I'll go to hell for this.'

Nuzzling into her neck, he weighed her breasts in the water. 'So long as you're in seventh heaven now.'

She tried to turn and kiss him but the foam got in the way and they both laughed, so that clusters of it flew up and landed in their hair.

· 'Pass me the soap,' said Fergus, 'and I'll do you all over.'

'You can't use soap!' protested Layne. 'All my fluff will disappear.'

He grinned. 'That would be the end of the world, wouldn't it?'

Layne rolled sideways and bounced the frog sponge on his head, trying not to drown in the process. He wrested it from her, lifted her head and shoulders out of the water and kissed her hard, before taking the frog on a sightseeing tour of her body.

Lying in bed later that night, after Layne had discovered that her problem ankle proved only a minor obstacle to lovemaking, she said, 'What have you seen of the film? I don't know why I haven't asked before.'

'I haven't given you the chance,' he pointed out, which was close to the truth.

'Well?'

'It's in edit. I've seen some of the dailies, so far, that's all.'

'How did they strike you?'

Fergus pulled her close but she was disappointed to hear him say, 'I refuse to talk shop this week. This is strictly Personal Relationship Week and the topic of work is banned.'

'I only want a feel of how it's gone, Fergus.'

'It's no good wheedling. You won't get anything.'

'You're very mean,' she complained, about to roll away from him, but he held onto her.

'There's something more important,' he told her.

'More important? What?'

'A subject I wanted to broach before we see Hanna.'

Layne slipped an arm about his waist, lifting her head slightly to look up at him. 'Oh?'

'Don't think I don't know exactly what you're going to say because I do. I'm just asking you now so that you can mull it over during the week.'

'What on earth is it?'

'You're already my wife in everything but name.'

Layne went very still, staring into the darkness, only able to make out his profile, until he turned his head toward her, voice gentle and persuasive. 'I want you to marry me. I want you to have my children one day.'

'Fergus, no . . .'

'I told you I knew what you would say now.'

'I'm flattered, Fergus, but I couldn't possibly . . .'

He traced the back of a finger along the line of her nose and told her plainly, 'I'd flatter you over my knee if I thought I could whack some sense into you but you'd only think me more wonderful and less attainable than ever.'

Layne nearly exploded. 'You really are the most conceited man I've . . .'

He tapped her nose with a pleasant warning. 'Dialogue's slipping! Still, at least you've found one fault. That's good.'

'Not just one!' announced Layne.

'Even better. By the end of the week, you'll realize I'm just the everyday, boring johnny down the road and the marriage is no more or less likely to break up than anyone else's.'

'That's not saying much these days.'

'Exactly. So what difference? I'm saying, see how you get on with The Horrible, watch me doing a Dorian Gray and come to the right conclusion when the week's over.'

Layne rolled away. 'Oh, Fergus, I wish you hadn't asked. I didn't want you to ask that.'

He followed her. 'You're already taking a chance. This is one tiny step further, that's all.'

'Right now, I'm happy Miss Nobody. If we married, I'd be Filmstar's Wife.'

'You make sacrifices whoever you marry, one way or another. That's what it's all about, isn't it? I love you and I hope I'll be prepared to compromise, too, because I think you're worth it. I'm asking you, Layne, because I want you . . . warts, swollen ankle, broomstick and all.'

The humour won her round and she turned over to advise him, 'I think *you're* The Horrible. Not your daughter.'

'It gets better and better,' he acknowledged.

CHAPTER 17

The drive through the wild and beautiful North-umberland country drove proposals of marriage far from Layne's mind. It was a county she did not know and one whose secrets she soon wished to discover. This would have made her curse her restricted mobility, had she not had a sister with Lizzie's difficulties. If ever Layne had something physically wrong with her, she would try hard to acknowledge all the good things about life and, right now, the heavens were smiling.

Fergus's mother was a well-built, statuesque woman who came out of her house wiping flour-covered hands on her apron as soon as she recognized her son's car snaking its way down the gravel drive.

As it crunched to a halt, Layne urged him, 'You go on and say hello first. I'll try and get the blood circulating in this leg.'

Just as Fergus got out, Hanna appeared in the doorway and came running, arms outstretched towards him, calling, 'Daddy, Daddy, Daddy!'

He picked her up in his arms and swung her round, while his mother smiled on. The thought came into Layne's head that she must be mad not to jump at the chance of marrying him. Who else would think twice?

She rubbed some of the feeling into her leg and reached for the door handle, while Fergus greeted his mother. As the door opened, Layne could hear the frantic barking of dogs somewhere in the distance.

By the time Fergus turned back, Layne had both feet on the gravel.

Hanna came winging round him, anxious to see her visitor, and Fergus called, 'Careful Horrible. Laynie's got a swollen ankle.'

It hardly slowed her down but she did screech to a halt at the door. A pair of blue eyes, still lit with happiness at the arrival of her father, peered round at Layne with curiosity.

She smiled encouragement. 'Hello Hanna? How are you?'

'What've you done?' demanded Hanna, pointing at the root of the problem.

'I fell down some stairs and twisted my ankle. Silly, wasn't it?'

Hanna looked into her eyes and nodded brightly. Her father shifted her gently out of the way and took Layne's arm.

'It has eased, Fergus. I can manage,' suggested Layne, afraid of looking like the helpless
woman.

'Stop pretending to be superwoman and let me
get on with it. My mother has buns in the oven,' he
reprimanded her.

Indeed, his mother had to rush indoors and then
back again to greet Layne's arrival. She held out
some floury fingers and Layne shook hands with
her, using Fergus for support.

'Sorry to rush off like that. Nice to meet you,
Layne.'

'It's kind of you to have me to stay, Mrs Hann,'
smiled Layne, looking round her at a large garden
with fields either side, backing onto woods. 'This
is really beautiful.'

'I'm Mrs Frazer, actually. Made the mistake of
marrying again, dear.'

'Oh, I'm sorry.'

'Call me Verity,' insisted Mrs Frazer. 'If I'm
going to be your mother-in-law, then I think we
should start off as we mean to go on. It's dreadful
having to call anyone but your own mother
"Mother". I know. I did it for more years than
I care to remember.'

Layne's eyes had narrowed and wandered to
Fergus. He was pretending to scratch his head.
Mrs Frazer saw she had made some gaffe and
enquired, 'What is it?'

Fergus avoided Layne's eyes. 'Er . . . she hasn't accepted me yet, Mum.'

This seemed to make little difference to his mother, who stayed blunt and to the point: 'Oh, but you will be sharing a bedroom?'

Fergus dared to look at Layne, who scowled. 'I'm not so sure about that.'

Trying to keep the humour from his expression, he said, in his defence, 'I forgot to explain that my mother is the most tactless person I know.'

Verity was already rushing indoors to make some tea, and so remained blissfully unaware that she was under discussion.

'What else have you forgotten to explain?' enquired Layne. 'I didn't know you had a stepfather for one thing.'

'Had is the word,' confirmed Fergus. 'He left my mother for a younger woman.'

'That's a man for you,' sighed Layne, as if it explained her attitude to everything.

'You need a crutch!' announced Hanna out of nowhere, just as Layne was just trying to convince herself she did not.

They had tea in the conservatory looking out at the garden and woods beyond. Hanna flashed backwards and forwards, bringing things to show Fergus, pictures she had drawn or books she was reading. He made rude comments about them which her laugh. Layne decided she was very like Fergus. The picture of Darcey beside his bed in Greece came into Layne's head and she felt tears filling her eyes. To have had a child like Hanna and never known her did not bear thinking about.

Layne reached quickly for her tea and blinked them back, turning her attention to the garden and asking Verity if she did it all herself.

'No, I have a "little man". I wanted a "little garden" but Fergus preferred to throw his money about. I keep telling him I'm not getting any younger but it never sinks in. Do you have any objection to dogs, Layne?'

'No, why?'

'I think it's time Fergus put them out of their misery and let them out. They know he's here, as you'll have heard.'

'Please, go ahead.'

Hanna, who had been eavesdropping, jumped up off the floor. 'I'll go!' She flew out of the conservatory at top speed.

'What kind are they?' asked Layne.

'Hamlet's a red setter. Lear . . . well, we're not quite sure. He looks like a cross between an Airedale and a Scottie.'

Layne smiled, querying, 'Hamlet and Lear?'

'Oh, Fergus's idea of a joke. I've always said he'd never be a true actor till he played Hamlet or Lear. He turned up with the dogs and said the nearest he'd get would be to playing *with* them!'

Layne looked across at Fergus. He'd stretched out on a two-seater sofa with his long legs hanging over the arm, head laid back on a cushion, apparently reading one of Hanna's magazines.

'Of course,' she said. 'He doesn't like Shakespeare, does he?'

Verity dismissed the suggestion. 'Ach, it's just because his legs don't look good in tights.'

Fergus shook his magazine, pretending to ignore them, and Layne was about to make a facetious comment when Hamlet and Lear saved his blushes by rocketing into the conservatory and bouncing all over him, yelping and barking hysterically. Hanna ran in and jumped on him, too.

Layne was not too sure if he would come out alive, but Verity seemed totally unperturbed by all the ruckus and took no notice, making reference, instead, to Layne's ankle. 'Would you like a herbal compress on that? I can make you one.'

'Oh no. It's already feeling better than yesterday. It'll soon be all right.'

Verity got up. 'It's no trouble,' she assured Layne, snapping at her son as she passed by, 'Get that dog away from the hibiscus, Fergus!'

'Yes, Mother.'

Fergus pushed Hamlet to the floor and lifted Hanna off his legs grumbling, 'There's no peace for the saintly . . .'

Hanna corrected him, as he reached over to grab Lear's collar and reverse him from chewing distance of the hibiscus leaves. 'Wicked!' she shouted.

'I know you are,' Fergus teased her.

Deprived of one area of interest, Lear took to Layne's feet, subjecting the ankle in question to a frenzied sniffing inspection.

Hanna rushed over to inform Layne, 'Lear never stops sniffing.'

Layne smiled at Fergus. 'That would be a new way to play him.'

Fergus did not agree. 'If you did that with Hamlet, he'd be forever cocking his leg up lamp-posts!'

Layne laughed and was joined by Hanna, when she thought she saw the joke.

When Verity returned with the compress, she recommended that Fergus take the dogs and Hanna for a walk to use up some energy. Fergus swished at Hanna's head with the paper, complaining, 'A woman's work,' before getting to his feet and informing Layne and his mother, 'I shall know if you're talking about me because Hanna's ears'll go red.'

'Get off with you,' advised Verity.

Layne gave a small wave of farewell, while Verity helped lift the afflicted foot onto a table, before squeezing a cloth in a bowl of green-coloured water.

Hanna was tugging on her father's hand as he looked back and observed, '*Two* witches. I'm surrounded.'

Verity shook her head as soon as they had gone. 'No wonder you don't want to marry him.'

Layne was not quite sure what to say, so she just watched the former Mrs Hann wrap the cold compress round her foot. Not expecting any comment, Verity went on. 'I don't know what made me think I wanted another man. I'm not saying Fergus's father wasn't as good a husband as you'd get but you give such a lot up for them. I think of all the things I could have done if I'd been single.'

'You wouldn't have been without your children, though, would you?'

Verity did not look too sure. 'I suppose not. They've been good to me . . . but look what you miss out on. Then they move on. They have to. And what are you left with? You're unfulfilled.'

'I suppose it's a case of the grass is greener,' suggested Layne. 'Who's to know you don't still feel that, even if you please yourself? Perhaps you can sacrifice just as much to a career as to a man.'

'You're probably right, dear,' conceded Verity, finishing with the compress. 'There. Keep your foot up and let that soak in.'

'Thank you. What did you use?'

'Comfrey,' said Verity, adding, 'though you could try lavender as an alternative.' About to remove the bowl, she patted Layne on the leg. 'It's comforting to know, at least, he wants some permanence in his life. I was beginning to give up hope. I really think men need it more than women.' She picked up the bowl.

Layne touched her arm as she was about to leave. 'It's not that I don't love him. I'm scared of the responsibility.'

'What? Of Hanna or the rest?'

'The rest.'

'Well, all I'd say to that is, they won't be crowing about him forever in that business. He's not getting any younger. Another five years . . . probably less and he'll be yesterday's news.'

It seemed a bit harsh but Layne appreciated the cold blast of realism, though felt she should point out that that was not always the case. 'Some stars retain their magnetism. I can think of a few who have become even more attractive in their later years.'

'That's as may be, but women aren't exactly fighting over their underwear, are they?'

Layne smiled at the thought. 'I suppose not.'

'No,' declared Verity. 'The sooner someone younger comes along to take the viewer's fancy, the better for Fergus. He might take the job more seriously.'

Layne felt duty-bound to voice her opinion. 'I think he does.'

Verity disagreed. 'He's been pandering to them too long, playing the hero. He wants something he can get his teeth into . . . like this one of yours. Something that shows him in a really unattractive light. He'll be good at that.'

Layne couldn't help herself. She laughed.

Verity laughed with her. 'Oh dear. It doesn't sound too complimentary, does it!'

Having acquiesced over the bedroom situation, Layne retired to Fergus's room that night, after spending an hour being given a running commentary by Hanna on her toys, cassette tapes and her wallpaper. Fergus had finally arrived to intervene, offering to read to Hanna.

Feeling tired, Layne sank into Fergus's bed and gave a sigh of relief. Verity had made it up with pink cotton sheets and matching, frilled pillow cases, which, Layne suspected, were not quite to Fergus's taste. There were sweet-smelling flowers in a vase on the windowsill and a balmy night breeze from the open window rippled the hem of the curtains.

Suffused by a sense of contentment, she watched quietly as Fergus came into the room to undress. When he climbed beneath the sheets and drew her close, she felt cosy and at home.

'Are you all right?' he said softly.

'Yes. Are you?'

'Never better.'

'Good.'

Layne squeezed him comfortingly and said, 'I love you.'

Perhaps because they were in his mother's house, she had thought, somehow, they would both simply drift off into sleep but Fergus gently eased his body on top of hers and began to kiss her slowly and methodically, working his way from her forehead down along her face and neck, circling her breasts, on down and down.

His preparation of her was so beautifully executed that, for a long time, she had no desire to move, nor did he seem to wish it. Yet, when the time came, there was a frenzied desperation about their coupling, leaving both limp with a luscious exhaustion that swallowed them up in the depths of sleep.

When Hanna burst in, early the next morning, expressing the wish to join them, they awoke suddenly, naked and embarrassed. Fergus sent her away on some pretext to fetch something and, while she was gone, they dived out of bed, searching frantically for scraps of clothing to make them decent. When Hanna returned, she found them hysterical with laughter in the bed and demanded to know the joke.

Fergus announced that Layne would tell her and Layne hit him with a pillow. Fergus retaliated in kind and, caught up in the atmosphere of lunacy, Hanna jumped on top and joined in.

One day rolled into the next. Layne's ankle healed steadily and she felt a bond was being slowly forged between herself and the other two women in Fergus's life. Every night, Fergus reassured her with his lovemaking that she was special and needed. She left her work untouched, not even wishing to give it a thought.

She was amazed to learn from Verity, while helping her with dinner one evening, that Fergus had phoned his mother from Greece to say he had fallen in love at first sight. Verity had told him to act his age but, within six weeks, he was seriously considering divorce.

'It had been the first time he ever mentioned divorce to me through six years of torment over that woman,' said Verity, clapping her hands to her chest, 'and I thought "thank God" . . . at last the fool is seeing sense. He should never have married her in the first place.'

'He must have hoped she'd be a mother to Hanna someday.'

Verity opened the oven door to check the joint but shook her head. 'In his heart, that's one thing he knew all along . . . that the woman was a walking disaster, when she wasn't too senseless to walk, of course. He thought Hanna should be able to put a name and face to her mother, that's all.'

'It must have been awful,' Layne symphathized.

Satisfied the meat was cooked, Verity fetched some dinner plates from one of cupboards and put them to warm. 'He spent thousands and thousands of pounds on that woman's treatment, Layne. And for what? All because of a guilty conscience for persuading her to bear her own child. I asked him several times how he knew the baby was his, anyway.'

'Hanna must be.' There was no doubt in Layne's mind.

'Oh, I see it now,' agreed Verity. 'I see his own father in her too but, at the time, all he could say was that he just *knew* and I had to believe him.'

Layne felt sudden sympathy for Fergus's mother. 'You're still not free, are you, Verity? At a time when you should have no more children to consider, you have a lively youngster on your hands.'

'The dogs are a lot more trouble than Hanna but, I do admit, there are times that it makes me feel older than I am. It's not that Fergus wasn't prepared to make other arrangements for her. He can afford to. But . . . well, I suppose family's family. Who knows who she'd have been farmed out to.' Verity turned the heat off under the potatoes. 'Could you mash these, Layne? I'll go and find Fergus. The least he can do is a bit of carving. He's done nothing to help yet.'

By the Thursday, Layne was able to walk with Fergus and Hanna along the majestic sweep of wide beach dominated by Bamburgh Castle. The sky was a clear, cold blue, with only the occasional wisp of mist white cloud.

They all took off their shoes to paddle at the edge of the water but when Layne felt the cold of the damp sand beneath her feet, she guessed the water would be icy and watched the other two, instead.

'She's chicken,' Fergus told Hanna.

Hanna flapped her arms and said, 'Quack! Quack!'

Fergus shook his head at Layne and she tried not to smile.

Further on, they dropped down in the sand and Hanna began digging with her hands. Layne suggested to Fergus, 'Why not do one of Shakespeare's great roles here on your home ground? It's a wonderful location.'

Fergus leant forward and helped Hanna with her excavations. 'Why does it always have to be Shakespeare? Let's write something new, for goodness' sake, and not quite so convolutedly tragic.'

'Write. Who? The Royal "We"?' queried Layne.

'Any "We",' said Fergus. 'There must be something you can do with a castle that isn't horror, Hamlet or Hood.'

'Hood?'

'Robin.'

'What?' Layne smiled to herself. 'Because you'd still have to wear the tights?'

Fergus gave her a sideways glance. 'You shouldn't listen to my mother. She specialized in Latin and ancient Greek, so she's sure to lean towards relics . . . in or out of tights.'

Layne got to her feet and looked out across to the Farne Islands and the vast expanse of the North Sea. Taking a deep breath, she filled her lungs with the air. The break had benefited not only her but Fergus. To look at him now, no one could possibly mistake him for the fictional character, Joseph Lennox. She knew for certain she was not in love with an image any more.

He was squatting on a ridge of sand, looking down into the deepening pit Hanna had tried to create before hopping back to the water's edge for a second paddle. Unable to resist, Layne crept up behind him. The stronger of her feet made contact with the seat of his pants and Fergus overbalanced into the hole, followed by a minor avalanche of sand.

For a few seconds, Layne stood over him laughing. Hanna ran up and joined in, pointing at him. 'Laynie kicked you in the bottom! Get out of my hole!'

Fergus lay on his back, slowly wiping the sand from the side of his face. Though a trace of humour could be detected in his eye, there was something about his expression that made Layne try to control her laughter and say, 'I'm sorry. I just couldn't help it!'

Fergus kept on looking at her but enquired, 'Did you say "kicked", Hanna?'

'Yep.'

'Oh dear,' he said.

'Errr . . .' was all Layne could manage, seeing he was quickly gathering himself together.

She turned tail and ran off up the beach as fast as her ankle would take her. Behind her, Hanna screamed with excitement. Layne was no match for Fergus and was already breathless when he caught up with her. She doubled up, knowing she was beaten.

An arm draped itself over her shoulder. 'Hanna said you *kicked* me, Laynie.'

She straightened up, daring to look him in the eye, but shaking her head in denial. 'No. I barely touched you. Honestly. You just seemed to . . . slide over.' The replay in Layne's head made her cover her smile with one hand.

Fergus appeared to consider this a final straw. He swept her up in his arms and carried her out to sea. The sudden realization of his actions changed Layne's demeanour. 'What are you doing, Fergus?'

'What does it look like?'

'No, Fergus, it's cold in there.'

'A promise is a promise,' he said.

'No, please. I'm sorry.'

The water was up to his knees and already wetting the hem of her skirt, which was trailing in the water. Incoming waves were threatening to lap higher and higher round them. 'Turn back, Fergus, please!' pleaded Layne, her arms reaching to cling round his neck.

'Why should I?' He took two more steps forward.

'Look, I've said I'm sorry,' she assured him, beginning to realize he was serious.

'I'd say the same in your position,' was all the response she got.

'Well, what else is there?' He gave her a long, hard look and comprehension began to dawn. 'You want me to say I'll marry you?' she said.

An eyebrow hovered. 'Do I?'

A wave splashed ice water up his thigh and across her knees. 'I'm going to have to let go, Layne. You're slipping,' he warned her.

'I'll marry you,' she said hastily.

'Mmm? What was that?'

'I said I *will* marry you,' she repeated, louder.

'Is that a promise?'

'Yes. A promise.'

'Cross your heart,' he said.

Layne nodded.

'No,' insisted Fergus. 'Cross your heart properly.'

She dared to release one hand to do as he said. Layne had just completed the manoeuvre when all support disappeared from under her. The last thing she saw before hitting the water was a smile of satisfaction on his face.

Once she had resurfaced, the shock left her gasping. He had not even waited to check if she had drowned but was at the water's edge with Hanna. She was not to know that, when Fergus had been about to warn Hanna not, under any circumstances, to laugh when Laynie emerged from the water, Hanna had pre-empted him by declaring, 'That wasn't fair!'

Fergus had informed her in mock serious tones, 'You can be kicked once too often.'

'It was a *gentle* kick,' he was quite firmly told in response.

He watched Layne drag herself from the waves, blonde hair glued to her shoulders, breasts pronounced beneath the wet top, skirt clinging about her knees. She turned aside, trudging her way back, parallel to the shore, determined to have nothing more to do with him ever again. At least, not until he had done sufficient penance.

Fergus told himself this was his wife-to-be. Life promised to be stormy but interesting. He began to prepare himself mentally. The wrath of two women was already upon him. What would happen when his mother found out?

The first thing Fergus's mother did was to order him to run Layne a hot bath. While he did so, Layne sat in the warm kitchen, shivering in a travel rug.

'It wouldn't be so bad,' stuttered Layne, 'but I said I'd marry him and the swine dropped me in the drink, anyway. It's positively freezing in there.'

Verity shook a teaspoon in the air. 'If he'd done anything like that when he was a lad, he'd have known about it from his father.'

'I know what I'd like to do with him,' grumbled Layne.

When he pronounced her bath ready, Fergus also offered to carry Layne upstairs. He was on the receiving end of an arctic glare to match her temperature.

Once alone with his mother, Verity shook her head at Fergus and warned, 'You know well that you can't hold the girl to a promise of marriage under duress.'

'Watch me,' recommended Fergus, with a wink. 'It could all fly back in your face.'

'I think that could well be tonight, so get your earplugs ready.'

If Fergus had been looking forward to fireworks, he was disappointed. It was an exceptionally quiet night. Layne was still giving him the silent treatment.

She had known, as she lay there luxuriating in the welcome heat of the bath, that she would not back out of her promise. That decision had been taken the night Layne learnt he had talked about divorce from Darcey, the same night he had made the most exquisite love to her. The threat of dropping her in the North Sea had not made up her mind, only hastened her acceptance.

But the sin had yet to be forgiven and Layne intended to take her time. She was still shocked that he could do such a thing and it had doused the flames of her natural fiery response.

She had to give him his due though. That night, he had tried to make her laugh, he had tried reason and he had dared to make a loving overture. Layne had remained unaffected, limp and uninterested. She particularly noticed the one thing he did not attempt was an apology. This unusual way of proceeding, however, had made for a restless night's sleep and, whereas, Fergus soon accepted the inevitable and drifted off, Layne lay awake, trying to envisage life as Mrs Fergus Hann and failing. It was a long, long time before she, too, succumbed.

Much to her shame, she awoke early next morning curled up in the warmth of his arms, just as if nothing had happened, her head gently moving with the rise and fall of his chest. She tried to unravel herself with care but found she was held in a vice-like grip. Tipping her head back slowly to look at him, Layne found herself being watched by a pair of amused blue eyes.

'Going somewhere?' he asked.

She tried not to look guilty. 'I was trying to turn over.'

He looked smug. 'I think you're still trying to avoid me.'

Layne pushed against his chest, but Fergus slid down and brought her closer than ever.

'What do you expect?' she complained, 'When you're still playing John Wayne! You knew it would be freezing in there.'

'Be honest,' he said softly. 'I think a short saltwater swim was pretty fair recompense for two slapped faces, two kicked shins and a boot in the behind, don't you? Besides, I wanted you to know I'm a man of my word.'

Layne was still trying to separate herself but his words were sinking in. Had she really subjected him to all that? She had no option but to admit to it, and possibly more.

'I wouldn't expect any less from you. I mean, I did hear you accept the job of wife, didn't I?'

Her features began to relax. She nodded. He assured himself, 'Wife to me, that is.'

Layne slid a hand about his waist. 'If you still want me, after all that physical abuse.'

There was promise in his smile. 'I've never wanted you more, witch.'

He leaned across her, pinning her arms to her sides, and kissing her hungrily. In no time at all, the bed seemed to be bouncing up and down along with them, causing Layne's voice to wail, 'The bedsprings!'

'Concentrate,' ordered Fergus, speeding up.

Helpless tears of joy sprung from Layne's eyes and soaked into the pillow slip. When it was over, Fergus found the strength for a final kiss, exclaiming, 'I love you, wife-to-be!'

Wearing an ecstatic smile, Layne clasped his head to her breasts and practically suffocated him.

They drifted back into blissful sleep, only to be awoken an hour later by a knock and voices at the door. Fergus struggled into a sitting position and called, 'Come in.'

Hanna ran forward first and threw a gift-wrapped parcel onto the bed, shouting, 'Happy Birthday, Daddy!'

She was closely followed by Verity with a breakfast tray of coffee and hot toast, which she slid onto the dressing table while Hanna waited for her father to admire his surprise.

Layne blinked, still half-asleep and trying to pull the sheet up to a minimum level of decency.

Impatient, Hanna helped Fergus rip off the paper and then watched his expression, as he examined her box of chocolates and held up the garish tie for comment. 'My favourite chocolates!' Then he gave her a huge smile. 'And what a positively hideous tie!'

Hanna was delighted. 'I knew you'd like it!'

'Come here, Horrible,' he said, holding out his arms.

His daughter caught him round the neck and hugged him tightly. Fergus kissed her soundly on the cheek and then advised her, 'You'd better give Laynie a kiss too, or she'll feel left out.'

Hanna did not hesitate to hug Layne in turn and give her a smacking kiss. Layne held onto the wriggling child but complained, 'I didn't know it was Fergus's birthday. Nobody told me.'

Verity, who had been standing over them, watching, with folded arms, revealed, 'He swore us to secrecy, didn't he, Hanna? And it took an awful lot of will-power to keep quiet, didn't it?'

But Hanna's attention had been distracted. She

pointed at Layne and Fergus, concluding, 'You're not wearing anything.'

'We were hot,' announced Fergus quickly.

Verity clapped her hands. 'Come on, off there, Hanna. This breakfast is going cold.'

Hanna scrambled to hinder Verity with lifting the tray. They managed to get it between Fergus and Layne without upsetting the coffee.

Fergus caught his mother's hand and kissed it. 'My ministering angel,' he declared.

She pulled it away. 'Behave yourself. Your present's downstairs if you want it. And don't be too late up, we're having a birthday lunch. Come on, Hanna. You can make flowers with the serviettes.'

Fergus watched them go, then turned to find his wife-to-be viewing him with concern. 'Why didn't you let them tell me, Fergus? I feel awful now. I haven't got you anything. Not even a card.'

He slipped a hand into her hair and kissed her cheek gently. 'You gave me my birthday present an hour ago. What more could a man want? Come on, let's dig into this before it goes cold.'

Later, when Layne was helping out with the lunch preparations, Verity said, 'Hanna's bursting to tell him we're having company. She's never had to keep so many secrets. She'll probably explode.'

'I thought there seemed a lot of food. Who's coming?'

'There'll be my daughter, Trina and her partner, Kevan, and Aidan, Fergus's elder brother, and his wife Catherine and their two boys. I hope you won't feel overwhelmed.'

'I'll look forward to meeting them.'

Verity wiped her hands on a tea-towel and admitted to Layne, 'I invited them over the phone at short notice and told them you were here. I thought they should meet you, Layne, with you and Fergus being so close. You must forgive them if they make you feel you're in a goldfish bowl but Fergus hasn't brought a girl home since he was in his early twenties. So you're a curiosity.'

Layne looked up from slicing one of Verity's home-made confections and smiled. 'I suspect I'll have to get used to much worse. This will break me in gently.'

Neither Verity nor Layne knew that, at that moment, Hanna believed she was being entrusted with yet another secret. Fergus had prepared the ground for Layne's arrival by telephone with Hanna and, on their walks with the dogs, made it seem as natural as he could that they should be sleeping in the same bed.

It had seemed understandable to Hanna that her father should want to cuddle up with Layne in bed. She had felt the same way herself in Greece.

Even then, Layne had already been sleeping in her father's bed.

Now, she had just learnt that her father wanted to marry Layne. This apparently meant that Layne would become one of the family and, not only might Hanna see a lot more of her, but people may come to think of her as Hanna's mother. Would that worry her?

She told Fergus she did not think so. She could always tell them the truth. Fergus had scratched his head. He said that, eventually, Hanna might come to think of Layne as a mother and then the truth would not be very important, would it? Hanna reminded him that the truth was always important. It was the one thing, she remembered, he insisted on.

There were different kinds of truths, he said. 'Like what?' had been Hanna's response. Her father had put his head in his hands and given a big sigh but, at last, he had explained that, if, for instance, someone did something wrong, like stealing, they should tell the truth. They would get into trouble but that was only fair. Stealing was bad.

On the other hand, no one knew the truth about Lear. Was he really a cross between an Airedale and a Scottie? Hanna did not know. No, but it didn't really matter, did it? What mattered was that Lear was one of the family and Hanna loved him. No one really knew who his parents were.

Hanna had smiled. Now she understood.

The birthday lunch turned out to be an exceptionally happy event. Since Hanna's hint-dropping had been about as subtle as hurling bricks, Fergus pretended to be surprised by the arrival of his brother and sister. His family turned out to be welcoming, if fascinated by the mystery surrounding his new girlfriend. When Fergus got up at the end of the meal and told them he had an announcement to make, Hanna had jumped up too and shouted, 'Can't I tell them, Daddy?'

He looked across to Layne for help. She smiled and nodded, so he stood Hanna on her chair, straightened her party hat and resumed his seat.

'Because,' she announced with a sweeping gesture that demonstrated the inheritance of the Thespian gene, 'Laynie doesn't have any parents, like Lear, Daddy's going to give her a home.'

There was a general mumble and a few sniggers from the assembled company. Layne looked to Fergus, who looked to his daughter. 'Horrible,' he informed her. 'You're talking tripe. Get down.'

She folded her arms, shrugging away from him. 'That's what you said!' she insisted. 'You want to marry her. That's what you said, isn't it?'

'Yes,' he agreed.

Hanna nodded firmly. 'Yes. And no one needs

to know the truth about Laynie because it doesn't matter.'

Layne stared at Fergus. 'What truth? What on earth have you been telling her?'

Fergus got wearily to his feet. 'As you were, ladies and gentlemen.' He put his hands on his daughter's shoulders. 'I'm afraid you speak words into Hanna's ears and she minces them in the middle, so that shapeless dollops of misunderstanding emerge from her mouth.'

Hanna looked as if she would like to hit him. 'The gist of this announcement is, in fact, far less interesting; that is that our Laynie has foolishly consented to join the Hann clan and be my unfortunate wife.'

There was a burst of applause. Fergus waved it down. 'And just to put the record straight, she bears no resemblance to Lear in any respect. She has parents and a perfectly acceptable pedigree . . . and I hope she and Hanna are on the same wavelength because I'm obviously in need of some fine tuning.'

'Where's the ring?' demanded Trina.

'Ring?'

'Engagement ring, Fergus, for goodness' sake?'

'I . . . er . . .'

'Where will you marry?' asked Catherine. Fergus again looked to Layne for help. All she did was shrug.

Fergus floundered. 'I don't . . .'

'Can I come?' enquired Hanna.

That night in bed, Layne said, 'You could be forgiven for having second thoughts. If you want a wedding to go ahead, we're going to have to wake up and start planning.'

CHAPTER 18

Two months later, there was a long silence during the wedding ceremony at Verity's tiny, local church of St Peters.

Fergus had invested the vicar's words with heavy meaning, as befitted an actor of his standing, his blue eyes fixed on Layne throughout. She was dressed in a pale green silk dress and jacket and stood a little taller than usual in high heels. Her blonde hair had been swept up and fastened beneath a matching pill box hat.

'I, Layne . . .' said the vicar.

Fergus felt Layne's hand flutter inside his own. There was a barely perceptible shake of her head and he could see her eyes filling with tears. Fergus shifted on the spot. There was an outbreak of throat-clearing in the small congregation.

'I, Layne . . .' repeated the vicar, deeming it wise to clear his own throat, too.

A tear slid from the corner of Layne's eye down the side of her cheek and Fergus felt the colour drain from his face. Layne was about to refuse him. His composure began to fail.

Fergus moved closer and pleaded with the sad, green eyes. He bent to whisper in her ear, 'For Christ's sake, don't change your mind, now!'

The vicar heard and looked displeased.

Layne seemed to blink herself back. She suddenly recognized the pain she was inflicting on Fergus and sniffed back the tears. At the same time, Hanna sneezed explosively into the posy that matched her flouncy, rose-coloured dress. Layne smiled gratefully in Hanna's direction, then turned back to Fergus, squeezing his hand, as she spoke, 'I, Layne . . .'

There was a relieved outbreak of coughing.

As they signed the register some time later, Fergus complained, 'You frightened the life out of me.'

'I know. I'm sorry. I didn't mean to.'

'You are sure, aren't you?'

Layne kissed his cheek. 'Of course I'm sure.'

'Well, don't ever do that again!'

'I don't expect to have to,' she warned him, as they left the church hand in hand.

A group of pubescent schoolgirls screamed at Fergus as he waited to climb into the car, and Layne had smiled into one camera before realizing it belonged to the press. So . . . this was the start, she thought.

Waiting at their hotel three days later for the taxi to take them on honeymoon, Layne read a newspaper report on their marriage. It read:

On Saturday, screen heart-throb Fergus Hann married Layne Dendran, screenwriter on his latest film, "The Thorn Field", due for release early next year. His eight-year-old daughter Hanna was a bridesmaid . . .'

Layne threw the paper to Fergus to read. 'Just look at that!'

Fergus said, 'Hanna will be pleased. They've notched her up a year.'

'You know what I mean. Layne "Dendran", indeed!'

He grinned. 'Good job you're not called Rhoda.'

Throwing the paper aside, Fergus shook his head. 'I'm still not sure it's wise to bring The Horrible on honeymoon, Laynie. We won't get much time to ourselves.'

'I don't want her to feel I'm pushing her out . . . coming between the two of you. I think we should bond as a family unit. She'll feel bad enough when we expand.'

'With a bit of luck she'll be a teenager by then.'

'That's unlikely,' said Layne.

'Well, it's up to you, of course.'

'No. I'm afraid it isn't.'

He searched her face.

'What?'

'The die is cast, so to speak.'

'You're not saying . . .'

She nodded emphatically.

'Yes. I *am* saying . . .'

'God. I'm sorry.'

'It takes two,' she reminded him.

'Yes, but I am sorry, Layne. It's not as if you haven't got enough on your plate.'

She smiled reassuringly.

'I'll manage.'

'I don't know what to say.'

'Well, that's a first.'

'You'd better put me down for the operation.'

'That would be a crime.'

'You're beautiful, have I told you that?'

'Once or twice.'

'On honeymoon . . . will we be able to . . .?'

'It would be a shame not to, on honeymoon. Fergus?'

'Yes?'

'Can I ask you something?'

'Anything.'

'If it's a girl, can we call her Lizzie?'

THE EXCITING NEW NAME IN WOMEN'S FICTION!

PLEASE HELP ME TO HELP YOU!

Dear *Scarlet* Reader,

As Editor of *Scarlet* Books I want to make sure that the books I offer you every month are up to the high standards *Scarlet* readers expect. And to do that I need to know a little more about you and your reading likes and dislikes. So please spare a few minutes to fill in the short questionnaire on the following pages and send it to me. I'll send *you* a surprise gift as a thank you!

Looking forward to hearing from you,

Sally Cooper

Editor-in-Chief, *Scarlet*

P.S. Only one offer per household.

QUESTIONNAIRE

Please tick the appropriate boxes to indicate your answers

1 Where did you get this Scarlet title?
Bought in Supermarket ☐
Bought at W H Smith ☐
Bought at book exchange or second-hand shop ☐
Borrowed from a friend ☐
Other _____

2 Did you enjoy reading it?
A lot ☐   A little ☐   Not at all ☐

3 What did you particularly like about this book?
Believable characters ☐   Easy to read ☐
Good value for money ☐   Enjoyable locations ☐
Interesting story ☐   Modern setting ☐
Other _____

4 What did you particularly dislike about this book?
_____

5 Would you buy another Scarlet book?
Yes ☐   No ☐

6 What other kinds of book do you enjoy reading?
Horror ☐   Puzzle books ☐   Historical fiction ☐
General fiction ☐   Crime/Detective ☐   Cookery ☐
Other _____

7 Which magazines do you enjoy most?
Bella ☐   Best ☐   Woman's Weekly ☐
Woman and Home ☐   Hello ☐   Cosmopolitan ☐
Good Housekeeping ☐
Other _____

cont.

And now a little about you –

8 How old are you?
Under 25 ☐   25–34 ☐   35–44 ☐
45–54 ☐   55–64 ☐   over 65 ☐

9 What is your marital status?
Single ☐   Married/living with partner ☐
Widowed ☐   Separated/divorced ☐

10 What is your current occupation?
Employed full-time ☐   Employed part-time ☐
Student ☐   Housewife full-time ☐
Unemployed ☐   Retired ☐

11 Do you have children? If so, how many and how old are they?
_____
_____

12 What is your annual household income?
under £10,000 ☐   £10–20,000 ☐   £20–30,000 ☐
£30–40,000 ☐   over £40,000 ☐

Miss/Mrs/Ms _____
Address _____
_____
_____

Thank you for completing this questionnaire. Now tear it out – put it in an envelope and send it before 31 April, 1997, to:

Sally Cooper, Editor-in-Chief

SCARLET
FREEPOST LON 3335
LONDON W8 4BR
Please use block capitals for address.
No stamp is required!   STARS/10/96

Scarlet titles coming next month:

THE JEWELLED WEB Maxine Barry
Reece Dexter only has to snap his fingers and women come running! Flame is the exception. She doesn't want Reece to give her his body – she wants him to give her a job!

SECRETS Angela Arney
Louise, Robert, Michael and Veronique all have something to hide. Only Daniel is innocent, though he is the one who binds them all together. It is Louise and Robert who must find the strength to break those invisible ties. Yet their freedom _and_ their love carry a dangerous price . . .

THIS TIME FOREVER Vickie Moore
Jocelyn is puzzled: 'Who does Trevan think he is? He seems to know everything about me, yet I'm sure we've never met before . . . well, not in this lifetime. I can't believe he wishes me harm – but someone does! Can I afford to trust Trevan?'

THE SINS OF SARAH Anne Styles
But Sarah doesn't think she's committing any sins – all she's guilty of is wanting the man she loves to be happy. Nick wants to make Sarah happy too – but there's a problem! He already has a wife and Diana won't give him up at any cost. Throw in Nick's best friend Charles, who wants Sarah for himself and the scene is set for a red hot battle of the sexes!